Crow's Cottage

By John Bowen

For

Joanna Franklin Bell and Joel Hames-Clarke.

Those times when the writing is hard and drives
me crazy?
It's nice to have friends in the asylum.

Also
by John Bowen

 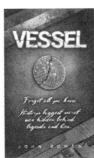 

Chapter One

The video opens abruptly, clearly a clip culled from a longer recording.

Three figures sit cross-legged on a checked blanket, outside at night, surrounded by darkness and tombstones. The video is compressed, reducing the subtle gradients of the night into twitchy, geometric bands of grey and black.

The low-light-amplified, night vision, monochrome palette will be a style of video familiar to fans of ghost hunting shows, as will the otherworldly appearance it lends its subjects. The two young women and the young man sitting on the blanket, dressed in a mixture of hoodies, jeans, boots and sports shoes share the same glowing cat's eye pupils and milky complexion.

The person behind the camera shifts position to get a better view of the three and the item that lies between them. As the shot moves in and steadies, it becomes possible to identify what the item is. The board's markings swim into focus, revealing words, numbers and letters: YES and NO, the alphabet arranged in two rows, and one to nine ending with zero below, and beneath this the word GOODBYE.

It is a Ouija, or spirit board.

The youths lean in, closer to the board, place their fingers on the planchette resting on it. One of the women begins to speak. The expression on her face, framed by wild, curly, shoulder-length hair, is deadly serious. "Spirits," she says, Yorkshire in her voice, "we are not here to offend, anger or disrespect. We seek only to communicate, to learn—"

The trio flinches as one as the planchette suddenly darts forward, taking them by surprise. They clearly hadn't expected as immediate a response. The planchette claims a letter. The camera moves in closer still. Everything briefly devolves into a blur. When focus returns it finds the planchette again in motion.

It zigzags around the board, pausing only for a beat before moving on. The girl calls out each letter as they come.

"L. E. A. V. E. T. H. I. S. P—"

The young man shoots the girl an anxious glance, but she appears oblivious to it. Her eyes are on the board, her steady voice continuing to call out each letter claimed.

"L. A. C. E."

Then the planchette stops. It does not ease, slow or slide to a rest. It stops dead, like someone hit the brakes or pulled the power.

The trio seems frozen, perhaps waiting to see if the planchette will spring back to life and offer them more.

As the seconds pass, it appears not. The young man starts to open his mouth, but while his lips part the words never make it out. He sees something which causes his eyes to widen and makes him scramble backwards.

The spirit board flips into the air. The planchette upon it is hurled into the jumping bands of square edged, digital darkness, and in the void behind the girl with the wild hair a shape, amorphous and pale, spills into being. As it gathers form, the other girl joins the young man in taking flight. Both are reduced to blurry grey shadows as they scatter from the camera's gaze. Only the girl with the wild hair holds firm, but then vanishes from view too, when the camera operator joins the ones who ran.

At this point, the video freezes, and then the last few moments are repeated, but in slow motion.

The spirit board lifts and twists step by step. The launched planchette becomes a pale smudge for a few frames, and then the shape appears. Presented as static pictures, robbed of fluidity, the shape is less distinct, far more a chunky collection of compression artefacts, possessing as few as two more shades of grey over the three which comprise the darkness from which it emerges. It is blocky and vague, but not formless.

It has two pockets of shadow one could read for eyes, one more for a nose, and one more for a mouth...

It looks like a face.

It looks like a figure.

If you really want it to, and are prepared to squint a bit.

-

Behind his desk, in his office at Bennett White Productions, Charles McBride, *Where the Dead Walk* producer, presenter and medium, clicked the pause icon on the video titled CHLOE HARKER - GHOST IN GRAVEYARD! CAUGHT ON CAMERA! before it could autoplay something else.

He had been checking in on the *Where the Dead Walk* YouTube channel and Chloe's video had appeared in his suggested feed. The internet, particularly YouTube, seemed single-minded about serving him more of what he had either already watched, or things very much like the things he had already watched. Technology and computers and whatnot were not really his strong suit, but he was trying to develop his skills and overcome his ignorance. When he had commented how YouTube seemed to be ninety-nine percent ghost videos and he hadn't been aware the topic was so popular, someone had kindly explained the mechanics to him.

The internet and digital media platforms were rife with algorithm thingies, constantly at work, determined to serve him another slice of the unfathomable ocean of content which now existed in the digital ether, too much for any human being to consume and expanding every day, something attractive enough to make a fellow sit through an ad or two to get to.

Where the Dead Walk were now direct contributors to this ocean of content too. The show's YouTube channel featured hours of video, popular clips and exclusive bonus content, and boasted very good 'metrics', apparently.

Charles was old enough to remember when television meant three channels, which all stopped broadcasting at midnight, and a video was something he fed into a VHS machine the size of a briefcase. It was sufficient to make one feel ancient.

He saw Chloe's video had now clocked up an impressive 614,678 views.

Seven months had passed since Chloe Harker had joined the *Where the Dead Walk* crew. With the next series closing in on completion, just one more location to be filmed, everyone agreed bringing her on board had been a good move. The crew had warmed to her almost immediately, and Charles was confident *Where the Dead Walk*'s audience would too. Despite this, he knew Chloe was anxious about her reception, but maybe that came from what she was used to.

Chloe's YouTube clips and shows had considerably more 'thumbs up' than 'thumbs down', but if he looked there were still 'haters', as he believed the terminology went.

Even on the infamous graveyard clip, a scroll down to the comments section demonstrated not everyone was convinced a 'ghost in graveyard!' had indeed been 'caught on camera!' A few negative comments peppered the first dozen.

One KittyG expressed the concise and candid view of *Fuk1n Bullshit*, while a chap going by the name of Barry_loves_biscuits left the no less sceptical, and even more concise, *FAKE!* A little further down Big_Harry_Butt, a boy who should perhaps have concentrated more in English class, was happy to elaborate further: *Congraduations,* his comment read, *u are all great at working out ghost is not real. The Paranormal Activity movies is not real either in case u couldn't work that out morons.*

Scepticism was to be expected, naturally. Paranormal investigation shows had been a part of the televisual buffet for well over a decade, and yet incontrovertible evidence of ghosts remained elusive. In practice, capturing hard proof of the paranormal on camera was tough.

As someone who had first-hand experience of the paranormal, Charles knew only too well how things which seemed astonishing in the moment had a way of looking less remarkable once reduced to a flat rectangular image and recorded sound. Changes in atmosphere, air pressure or temperature, the sudden appearance of scents or a plethora of subtle sensations only detected in person were lost. The show hadn't stopped trying though, even if things had been in doubt for a while.

Two years ago, *Where the Dead Walk* seemed in danger of seeing its final episode, despite commanding healthy ratings. After several series the original creators and producers, Kate Bennett and Henry White had voiced their desire to quit the show. With Kate being not just its co-producer but also its lead presenter, everyone assumed it signalled the end. Thankfully, Kate and Henry didn't.

They argued Charles and *Where the Dead Walk*'s lead researcher, Ray Darling should take the reins. The show would still be a Bennett White production, but Kate and Henry would not be creatively involved.

Once digested, Charles conceded the proposal made a lot of sense. *Where the Dead Walk* had been a lean operation from day one. When attempting to capture manifestations of the paranormal, having dozens of people tramping around wasn't helpful. A small crew with a handheld video approach was not only more practical and a lot more atmospheric, lending proceedings a feeling of immediacy, intimacy and authenticity, it also happened to be an excellent way for a fledgeling production house like Bennett White to make a television show on a shoestring budget.

Of course, the small crew approach only worked if the crew in question were versatile folk who, in addition to their primary roles, were up for doubling as presenters and investigators too. The core *Where the Dead Walk* crew had featured on camera since episode one and thereby become personalities in their own rights. Fans of the show grew to know and like them, had their favourites. Charles, as the crew's resident medium, had, of course, always featured prominently, so the shift to lead presenter was mostly just a step to the fore.

The crew all wanted to continue and were rewarded for their efforts when the first Kate-and-Henry-free series of *Where the Dead Walk* ratings held steady. The shift brought changes beyond the crew. Charles acting as lead presenter placed a greater emphasis on the spiritual aspect of investigations, while on the other end of the spectrum, former police officer Ray tightened the focus on the factual side, diving deeper into the history of places they investigated, and the figures connected there. The polarisation seemed to work, satisfying sceptics and believers alike.

And yet, a second series without Kate and Henry confirmed a nagging feeling something had been lost. Charles, in particular, felt Kate's absence. He suspected he worked better positioned one step back, with someone to play off. He and Ray discussed bringing in a new co-presenter, and then took the idea to the rest of the crew.

It had been Claire Montgomery, the crew's logistics queen, who had found Chloe Harker, or rather Claire's thirteen-year-old niece had. The girl followed several amateur paranormal investigators on YouTube. Chloe Harker was her favourite. She showed her aunt the infamous graveyard clip, which had 'gone viral' (something which sounded unpleasant as far as Charles was concerned, but could actually be a good thing and meant lots of people had ended up seeing it) and taken Chloe Harker from having a couple of thousand subscribers to tens of thousands.

Claire had checked out the rest of Chloe's channel, where she found full episodes of her investigations.

They were good. Well thought out, nicely paced, and confidently presented.

She had presented them to the crew, and they contacted Chloe to arrange a meeting. Chloe, it transpired, was a committed *Where the Dead Walk* fan, going right back to the first series which she had watched 'when she was a kid.' By which she meant, Charles realised, in her mid-teens rather than the Methuselah-like twenty-two she was today. He and Ray told her they were planning to expand their online presence and intended to film a short web-only special, along York's famous Ghost Walk tourist trail. Would she be interested in taking part, as co-presenter? Chloe's answer was a very, very enthusiastic yes. The shoot hadn't just gone well, it had gone great; Chloe Harker was perfect, succeeding in coming across as both earnest and fun, and a tremendous foil for Charles.

When they asked if she would be interested in joining the show as co-presenter on their next series she had said yes, in quite a lengthy and excited fashion.

Charles' attention was captured by a rap on his office door.

He looked up. Speak of the devil.

Chloe was at the threshold, next to his co-producer, Ray Darling. They couldn't have presented a greater contrast. Ray: solid and stocky, greying hair, polo shirt, chinos and desert boots. Chloe: lean, almost wiry, and afflicted with the sort of wild, curly hair brushes and combs probably told stories about to scare one another on Halloween. She was dressed almost entirely in black. A sweater hung off one shoulder, exposing a vest top, and under these a pair of skinny jeans, and finally the exception: a pair of white Converse All-Stars, the only sartorial choice set to ruin her odds should she wish to successfully infiltrate somewhere at night.

"Raymond. Chloe. Something I can help you with?"

"Maybe," Ray replied.

"Got a question for you, boss," said Chloe.

"Then, by all means, ask away."

"Ever heard of something called the Mephisto Arcane?"

Charles had. It wasn't a story he had heard lately, but he had heard it more than once over the years.

Chapter Two

"The Mephisto Arcane," said Charles, "was said to be a device, engineered through a mixture of skill and magic, to observe and commune with the spirit world." He corrected himself. "Well, two devices actually, one a few centuries old, one a few decades, both equally unlikely to have ever truly existed. If the legend is to be believed, the original Mephisto Arcane was destroyed, burnt to ash at the feet of its unlucky creator in the 17th century, during the English witch trials."

"And the second, more recent one?" Chloe asked.

"Was said to be a recreation of the original device, that comes with its own story. Why do you ask?"

"Can we hear the story first?" said Chloe.

Charles was curious but decided to play along.

"The second Mephisto Arcane was the work of three men who belonged to a group called the Longwood Society, or 'Longwood Occult Society' as some later referred to it, first formed in the early seventies, and made up of individuals active in spiritualist and parapsychology circles. It was founded by the late sensitive John Bartleholm, his wife, the psychometrist Eleanor Bartleholm, and their close friend, the occult artist Samantha Carrington.

"By the eighties, this version of the Longwood Occult Society was no longer active, but clearly not forgotten," said Charles. "The medium Edward Needham, an occult scholar named Hubert Langley, and a stage magician named Damien Faulks sought to resurrect it. These were the three men who were supposed to have crafted the second Mephisto Arcane. The group's revival was to be short-lived, however, due to an unfortunate event the three were connected to. Ray, you might even recall it, a famous pop music producer committed suicide?"

Ray didn't appear to. Which almost guaranteed Chloe wouldn't, given she had been approximately a decade away from being conceived at the time.

Charles continued. "Edward Needham and Hubert Langley were at a party thrown by Damien Faulks. If the stories are true, Faulks' gatherings comprised an eclectic crowd, not just performer and showbiz types Faulks knew, but members of this Society, and one or two slices from the upper crust too; Hubert Langley himself was minor aristocracy, a baron or something.

"Whatever went on at Faulks' parties, it was all private and blissfully discreet, until one of his guests decided to leave and go kill himself. The chap was the brains behind a string of hit pop songs, so his suicide became front page news. What had happened at the party to cause him to top himself? The tabloids seemed to be keen to unearth whatever miscellany of debauchery they could dig up, sex or drugs, but the story which emerged in spiritualist and paranormal psychology circles was more concerned with the paranormal. Given the mystique Faulks, Needham and Langley had woven around themselves, of which the Mephisto Arcane was simply one thread, tales about what had really happened to the chap that night grew rather... imaginative."

"Go on," said Ray. He and Chloe abandoned the doorway. Chloe parked her bottom on the edge of Charles' desk and Ray set his in the spare chair.

"The most common version has the record producer and a girl investigating the house, perhaps intending to make athletic and debauched use of one of the guest bedrooms, only instead they stumble upon the Mephisto Arcane," Charles said. "Drunk, possibly even high on drugs, they begin to fool around with the curious device. What they don't know is that in the wrong hands something like the Arcane can prove dangerous. The device was crafted to observe and commune with spirits, and there are those who believe not all spirits are derived from man. Some spirits are older, ancient, hail from an age before man existed, before even the material realm we inhabit existed. I talk, of course, of demons. It is such an entity the couple inadvertently called forth, and one does not summon a demon without providing it with an offering.

"The demon, powerful and hungry, takes what he assumes his offering to be: the girl. He claws her back into the unspeakably vile dimension from which he came while the record producer watches helplessly in sheer horror. Shaken loose of sanity, the man flees the scene and takes his own life.

"In the aftermath, our magician, medium and occultist, finding the device disturbed, and suspecting the truth, elect to destroy it on the spot, burn it, reduce it to ashes like its predecessor—and henceforth cease to meddle in matters no mortal man should…" Charles trailed off, one eyebrow firmly raised.

Ray took a moment to digest the story, before asking, "The record producer guy did top himself, though?"

"He did."

"And a young woman? Did one really go missing?" Chloe asked.

"That I'm less sure about."

"And the device? The Mephisto Arcane?" Chloe asked.

"As I said, likely never existed at all, in either incarnation. Where did you hear of it?"

"As part of a conversation I had this morning," Ray said, "with a man who recently inherited property from his late uncle. He's had tradesmen in to carry out a bit of maintenance, and with an eye to doing some remodelling. One of them found something hidden behind a panel in one of the bathrooms, an odd-looking box with a big metal disc on top. It has three words inscribed on its base, *The Mephisto Arcane*."

Charles was dimly aware his mouth was quite possibly hanging open.

"Since its discovery a few of the tradesmen have reported hearing things, seeing things. Then the owner, the guy I spoke to too," said Chloe.

"Things?"

"Unaccountable noises from empty rooms," said Ray, "and a figure, a dark shadowy figure."

"This house would be where?" Charles asked.

"In Surrey. It's called—"

"Crow's Cottage?"

"Is that the house from the story you just told?" asked Chloe.

Charles nodded.

Ray couldn't help smiling. Chloe looked like she might begin to jump up and down.

"One of the witnesses suggested the new owner, Giles Langley, contact us," said Ray. "I said we'd be happy to come and see him this morning."

Chapter Three

Chloe watched the world roll by from the back seat of Ray's Range Rover. Not even an hour from central London, Crow's Cottage was situated in Surrey's leafy greenbelt of rolling countryside. Up front, Charles and Ray were debating the practicalities of squeezing another location into the current series, and whether it was worth the crunch. As things stood, they were nicely on schedule, with just one location left to shoot and five weeks before final edit.

She would have said yes to half a dozen more. The novelty of being part of the show wasn't even remotely wearing off. For the first time in her life, she found herself in a position where being a ghost geek wasn't a weird hobby she had to justify or get embarrassed about. Even though she was stunned at the YouTube viewership she'd racked up on her own, this was a job. She was actually being paid to do it.

It wasn't just the work she loved, though. The job had come out of nowhere like a magic escape hatch, and allowed her to move halfway across the country which was exactly what she had needed. Once away she realised how suffocating home had become. Her own place, her own space, a nice cosy flat in Woking, good links to London and work, independence, somewhere she could breathe, somewhere her sister Kara didn't suck the oxygen from the room and leave her feeling like dark clouds were permanently brooding overhead.

Ray began to slow. They had reached a break in the trees and hedgerows beside the road, a giant leaf-fringed mouth yawning from the foliage where a narrow road cut in. The sat-nav confirmed they were nearing their destination. Ray steered the Range Rover into the leafy maw and trundled down a rough driveway into dappled shadow beneath a canopy of tall trees which blotted out the late afternoon sun, but not for long. Soon enough the gloomy tunnel opened back out into sunshine and upon a charming cottage.

The building was picture postcard stuff, red brick and slate, exposed wooden beams, and wonky square windows, more like a secret tucked away than a home. There was a grey Bentley parked outside. Ray drew the Range Rover up beside it.

"Crow's Cottage," announced Charles.

Once outside they found the cottage's door open. Ray nudged it wider, barking a gravelly, "Hello?" from the threshold.

A head appeared from around a doorway across the room, topped with a mop of fair hair so pale it reminded Chloe of the type usually only seen on toddlers. The rest of the man followed a moment later, building up momentum as he approached. Tweed jacket, corduroy trousers and cherry brogues, rosy-cheeked, chubby build—the man's every fibre screamed upper class. He practically bounded to meet them, one pudgy hand extended.

"Hello, I'm Giles Langley! You're the paranormal investigations people?"

"We are. Ray Darling, Charles McBride, and Chloe Harker."

Ray suddenly found himself on the business end of an ebullient, meaty handshake, and then Charles too. Chloe braced herself, but Giles Langley deftly shifted into 'dealing with lady' mode, and instead of a vigorous handshaking Chloe received a genteel clinch of her fingers and a small nod.

Unaccustomed to dealing with posh people, she successfully fought the urge to curtsy.

-

Giles Langley was obviously warming up to give them the tour, guiding them through a large low-ceilinged lounge with four sofas and several armchairs. He progressed as far as, "As you can probably see, this part of the house is the original Jacobean cottage. Everything beyond belongs to the Georgian era wing added by the Third Baron of Loncombe," before Charles interjected, and politely asked if they might be able to take a look around unaccompanied. He explained that it helped them arrive at a more objective impression, and gave him room to better pick up on any resident energies.

Giles Langley said of course and invited them to convene with him once they were ready.

Prior to the first location assessment Chloe had joined them on, Charles and Ray had talked about what they looked for, and what they felt helped going about identifying it. Beyond the obvious question of whether a location was actually haunted, there was the broader question of how it might work on the show. Did the location have a good visual atmosphere? Did it have a distinct identity, whether it be opulent and grand or distressed and disintegrating? Did it feel spooky? Most places held the potential in the dead of night, especially if one was there with the mindset of capturing something paranormal, busy creeping around alone actively alert for bumps, creaks or strange lights or shadows.

Charles and Ray argued the sober soak of daytime offered a suitably stiff test. If roaming someplace alone in daylight felt eerie, then roaming through in the wee hours of darkness was sure to. Hence, splitting up for the initial walkaround. They would pick different starting spots, as far apart as possible and swap over as they went. Ray took the ground floor, Charles the top with the attic rooms, leaving Chloe with the middle floor.

Chloe and Charles left Ray downstairs and headed for the staircase. Chloe stopped on the landing, watching Charles' feet continue upward. Once alone, she took in her surroundings. A hallway stretched before her. Half a dozen doors ran its length before it reached an end and turned right. She started walking, slowly, toward the first door, trying to not to think but to feel Charles' advice: *Invite a space to make its impression on you. Don't think, feel.*

Most of her amateur paranormal investigations had been in spaces open to the public, or abandoned buildings, which were sort of open to the public if one was a member of the public who was prepared to ignore Keep Out signs to climb a fence or squeeze through a locked gate. While strictly speaking this was trespassing, Chloe reckoned if someone couldn't be arsed to keep glass in the windows of a property they owned or were responsible for, or locks on the doors, they couldn't be too bothered if someone got in.

Being invited into a property was a lot simpler for sure, no concerns about a run-in with the law, but it didn't necessarily mean fewer complications. Whether Charles and Ray instigated an approach, or a prospective property was brought to them, someone was usually hoping to benefit in some respect. Ray split them into three main camps: historical, entrepreneurial, and delusional.

Historical was the least complicated, Ray reckoned, explaining it to Chloe soon after her hiring. At worst they were places hoping for a little free publicity to encourage visitor numbers, castles, country houses, museums... Benign as far as motives go, and usually a fair trade; a wealth of history meant lots of background material, which Chloe and every viewer could see that Ray loved, and folks simply felt that ghosts should be found more readily in historical sites.

Entrepreneurial was not so straightforward. While also after a little free publicity, the entrepreneur's motivation was decidedly more mercenary. Appearing on television doubled as a wonderful free advert, and a pet ghost could prove surprisingly lucrative. Pubs, bed and breakfasts, or hotels boasting a resident spirit could do well out of such an approach. Some even charged special rates for their most haunted rooms...

Delusionary was the most common. When you made it your business to investigate the paranormal, and let the world know you did, there was no shortage of folk ready to get in touch to tell you they lived somewhere haunted. Sadly, most wound up being hard to take seriously. To put it bluntly, a large proportion were oddballs, nuts, kooks, gals and guys who liked to set their tin foil hats at a jaunty angle while they tugged at their generously loose tether on reality. They were very keen, often certain not only of the existence of ghosts but also of Bigfoot, Men in Black, shadowy lizard overlords, aliens—and most likely the ghostly essence of deceased Bigfeet, Men in Black, shadowy overlords and aliens, which made them terrible subjects for the show. Viewers are unlikely to believe something which comes from someone who will believe anything.

There was, however, said Ray, a far rarer fourth camp out there looking for answers or help: sober, ordinary folk whose lives had been turned upside down by experiences they were at a loss to explain, dealing with phenomena which ranged from unnerving to downright scary, and appeared genuinely inexplicable.

Anyone who watched the show knew the *Where the Dead Walk* crew believed in the existence of spirits and ghosts, and that save for Charles this had not always been the case. At the outset, most evident in series one, most of the crew had been sceptics. This was the show's stance behind the scenes, guided by a mission statement which argued the credibility of the show rested upon securing its viewers' trust. Investigations had to be serious and stringent. The most rational explanation for strange phenomena sought first, with the aim that if the crew did encounter things which were tricky to explain away the credibility earned lent those moments greater impact. If the audience grew to suspect the crew was a bunch of gullible twits anything they captured would be in question.

It was experiences like these which had changed the crew members' minds, one investigation in series two in particular. The crew were now as one; ghosts, hauntings, the supernatural, while not common, did exist, even if hard evidence to support the view still escaped them.

Chloe reached the first doorway. It was a bedroom and shared the same shag pile carpet covering the landing hallway. The walls were decorated in pale blue and cream stripe wallpaper. A large brass-framed bed, mattress bare, two tall wardrobes and a dressing table made up the furniture. Like the rest of the house, there was a forgotten feel to the space, as though it hadn't been inhabited properly for a long time. It was old-fashioned too. Not old-fashioned like *old* old-fashioned, Victorian, Edwardian, Georgian or anything like that, not centuries, but old-fashioned in the way her nan's house had been old-fashioned, a few decades out of step.

Chloe almost smiled, recalling how it used to drive her mum crazy how Nan flatly refused to redecorate, arguing the upheaval would bother her much more than the existing décor did. In retrospect, once Nan was gone, Chloe came to suspect there was more to it than that. She wondered if her nan just prefered to keep things as they had been when Granddad was still around, to keep as much of him as was left. The clues were there, if Chloe paid attention, like the ashtray still there beside his old armchair, even though Nan didn't smoke, and no longer allowed anyone else to in the house, or the Wilbur Smith novels next to her Catherine Cooksons on the bookshelf.

Mum never won the battle to redecorate, and it probably hadn't helped that neither Chloe nor her sister Kara were interested in adding weight to her campaign. They spent a lot of time at their nan's, often sleeping over when their mum was working late shifts at the hospital. Chloe secretly loved the spare bedroom they slept in, Mum's old room. It was like a time capsule, still full of stuff which belonged to Mum back when she was a teenager. There was an old boom box with a CD player *and* cassette decks and a tower of CDs full of bands whose members could be granddads now. Taking up one half of the surface of a chest of drawers, a chunky portable TV/VHS combo, which was around ninety percent box and ten percent screen, and portable only in the sense one person might move it a short distance without requesting assistance or risking a hernia. Kara was probably not as fond of these things, or possibly against redecorating; she just generally opted to be a contrarian whenever the opportunity presented itself.

For Chloe the unchanging nature of Nan's house made it feel comfortable and safe, a fixed point, a small island among the churning, rolling rapids of life, and while it may have been dated, more so with every passing year, it was never untidy and always clean, right to up until the day Nan spent her final afternoon in front of the telly, not dozing with her mouth open as she sometimes did, but gone. Chloe remembered the phone call, the way she knew something was wrong from her mum's voice, even before she broke the news.

Chloe moved on, to the next doorway on the other side of the hallway, found another similarly dated and forlorn bedroom. This time she entered and strolled to the window. It was a huge timber-framed affair, like the others in the newer, although still very old, Georgian extension to the original cottage, and not far from the size of a small door. She looked out onto a garden, with hedges bordering a lawn, themselves fringed by trees. At the far end lay a wooden gate, with access to the woods beyond. She turned, ready to move on, and caught a glimpse of something moving past the doorway.

Had Charles or Ray finished looking around their area already, and moved on to hers?

"Charles, that you?"

No reply.

"Ray?"

She reached the landing in time to catch a whisker of someone slipping into the next room along.

She frowned, tried again, "Charles? Ray?"

Still no reply.

She advanced, reached the doorway and stared into the room, expecting to find Charles studying his surroundings in that way he had, lost in his head, as though he were trying to gauge the temperature or humidity rather than look or listen, or Ray studying some detail or other.

Only the room was empty.

Chloe entered, slowly turning to look around, and wondered, even though the idea was ludicrous, if one of them were hiding, squeezed into one of the wardrobes along the side of the room or slotted themselves beneath the bed. Even knowing it was ridiculous, and not really expecting to find one of her colleagues folded into an awkward ball inside, she pulled the mirrored doors of the wardrobe wide one by one, but save for a handful of lonely coat hangers the wardrobe was empty. If checking here hadn't been crazy, she figured, why not go the whole hog? She peeked under the bed and was equally unsurprised not to find either of her bosses splayed out beneath.

But she was sure she had seen someone—

The floor behind her creaked.

She turned, and there he was in the doorway, Charles, as neat and collected as he always was.

"Everything alright?" he asked. "Thought I heard you call me."

"Erm, yeah. I did… But it was nothing, I think, I just…"

"What?"

"I… thought I saw someone come in here."

"Go on."

"It was just a glimpse. Probably nothing."

Charles seemed to think about this. "Perhaps. Perhaps not? I'm almost done with the attic rooms. Why don't I go finish up and then we can switch around?"

"Yep. No rush. Looks like I've still plenty to check out here."

Charles nodded and headed back out into the hallway. Chloe went to join him, casting a parting look into the room, which caused her to collide with him an instant later. For some reason, he had stopped dead just outside the doorway. She was about to ask when she saw him staring down the corridor and tracked his gaze.

There was something there at the bottom of the landing, at the head of the stairs, a figure, dark as a shadow, there, but not there. Before her eyes and brain could really process anything beyond that it turned and took a step down the stairs, out of sight.

Charles looked back at her.

An instant later they were racing to the top of the staircase. They arrived there together and stared down.

There was nothing there.

"Um, Charles? Please tell me you saw that too."

"I saw it."

"Ho-ly fffffudge cake…"

Chapter Four

They were all with Giles Langley in the lounge, Chloe trying her best to focus on the present and put a lid on her excitement. Charles had cautioned her to keep what they had seen to themselves for the time being. Easier said than done. Part of her was fighting the urge to yell, "We just saw the ghost!"

Crow's Cottage, already interesting enough, had instantly become an immensely exciting prospect. All the more reason to tread carefully, said Charles. As it stood, Giles Langley was the one inviting them to investigate, and it could be preferable to let the balance rest that way until they knew more. "What about Ray?" she had asked. Charles had argued they should hold off telling him what they had seen until they left. Right now, Ray was, perhaps, the only one of the three of them thinking straight, certainly the most objectively. He would be focused on the house and how it might play on the show, haunted or not.

From an aesthetic standpoint, the cottage had the goods. Its crooked walls and low ceilings screamed ye olde, and darkness would lend it a claustrophobic feel which would work well on camera. The later Georgian expansion was strong too, also offering plenty of period detail tucked in around the whole middle of the road, upper-middle-class eighties vibe. This aspect was inescapable, evident throughout, in the various bedrooms, the two lounges, the kitchen, and dining room, the games room replete with a billiard table and a bar… The decade was draped over everything like cobwebs.

Crow's Cottage wasn't run down. Far from it. It was clean enough, but had an abandoned vibe. Giles Langley explained to some extent. Apparently, his late uncle, Hubert Langley, had owned a portfolio of various properties. Most were investments under long-term leases, but a few he retained for his own use, as seems to have been the case with Crow's Cottage. Yet it was hard to believe Hubert Langley had used it all that often, given he hadn't felt moved to spruce the place up in decades. It certainly didn't scream of somewhere much loved, or much lived in.

Giles told them the inheritance had come as a complete surprise, a provision dating back to when he was a child. His brothers had been beneficiaries of properties too. Hubert had no children of his own and had never married.

The item that had been discovered, the Mephisto Arcane, sat on the coffee table before them. To Chloe, it looked exactly how someone might expect an occult device to look. It was a sort of wooden box, around three times as tall as wide, and tapered near the top, reminiscent of an antique metronome, only with a polished circular metal disc affixed to the head. The dark-stained casing was inlaid with strange symbols. On the front at the base was a brass plate with the name from Charles' story etched in fine script: *The Mephisto Arcane*. The thing was rather attractive, in a creepy Victorian back-alley curiosity-shop type way.

"Can you tell me how and where this item was discovered?" asked Charles.

"One of the tradesmen checking the place over found it," said Giles. "He was investigating some minor water damage on the ceiling below one of the first-floor bathrooms and went to check the pipework. When he pulled the panelling away from the bathtub, he found the thing sitting there. I assume it's been there for some time. It was a day or two after that one of the other tradesmen asked me directly if the cottage was haunted. He said he had seen a dark figure. I admit I didn't really take the fellow seriously, until a few days later when I saw it too."

"Could you describe the apparition?" Charles asked.

"It looked like a shadow. There for a moment, then just as quickly gone."

"How do you feel about what you saw?"

Chloe thought Giles Langley looked quite pleased.

"Truth be told, now it's had a chance to sink in, I think it's rather exciting. Lots of people inherit houses, far fewer a ghost. Do you think it's possible the spirit belongs to my uncle? Woken by the discovery of this thing perhaps?" Giles gestured toward the box.

"Do you have any knowledge of what this object is?"

Giles Langley shook his head. "I've not the foggiest, but I assume it must have belonged to my uncle Hubert, given his... interests. One cannot be related to an outrageously black sheep like my uncle Hubert without tales of his black sheepery entering family legend. I gather he had a lifelong fascination with the occult. I strongly suspect it to be the source of the friction which rendered him so distant. Uncle

Hubert, an occultist! Scandalous, and naturally hugely embarrassing to my grandfather and especially my father. The rift was deep enough I never got to meet him. My grandfather maintained tenuous contact, but Hubert and my father had ceased any sort of interaction long before I was born. My father seemed determined to pretend he didn't exist, and I expect the feeling became mutual. I would have liked to meet Hubert. I'm more than aware my father can be somewhat inflexible. Now I regret I never made the effort and weathered his inevitable displeasure. I can't but feel a certain kinship with Uncle Hubert, being something of a black sheep myself."

"Really?" said Charles. "How so?"

"Well, I'm not an occultist, granted, but unlike my brothers who followed my father into law, I greatly upset him by pursuing a career in publishing. I own a small publishing house. We specialise in poetry. My father is not one for the arts, flowery prose, metaphors or similes, existential musings, language devoted to the senses and emotions. He prefers the dry precision of clauses and amendments, exemptions, terms and conditions… I believe my choice irritates him still, although thankfully he hasn't gone as far as disowning me. Yet." Giles smiled.

Charles reached for the Arcane. "Would you mind if I take a look?"

"Not at all."

Charles picked the box up. Chloe leaned in for a closer look. Ray too. Charles turned it slowly, studying each facet. The bottom was clad in felt, the metal disc affixed to the top polished to a high sheen, creating a dull mirror. The symbols that decorated the case were beautifully done, inlaid in a lighter shade of wood, and polished so smooth the surface was seamless. Chloe had no idea what the symbols represented. They didn't look like any she was familiar with.

Charles raised his eyes to Giles again. "There were no sightings of the apparition prior to this being discovered?"

"Not that I'm aware of."

"If we investigate," Charles asked, "what are you hoping we might be able to do or discover?"

"I'm not well-versed, but the chap who suggested I contact you said you're sometimes able to help spirits find peace, move on? If the spirit haunting this house is trapped and unhappy, this would obviously be most desirable, especially if it belongs to my late uncle."

Charles nodded. "Assisting a spirit to continue its journey is sometimes possible, but also not something I can guarantee, and it's not always necessary. Malevolence is the exception. Most spirits are quite harmless. Many people find that once accustomed to their minor disturbances they can live happily with one."

Giles smiled. "While I'm sure that's true, my good lady wife may disagree. If you agree to investigate, what would that entail?"

"We would carry out research into the property, events that may point to a source of attraction for such an entity, individuals closely associated with it, your uncle in this case, and others who may have spent significant time here. These may offer clues to the spirit's identity, and finally, once we felt adequately prepared, the investigation would culminate in a night-long vigil."

"Well given what little I do know about my uncle Hubert I'd welcome learning more. I suspect he may have been quite the character."

"I suspect so too," Charles said, then added, "and obviously the device you found certainly warrants further investigation. If you were to let me keep hold of it for a while, I know people who might be equipped to tell me something about it. Even if it turns out not to be directly connected to the apparition it was almost certainly connected to your uncle."

"Of course. Whatever you think best."

-

Charles and Chloe had agreed to wait until they got back to Bennett White Productions to tell him what they had seen, but Ray's radar was too good for that. He quickly rumbled he was missing something.

They got around a mile down the road from Crow's Cottage before he pulled into the side of the road and said, "Okay you two, let's have it. Has to be something worth hearing because Charles here is far too quiet, and you," Ray craned his head around to get a look at Chloe, "look like you've drunk too much fizzy pop."

"You gonna tell him," Chloe said, "or shall I?"

"Go ahead."

So, she did. Only she got a bit wound up and overexcited and sort of started to babble by the time she got to the part where they saw the apparition. Charles helpfully took over and described what they'd seen in a more restrained fashion. Chloe had anticipated some degree of scepticism, but Ray never batted an eyelid. Not for the first time she wondered what he and Charles had encountered in the course of previous investigations; things that maybe hadn't ended up on screen.

"You both saw it?" Ray asked. "The same thing?"

They nodded.

Chloe tried to fix the instant in her mind, recall the figure, the way it stood at the end of the hallway like a swatch of shadow despite the daylight flooding in, and how it had suddenly stepped from sight down the stairs and vanished.

Ray nodded. "Charles, did you get any other impression of it?"

Charles shook his head. "No, nothing at all."

"A ghost and a device designed to view and contact the spirit world," he said. "And a whole new location to research and shoot on a very tight deadline."

Chapter Five

Chloe was in the lounge, shower-fresh, her dark unruly hair towel-dried and cowed from two rounds with a hairbrush, although, as usual, the result was closer to a draw than a victory.

They'd swung by Charles' first, dropped him back home. He had waved to them as they pulled away, *bye*, the creepy-looking box tucked under his arm. Then Ray had dropped her back at her flat. They planned to get the rest of the crew together first thing in the morning, tell them all about Crow's Cottage, the whole tantalising mess, the apparition, the discovery of the Mephisto Arcane, the magician, the occultist and the medium responsible for it, a dead record producer, a vanished woman, and the job of squeezing one more location into the present series.

Chloe was on her way to the kitchen when her phone, charging on the bookshelf, started to buzz and ring, or more accurately shriek. Her personalised ring tone was set to the Wilhelm scream, the beloved audio in-joke of many a film director. The overdramatic scream played out in its entirety and started to loop around by the time she doubled back and reached it. She looked to see who was calling, paused and grimaced.

MUM.

She considered leaving it to go to voice message, and then forced herself to answer.

"Mum?"

"Hello, sweetheart. Everything okay?"

"Yep. All fine."

"Good, good… Only when I called the other day you said you were going to call me back, and… well, it's been a while."

"Yeah, sorry. Slipped my mind."

"Everything good at work? Still enjoying it?"

"Yep. It's great."

"That's wonderful. I thought I might—"

"Look, Mum, this is going to sound rude, but I was just heading off to bed. Things have been super-crazy busy, we did a night shoot a couple of days ago and my body clock still isn't happy. Would you mind if call you back tomorrow?"

"Tomorrow?"

"Yeah. Tomorrow."

"Chloe, I…"

"Yeah?"

There was silence on the line, then, "Nothing. I'll speak to you tomorrow then. Go get some rest."

"Bye."

Chloe ended the call and set the phone back down to charge. She resumed her journey to the kitchen and collected a tumbler, a two-litre bottle of Pepsi from the fridge and a bag of Doritos and returned to the lounge. She slumped into the sofa, reached for the remote, woke up the TV and launched Netflix.

Now, what was the name of that series from the trailer she had seen, the one about some family being chased by the mob?

Chapter Six

For the purposes of research, Ray was ready to admit the internet was invaluable, once he accepted much of what lived there was a generous brew of nonsense, lies and utter inanity, occasionally diluted with a splash of hard fact.

For gaining a quick and dirty snapshot of almost anything, it was hard to beat. It depended on the subject, of course. If he wanted pictures of cats or the news, or latest opinions on the news, or pictures of cats, or pornography, or pictures of cats, or a wealth of information covering almost any aspect of pop culture really, the internet had him covered. What was there wasn't spread evenly though. Some topics were in leaner supply. Popularity was a factor, but so was time, especially when it came to news and how long ago the thing you were hunting for had occurred. News coverage from a pre-internet era was far less evident. Some big outlets had worked to get archive material available, but fewer than he might expect. The deeper beyond the millennium he grasped, the sketchier reputable information became.

In terms of internet geology, the 1980s was comprised of a fragile, ancient sedimentary crust of reclaimed and digitised old media, a mess of fragmentary fossils, debris culled from old news stories, radio clips transferred from audio cassettes, video transferred from home recordings of broadcast television, often at postage stamp resolutions. Much of this material was only there because some random fanatic had used it in a blog, or entered it into some wiki or built a rickety fan site to host it.

The internet was wonderfully democratic. Everyone could contribute, but unfortunately, everyone didn't fact check information, and once emboldened with a hyperlink, be it rumour or a total tissue of tripe, fancy could easily strut around dressed as fact. Ray preferred to trust in the work of journalists and documentarians, with reputations to maintain, official bodies with legal responsibilities to adhere to, or talking face to face with real people whose trustworthiness he could judge for himself. In short, he preferred his research, and the information collected, to have rigour, but this took time.

A Google search took seconds.

He soon found a handful of references to the scandal at Crow's Cottage, primarily through the deceased record producer, whose name turned out to be Len Arkin. The name was familiar. The top search result was Len Arkin's Wikipedia page.

Arkin had been half of the eighties pop hit production duo, Moore & Arkin, responsible for, or guilty of, a string of hits with fresh-faced artists. Ray struggled to recall any. He scrolled down the page. A couple listed rang a bell. Gary Swift's "Won't Break Your Heart (Again)" was a big one, and The Hope Sisters' "We Can Weekend" another.

Ray wasn't averse to pop music, but Moore & Arkin's brand hadn't done much for him at the time and was unlikely to have improved with age. Ray struggled to recall anything he would even be able to hum. It all blended into a bland melange of pop dance drum beats and cheesy choruses. Then and now he would list Moore & Arkin's song catalogue alongside piercings, sewage contaminated sea water, and pregnant insects among things he would prefer didn't get into his ears.

The date of Arkin's death was there though. Ray would, of course, confirm the date later, but according to Len Arkin's page he had been born in 1956 and taken his own life in 1988. Ray was not shocked to find the page made no mention of Crow's Cottage, or anything about a missing young woman, or indeed an occult device called the Mephisto Arcane.

The page instead confined its sparse few paragraphs to covering Arkin's successful collaboration with Dave Moore as Moore & Arkin. Ray hopped a link to the Moore & Arkin Wikipedia entry. It covered the formation of their partnership in 1984, their cultural impact, their pop music production-line-style hit factory, and their catalogue of chart successes. They were behind over seventy U.K. top forty hits, over thirty million records sold, earning them an estimated fifty million pounds. After Arkin's death, Dave Moore continued to write and produce, but to far diminished success.

While Ray recalled the pair's musical crimes, attaching faces and personalities to the men was trickier. He turned to YouTube in search of Moore & Arkin interviews. The pickings were slim, or those featuring Len Arkin were.

In every one Dave Moore did almost all the talking. Len Arkin was obviously the quieter and more reserved of the duo, relegated to adding nods and mumbles of affirmation to what Moore had just said. An ever-present pair of aviator shades served to render Arkin even more anonymous and forgettable.

Ray turned it all over in his head: Moore & Arkin, Crow's Cottage, a ghost, the Mephisto Arcane, and a story about summoning a demon that had to be nonsense.

Didn't it?

It was certainly possible something had happened to Arkin at the party at Crow's Cottage to cause him to take his own life, but something supernatural?

Hubert Langley, Edward Needham, and Damien Faulks, all members of some occult club, the Longwood Occult Society.

Occultist.

Medium.

Magician.

Ray googled "Damien Faulks".

A string of links to various websites populated one side of his browser, and a potted bio from Wikipedia with a handful of pictures of Faulks the magician appeared on the other. All the shots hailed from the eighties, Faulks arranged in a variety of poses and outfits, ranging from svelte black polo neck sweaters to jet black suits with the shoulder pads of the era. The conjuror's image was clearly shooting for moody and mysterious. A favourite pose seemed to be one where his pale blue eyes gazed intensely up from beneath tipped brows, his hands sometimes posed in front of him as though he were about to conjure something from thin air. On one hand he wore a distinctive silver double ring that united his ring and pinky finger. Faulks had been objectively good-looking. All the key elements were there, the classic Don Johnson/George Michael stubble, the sunbed tan, the big hair, set with enough hairspray to deflect a small calibre bullet...

Ray heard a polite cough.

Behind him he found Julia leaning in the study doorway, her face artfully arranged into an expression of mock confusion.

"Excuse me? Are you my husband?" she said. "Only you look like him, but my husband said he would be down shortly, and that was over two hours ago. If you see him can you ask if he wants a cup of tea before I turn in to read a few chapters of my book?"

"Sorry, love. Lost track of the time."

"Work all day and all evening?"

"I was just checking on something."

She came over and stood beside him, looked down at the laptop's screen.

"I remember him. Damien Faulks, the magician? What are you looking him up for?"

"Do you remember him being involved in some story in the eighties? Something to do with a record producer topping himself? The last place the guy was seen alive was a party Faulks threw. Some interesting guests, starting with his two close friends, an occultist and a medium. According to some stories that went around afterwards a woman at the party went missing the same night too."

Julia shook her head. "I just recall him being an occasional face on TV, the sort you would see on celebrity panel game shows and whatnot. Famous, but not *famous*, if you know what I mean. At some point, he did seem to just disappear. Which is quite fitting for a magician, I suppose."

"We've been invited to investigate the property where the party was thrown. There have been reports of an apparition."

"Sounds like the opening to a joke. A magician, an occultist and medium go to a party… Except a man committing suicide and girl vanishing isn't the funniest punch line is it?"

"No."

Julia sighed, leaned down and curled her arms around him, planted a kiss on his stubbly jaw.

"Try not to wake me when you come to bed?"

"Honestly, I won't be much longer. You'll probably still be reading."

"Hmm. Just try not to wake me, okay?"

Chapter Seven

Charles was thinking. The apparition had only been there for a second, but it had been there. Indistinct, dark as a shadow, but very real. Chloe had seen it too.

The Mephisto Arcane rested before him on the coffee table, looking every inch how one might expect an occult device should, from the arcane symbols skilfully embedded into its surface to the strange polished metal disc affixed to the head of the case. Charles rather suspected this was the intention. It was worth keeping in mind the man who had crafted it was a magician after all, all too aware of the power of appearance, accustomed to leading an audience to a conclusion of his choosing.

He picked it up again, gripped it firmly in both hands and closed his eyes, relaxed, emptied his mind and opened himself up…

Waited.

Even reached a little.

But, as with every previous attempt, received no impression at all.

His gift was modest and often mercurial, but for a device tales claimed had beckoned a demon, snatched a young woman into a realm of darkness and driven a man to insanity, it surely wasn't too much to expect to feel something, some vibration, some residual energy… He set it back down.

He had experience dealing with the occult, witchcraft, and its misuse. He had seen 'workings' employed, the ways someone gifted and schooled might attempt to marshal the spirits to do things for their own selfish ends. These things were real, but they were also uncommon, beyond most people's knowledge, and bound by rules.

He set the device down, headed for his kitchen.

Impression or no impression, there was no question the object was mesmerising and darkly beautiful in a baroque, gothic fashion. Crow's Cottage was not short of similar charms, and a property of its age always had some interesting history, but the object's discovery and the resulting presence of an apparition made the story about Arkin and the missing young woman a worthy candidate for fresh investigation. Damien Faulks, Edward Needham, and Hubert Langley's connection to the Longwood Occult Society was yet another tantalisingly rich seam to mine.

Charles had once met the Longwood Occult Society founding member, John Bartleholm, in the early 2000s, after being invited to an exhibition of occult art. Charles had been dating a collector who had agreed to lend a few of his pieces to the event. One of the works was by Samantha Carrington, a close friend of John Bartleholm and his wife Eleanor. Charles' date knew the three well and introduced him to them.

John Bartleholm had looked frail and not in the best of health. He was suffering from Parkinson's disease, and the signs of its advance weren't hard to detect. Nevertheless, he remained a striking and magnetic presence. His wife Eleanor and the artist Samantha Carrington flanked him like Swiss guards.

Seen as a key figure in forming and shaping the public's perception of the occult in 1970s Britain, John Bartleholm had been at the vanguard of the nation's growing interest in paganism, witches, black magic and the occult. Charles was familiar with the theory regarding what sparked this phenomenon, the repeal of the Witchcraft Act in 1951 coupled with the growth of a sixties' youth culture eager to shake off the previous generation's norms. Whatever the cause, there was no doubt a new curiosity about spirituality had emerged. The Beatles studied transcendental meditation with the Maharishi, others looked to Buddhism or Native American mysticism, and many British folk looked closer to home, to Anglo-Saxon England for answers.

These people began to practice forms of Wicca and witchcraft, enough of them for the mainstream to take note, birthing a wave of popular books and movies, such as the novels of Dennis Wheatley, Hammer Films' *The Wicker Man,* and the rediscovery of figures like Aleister Crowley

By the eighties, though, this interest in the occult was losing steam, and it seemed interest in the Longwood Occult Society faded with it. Some still remembered the name though, among them Edward Needham, Hubert Langley, and Damien Faulks. The three men had sought to resurrect the group. The unwelcome attention of the press surrounding Len Arkin's suicide may have ultimately led to their revival being short lived, but it had survived long enough for the trio to craft the Mephisto Arcane now sitting on Charles' lounge coffee table.

Samantha Carrington was still a working artist, her work desirable among those with a taste for occult art who could afford the increasingly rare pieces she put to market.

Charles finished fixing himself an espresso and returned to the lounge.

He turned the Mephisto Arcane so its polished metal disc faced him, caught his face reflected there, diffused and distorted by the disc's dull and not quite even surface, a combination of funhouse mirror and an impressionist watercolour—

And saw something which caused him to jolt back, a dark shape looming over his shoulder. His hand grazed his coffee cup, almost tipping it over. Some of its contents slopped over the lip across the table. He snatched the Arcane away from the spill and quickly whipped around.

Nothing was there.

He glanced back into the metal disc again but saw only his own expression thrown back, blurry, warped and bent with consternation.

No dark shape to be seen.

Chapter Eight

Light spilt through the large windows of the Bennett White Productions' meeting room, stencilling bright rectangles of morning sunshine onto the large table at its centre. The *Where the Dead Walk* crew were gathered around it, Charles, Ray, Claire their logistics queen, Mark the lead camera operator, Keith the secondary camera operator and technician and sound guy, and of course Chloe herself.

They were originally meant to have been covering outstanding tasks for the final shoot of the series, at a closed and crumbling boys' school, but the previous day's events had changed all that.

Ray told the other three about Giles Langley and Crow's Cottage, the reported activity, and of course the discovery of a strange object. Ray had asked Charles to repeat the story he had told them when they had first quizzed him about the Mephisto Arcane. They then recounted their visit to Crow's Cottage, what Charles and Chloe had witnessed, and their chat with Giles Langley.

The Mephisto Arcane was returned to the centre of the table, after being passed around. Everyone got a good look at it.

There were no dissenting voices. Everyone agreed Crow's Cottage was too valuable and intriguing to push out to next series, and there was a risk Giles Langley might be tempted to seek help elsewhere if informed the investigation wouldn't be carried out for perhaps another four to six months.

"We have a lot to do then, and not much time to do it in," Ray said. "I started looking into a few things last night and again this morning. Internet mostly, much of it to be confirmed or corroborated, but given that proviso allow me to present for your listening pleasure a tasty buffet of fact, supposition, hearsay and filthy rumour."

Ray stood up and collected the marker under the whiteboard fixed to the meeting room wall.

"As far as persons of interest go, let's start with Crow's Cottage's former owner, Hubert Langley, our host Giles Langley's recently deceased uncle."

Ray wrote HUBERT LANGLEY on the board.

"Seventy-eight years of age at the time of his recent passing, Hubert was honest-to-goodness English aristocracy, albeit lower rung. As the eldest of three sons, he inherited the mantle of the Seventh Baron of Loncombe in 1972, along with seventy-five thousand acres in northern England. He studied history at Oxford and travelled widely throughout his life, documenting the folk stories and the esoteric practices of different cultures. Which I think is Burke's Peerage's way of saying checking out 'weird occult crap around the world'. At some point in the eighties, he struck up a friendship with Edward Needham and Damien Faulks."

Ray wrote EDWARD NEEDHAM on the board too.

"Edward Needham? Middle class, home counties kid, studied English language and literature at university but was practising mediumship even then.

By his mid-twenties, he had enough of a reputation to fill large venues across the country."

Ray added DAMIEN FAULKS to the board.

"Damien Faulks? A name you might vaguely remember if you're old enough to recall the days when British TV meant a trio of channels and the test card after midnight. He was a stage and television magician. Never had his own show but was a frequent enough face on other entertainers' to justify sticking 'as seen on TV' on his tour posters. In the mid-eighties, if there was a royal variety performance, you wouldn't have been shocked to see him doing a five-minute turn somewhere between Keith Harris and Orville, and Lenny Henry.

"Langley, Needham and Faulks also happened to be members of a group called the Longwood Occult Society."

Ray added THE LONGWOOD SOCIETY to the list.

"The Longwood Society was a sort of club for people with an interest in the occult and the spiritual, parapsychology, Wicca, black magic, and the general paranormal," Ray said, waving a finger at the Mephisto Arcane. "The three were also responsible for the creation, or recreation of that funny looking thing on the table there.

"In 1988 Damien Faulks was living in Crow's Cottage, I assume renting the place from Hubert Langley. One evening he threw a party. A record producer named Len Arkin attended. When Arkin left it, he climbed into his car, drove to the coast, stripped down to his birthday suit, abandoning his clothes, a wallet containing cash, credit cards and his driving licence on the beach, waded out to sea and kept going until turning back wasn't an option. His body was never recovered, but he was officially declared dead in absentia a couple of years later.

"According to stories passed around after the event, a young woman who also attended the party was said to have gone missing, although I've found nothing to support that yet."

Ray added, THE MEPHISTO ARCANE, CROW'S COTTAGE, PARTY, LEN ARKIN, and MISSING GIRL?

"I think we have the makings of an amazing episode, but to get it in this series we're really going to have to hustle, sort fact from fiction, see if we can find out more about what actually happened to Arkin. The thirty-year gap's going to make that a challenge, but on the other hand, people who mightn't have been keen to talk at the time might have looser lips now if it feels like ancient history.

"We'll be looking to approach Edward Needham and Damien Faulks, see if they're willing to chat to us. On camera would be fantastic. If not, any information we can get out of them will still be welcome. Obviously, there'll be no chatting to Hubert Langley, but we can talk to people who knew him. I called Giles Langley first thing, asked if he might put me in touch with the lawyer who handled Hubert's estate. Someone from the firm called me back shortly after. Clearly Hubert was a valued, and probably valuable client. They confirmed what Giles told us. Hubert hadn't been in contact with any of his family for years. He knew he was sick for quite a time, fighting a losing battle with lung cancer. He had been living in various properties abroad for the last few years, but it seems once his condition reached a certain stage he returned to his home in England, to die, in private. For the last year or so of his life, Hubert Langley's nursing team provided not just his care but most of his company.

"I went back to Giles, and he was able to get hold of the contact details for the nurse heading Hubert's care team," Ray checked his notes, "a Nick Spokes. Chloe, fancy trying to see if you can arrange a chat with him? See what he might be able to tell us regarding what sort of man Hubert Langley was?"

"Consider me on it."

"Great. Charles, any chance you have any contacts who might wangle us a chat with Edward Needham?"

Charles nodded. "I well might. Leave it with me."

"Good. I'll see what I can achieve on the Damien Faulks front. Let's get busy then."

Chapter Nine

The outfit responsible for Hubert Langley's palliative care was located in Knightsbridge, a private hospice which looked frighteningly exclusive. Chloe got the impression it catered to a very specific sector of the sick people market, ones who had deep pockets.

Chloe had checked out their website before calling Hubert Langley's lead nurse, Nick Spokes. The site was slick, designed with a minimally expensive look which suggested even its pixels were more exclusive than the norm. Facilities and offerings were presented, and the extent of its services, how clients could choose to receive care in one of their private hospices or be provided with expert nursing teams to be cared for around the clock in their own home. Hubert Langley had obviously chosen option B.

She called Spokes after the morning meeting and explained that she was seeking to gather information about Hubert Langley for his nephew, Giles Langley. To Giles' surprise, explained Chloe, he had been one of the beneficiaries of Hubert's estate. Due to long-standing family tensions and a rift, Giles had never actually been able to meet his late uncle, now a source of regret. While eager not to tread on any family toes, he would like to know something about Hubert, and what sort of person he was. Nothing confidential, just to gain a general picture.

Spokes seemed sympathetic. Chloe asked if he would be willing to spare her a few minutes to chat face to face, maybe even today perhaps? He said if she could reach Knightsbridge around noon he could. He knew a nice park nearby to grab some air on his breaks. He gave her the address and said to ask for him at reception.

She arrived just after twelve, emerged from the nearest tube station and made her way to the hospice. The place matched her impression from the website: exclusive, expensive. Once inside, the building's reception presented more like the foyer of a space-age luxury hotel than a medical facility.

At the reception desk, an immaculate creature in a blinding white uniform, pristine hair and faultless makeup called Arabella Luddington (her name was stitched into her breast pocket) received Chloe with a glacial smile and asked how she could help.

Her accent was so refined Chloe felt her own northern one should come with a flat cap and a whippet. She explained she was here to meet Nick Spokes. He was expecting her.

Arabella, who was perhaps only a couple of years older than Chloe, but somehow seemed considerably more, dryly instructed her to take a seat. Chloe wondered if she might have earned a bit more warmth if she had spoken less like a shipbuilder and had been carrying a Louis Vuitton bag or wearing Jimmy Choos instead of Chuck Taylors.

She had fallen into musing the question of how long Arabella took to ready herself for work in the morning (to get even close to as polished Chloe would have required a crack team of beauticians beginning work around midnight) when a man she easily identified as being Nick Spokes descended a nearby staircase and approached her.

It was easy to identify him because, like Arabella Ludington, his name was stitched into the chest of his uniform, although his was of the scrub style and pale blue.

Spokes was lean and a little gangly, with a nice face and a crop of dark brown hair, cut into a short unfussy style. At some point, it might even have had a comb run through it. When he greeted Chloe, his accent was blessedly working class.

-

"What was Hubert like?" Nick Spokes said. "A complete gentleman, intelligent, educated, maybe a touch eccentric, although experience has taught me the upper classes often are. Friendly and well-mannered, even as things progressed and he was sometimes suffering a lot of discomfort. That always says a lot about someone for me."

They had found a pleasant spot in the park to sit down, a big wooden bench under an oak tree. Spokes was right, it was a lovely space, quiet, bordered by tall privet hedges. A slice of tranquillity built of plants, trees and grass. Chloe wouldn't have known she was in the middle of a big city unless she lifted her chin.

"How long did you care for him?"

"For around five months in all. Palliative care for late stage lung cancer. I was team senior."

"The cottage he left Giles came as something of a surprise. Crow's Cottage? I don't suppose he ever mentioned it?"

Spokes gave it some thought. "Sorry, doesn't sound familiar. I think he had several properties, but I knew his one in the city where we cared for him."

"Did you like him?"

"I did. Hubert was good company, very sociable."

"Lots of visitors?"

"No, not many. I meant he was very sociable with the team. I suspect he hadn't told people he was ill."

"That's quite a thing to keep to yourself, isn't it?"

"Not as rare as you might imagine. Everyone deals with the knowledge they have a terminal illness differently. I've learnt not to assume anything. Some people want to be surrounded by friends and family, spend as much time with them as they can, while they can. Other people choose a more solitary journey. My job is to respect and support a patient's choice, whichever it is, trust it's one which allows them to meet death feeling ready, or at least without fear or bitterness."

"Did Hubert seem ready?"

"I hope he was," said Spokes. "Knowing you're about to die is hard to absorb. Not just that you're going to perish someday, but sometime soon. In months, weeks, days."

Chloe didn't doubt it, although perhaps death had to be less scary for people with faith, a belief that death is not the end?

"According to his nephew, family stories paint Hubert in a... colourful light. Giles was led to understand he was, sorry, there's no real way to say this without it sounding melodramatic, an occultist?"

Spokes smiled. "I'm not sure he was an *occultist* as such. I struggle to picture him surrounded by pentangles, daubing animal blood on captive virgins or cavorting around bonfires in a goat mask or whatever. He had an interest *in* the occult, but I think it was more academic than practical. I believe he spent most of his life travelling, studying and writing about occult beliefs, folklore relating to magic and the supernatural. All over the globe."

"Would he often talk about that type of thing?"

"Sometimes. My job is to make the people I care for comfortable. Attending to their medical needs is a large part of that, administering treatment, managing physical pain, preventing ancillary issues their condition might result in, like pressure sores, infections, but there's another aspect too, just as important. You're supporting someone who has a lot weighing on his mind, a lot of stuff to process, who facing death, may naturally be reflecting on his life. That means listening and talking. We discussed all manner of things, at length."

"But the occult was one of them?"

"It was. Hubert was keen to dispel misconceptions I had. It obviously bothered him the word occult is generally taken to mean something sinister or evil. Apparently, in Latin, it translates as 'knowledge of the hidden'. He felt the stigma prevents people understanding and discovering older views of the world, of spirituality and reality, that pop culture today just perpetuates centuries of propaganda. Belief systems predating Christianity or Islam were literally demonised in an attempt to stamp them out. Old meant evil and bad, new meant right and good. It wasn't a gentle campaign either. According to Hubert, fifty thousand people were executed during various witch trials in Europe. Does sort of beg the question which side was good, and which side was really evil, eh?"

"I don't suppose Hubert ever mentioned any old friends who shared the same interests? Maybe a Damien Faulks or an Edward Needham, or a club he once belonged to, the Longwood Occult Society? Maybe something called the Mephisto Arcane?"

"The what?"

"The Mephisto Arcane. It's a wooden box with a shiny metal disc fixed to the top, lots of strange symbols all over it."

Spokes shook his head again, but a wariness had crept into his face. Chloe sensed if she wanted to know more, she was going to have to explain why. She wasn't sure if honesty was always the best policy, but it was a policy which had the merit of coming with the fewest and simplest terms and conditions.

"There was clearly a lot more to Hubert than his interest in the occult, but there is a reason why it's of particular interest to his nephew Giles," she said. "The place I mentioned, Crow's Cottage? Since Giles took ownership there have been sightings of an apparition. They seem to have begun after an object was discovered, it appeared to have been deliberately hidden. Hubert allegedly had a hand in making it."

"This Mephisto Arcane thing?"

"Yeah. It's supposed to let someone view and communicate with spirits. The one which was discovered in Hubert's old cottage is alleged to be a replica of one destroyed a few centuries ago."

Spokes was still smiling, but a little more uneasily now. "And... does it?"

Chloe smiled and shrugged, trying to keep it light. "Maybe if you know how to work it?"

"O-kay. So… Hubert's nephew is afraid he's put some black magic on the house he left him?" Spokes' uneasy smile persisted, as though he had somehow found himself in a different conversation to the one he thought he'd been having. "I have to say, even if I thought that sort of thing was possible, I couldn't see it. I don't think the Hubert Langley I knew had a mean bone in his body."

"I'm sure you're right. We're just trying to find out what we can. Obviously—"

A phone began to ring. Nick Spokes pulled his mobile out, saw the number and sat bolt upright. "Sorry, do you mind, I need to… Important call."

"Of course, go ahead."

Spokes left the bench, walked a few feet, turned his back slightly and stared at his phone's screen for a moment. Chloe detected an instant of hesitation before he hit accept as if he were girding himself. He was only a short distance away so it was impossible not to catch his side of the call.

"Hello?" he asked. "It is." He nodded, and some very interesting body language followed as someone on the other end of the call relayed information and Nick Spokes received it: stiff-backed apprehension, nodding understanding, followed by obvious elation when a small fist pump followed. "That's brilliant." He nodded again. "I am, very. You too. Thank you." He ended the call, let out a whoop, and then belatedly remembered he wasn't alone. He turned back to face Chloe looking slightly embarrassed, but still beaming like a loon.

"I did it."

"Congratulations."

He shook his head. "You know I'm not sure I can believe it. It feels like I've been working towards it for so long... I think it might to take a while to sink in, you know?"

Nick Spokes' exhilaration was infectious, Chloe found herself swept up in the moment and grinning too. She decided she should probably know why.

"Sorry," she asked, "would it be considered rude to inquire what exactly we're celebrating?"

"Oh right. Bit of a red-letter day. I just had an offer accepted on a house I'm buying my mum. Well, enough of one she won't find the remaining mortgage payments a struggle."

"You're buying your mum a house? What are you, some secret nurse millionaire?"

"Ha. No, just the nurse part, but one who worked hard and saved harder."

"Wow, you must really think a lot of your mum."

"She deserves it, trust me." He slipped the phone back into his pocket, wiped a hand across his jaw and collected himself. "Sorry, where were we?"

Chloe tried to think if there was anything else to ask. She seemed to have covered all the major questions. Maybe it would be wiser to leave it for now, but leave the door open to contact Spokes again if something came up later.

"You know, I think I'm all good. Really, thank you for sparing the time."

"No problem."

She fished out a business card, offered it to Nick Spokes. "In case anything we discussed should come to you later?"

Nick Spokes accepted it. Gave the card a quick look over. It was an almost black, matte dark green. The Bennett White logo, WHERE THE DEAD WALK, with her name and Presenter/Investigator set in crisp white type. Chloe loved her business cards. The novelty was yet to wear off. Having them felt official, like a warrant card or a sheriff's badge. So okay, it wasn't remotely like either of those things, but it was still pretty cool.

Nick Spokes accompanied her out of the park, and she thanked him once more for making time to see to her and congratulated him again on his good news. He thanked her and said he hoped he had at least been some help. They wished each other goodbye. Nick Spokes headed back toward the grand-looking hospice, and Chloe headed in the direction of her tube station.

-

Chloe was waiting on the tube platform when her phone started to ring. The number wasn't one she recognised, but she answered it anyway.

"Hello?"

"Hi. It's Nick? Nick Spokes? From around half an hour ago? Hubert's nurse? Loony who whoops in parks?"

Chloe laughed. "Of course. Did you remember something?"

"Ah, not exactly... Look, I was kinda of wondering if you might like to, and feel free to say no if you don't, I honestly won't be offended, I mean you're probably already with someone, but if not... Would you... fancy going out for a drink sometime? I know this might seem a bit, erm, forward, given we've literally only just met and—"

"Yeah."

"Yes?"

"Yeah. When?"

"Oh. Well, let me think. Are you doing anything tonight?"

"Looks like I might be now."

-

"Granted," Chloe said, "he didn't know Hubert Langley before he was sick, but according to Nick Spokes, Hubert was decent, modest, likeable and not at all overtly black magicky."

They were in Ray's office, Chloe was catching Charles and Ray up on her Spokes meeting.

"And Hubert Langley never once mentioned the Mephisto Arcane or even Crow's Cottage?" Ray asked.

"Nope. Nothing doing for Edward Needham, Damien Faulks or the Longwood Society either."

"Speaking of Faulks," Ray said, "I have an address and a number for him, a club he owns. I called. He wasn't there, but I managed to speak to one of his staff, asked if they could get him to call me back. The place is a restaurant magic show affair. You eat and drink and watch ladies get sawn in two or whatever, and in between they have people perform close magic at the tables. It's called The Effectary."

"The Effectary?" Chloe asked.

"I looked it up. Its stage magician terminology. An *effect* is the term for how illusion is perceived by the spectator. What seems to be happening versus what's really going on—the effect on the audience. You had any luck on the Edward Needham front, Charles?"

"I contacted a friend who's still in touch with him. She said she would speak to him, see if he might agree to talk."

"Okay, fingers crossed."

"I'm seeing Nick Spokes again later," Chloe added. "Maybe he knows a bit more about Hubert Langley than he realises."

Ray cast Charles a glance. Chloe caught it too.

"What?" She shrugged. "He asked me out for a drink."

"You're going for a drink with him because he might know more about Hubert Langley."

"Oh, no. I'm going out for a drink with him because he's a bit of a hottie. That a problem?"

Ray shook his head. "Nope, not at all. You have a problem with that, Charles?"

Charles raised his hands. "My dear, your romantic pursuits are entirely your own business. Although… as a young lady, I would hope you exercise an appropriate degree of caution when meeting someone you don't know well."

"Charles has a point," Ray added. "I'm sure this Spokes guy is fine, but just in case make sure you don't leave your drink unattended and be careful not to put yourself in a vulnerable situation."

"A sensible precaution," Charles agreed. "Stick to somewhere public, where other people are, and if you get a bad feeling about things don't be afraid to cut and run."

"Yeah, call a cab, tell him you're going to the ladies," Ray said, "and then duck out a side door."

"Better to be safe than sorry," said Charles.

Chloe nodded dutifully. "Yes, Dads. I'll pick up my extra spicy pepper spray." She swung her legs and hopped off the edge of Ray's desk. A few more steps and she was at the door. Behind her, Charles and Ray were both shaking their heads.

"Look, I promise I'll be careful."

"Then I hope you have a lovely evening," Charles called after her.

"You bet."

Chapter Ten

They arranged to meet at a bar called Brewdoo in Camden. The frontage featured a cartoon voodoo doll holding a pint of beer as large as its head. Perched on the corner of the street, the place had once been a traditional old London pub, but the cave-like interior had been thoroughly excised. Gone were the usual floral, beer-stained carpets and tables tanned so dark they looked like Viking shields, and in its place was a stridently modern-rustic aesthetic made up of huge windows, timber floors and exposed brickwork walls. Brewdoo was hip and trendy and consequently filled to the brim with hip and trendy denizens. Chloe's home city of Leeds was hardly a rural backwater, but the definition was more acute here. London was different, bigger, grander, older, hipper, richer. Its people reflected the character of the capital, a place more aware of itself, more than just another city in England—and they behaved accordingly.

The place struck her as an odd choice for Nick Spokes. Once out of his scrub style uniform he was dressed nicely enough, but not in the mode of the fashion-conscious crowd around them. Not one for fancy labels, Chloe probably looked similarly out of step.

They had managed to secure half a table and a couple of stools, in a spot where the sound system was distant enough to allow for conversation. Nick was currently in the middle of assuring her he didn't ask out every woman he met.

"In *ages*? I'm not sure I believe that." Chloe fixed him with a sceptical eye.

"I swear on my life, I haven't been on a date in… good grief, maybe six months?" Nick took a sip of his pint and brushed away a slim strip of beer moustache, a totally casual gesture, but one Chloe found inexplicably sexy. Maybe it was the lips. He did have sexy lips.

"I have to say I do find that surprising," she said. "I mean, you're conservatively the right side of repulsive, and being a nurse? Caring for the vulnerable and poorly? I'd have thought that's worth no end of brownie points with the ladies."

"You'd think so, right? And don't forget the dorky uniform and the intoxicating scent of hand sanitizer. I should be fighting women off." He grinned, and took another sip of his beer. "Sadly, nursing, especially the area I'm in, doesn't always fit well with a rich social life or a budding relationship. The hours are frequently unsociable and subject to plenty of unexpected overtime. Shifts, nights, evenings… And if a patient is approaching the end of their life, you can't just clock off and dash. It's not that sort of job. To do it well, you do actually need to *care*."

A tall, muscular guy had stopped behind Nick.

"And I suppose your pitiful dating record has nothing to do with you being a workaholic?"

Nick looked around and groaned. "Urgh. I should have known you'd do this."

"What? I'd totally forgotten I suggested this place. We were just passing by. Meet Sharon. Sharon, meet Nick. My friend, flatmate, technically my boss…"

"Hi Nick," said a woman trailing the talkative newcomer, blonde, pretty and clearly a recent acquisition.

"Hi, Sharon."

Before Nick had the chance to introduce Chloe, the man had turned his attention to her anyway.

"You must be Chloe?" he said. "Pleased to meet you. I'm James, James Barlow. Sharon. So, what are we drinking?"

The answer turned out to be 'lots'. James Barlow not only returned with a fresh round of drinks but shots to chase them with. He was lively and good fun though, and Chloe soon worked out what was going on. James Barlow had unilaterally invited himself along to provide his friend with moral support. Whether Nick wanted it or not. Perhaps to excuse himself he did end up buying most of the drinks, mostly because he ignored everyone's protests that they were still halfway through their current one to disappear to fetch a fresh round, accompanied by more shots.

On the topic of pairings, as friends went, Nick and James made for an odd combo. James was as confident as Nick was reserved. Nick was built like a violin bow, with a relaxed attitude to grooming, tidy enough, but a far throw from fussy. James was built like someone better equipped to put someone in a hospital rather than attend to them once they were there, obviously a gym bunny, muscular but lean, and just as obviously mindful of his appearance in every other respect too. His hair was impeccably clipped, waxed and styled, and every item of clothing he wore was a designer label.

And yet for Chloe, Nick Spokes was by far the sexier of the two.

She was having fun, unplanned double date or not. James' date Sharon was nice. As well turned out as James, well dressed, tanned and toned, but very friendly and down to earth. Clearly they'd met using the same internet-dating keywords.

Four people made for easy conversation, and it was nice to be part of a crowd. Chloe felt like she was part of a night out with her mates, something she hadn't done for a long time. They talked a little about work, and Nick admitted he and James had checked out *Where the Dead Walk*, A show they were both aware of, but never actually watched.

"You're on *Where the Dead Walk?* That ghost hunting TV show?" Sharon asked.

"Yep, I'll be in the next series to air."

"Nick told me about the stuff with Hubert, the cottage he left his nephew you're looking into," James chimed in.

Nick clarified. "James was on Hubert's care team too."

Chloe's ear pricked up. "Really? What did you think of him?"

Barlow shrugged. "Nice chap. I think he took to Nick more than me, but he was always friendly. Remarkably down to earth given he was aristocracy, minor aristocracy, granted, but still. This old cottage the nephew got is haunted?"

"There have been several sightings."

"Of a ghost?"

Chloe nodded. "They all describe seeing something similar, a shadowy figure. It seemed to start after an object was discovered in the place."

"This is the thing that looked like it had been hidden?" James said. "What did you call it Nick? A Mephisto-sumthin-or-other?"

Nick looked to check with Chloe. "The Mephisto Arcane?"

"Yeah, that." James said. "You think it's linked to this ghost?"

"Well…" said Chloe, "according to legend, the Mephisto Arcane is meant to be a device designed to speak with the dead. The one we have is a replica. Supposedly Hubert helped recreate it with two friends back in the eighties, based off drawings of an original which maybe existed centuries ago. One of the friends was a magician and the other was a medium. There's more though, another story that came later, a sort of urban myth, that meddling with the device drove a man to madness and suicide, and led to a woman vanishing without a trace."

"Wow, so where's the thing now?"

"My boss has it, Charles McBride. He's one of the producers on our show and its medium."

"A device designed to talk to the dead and a shadowy figure, eh?" James smiled.

Chloe was on the cusp of telling him she had seen the apparition herself, then thought better of it. She recalled Charles' first date advice, only flipped. In this version it was Nick who excused himself to visit the men's toilet and promptly did a runner. She reckoned it might be wiser to keep the 'I see dead people' to herself for the time being.

"You believe that stuff exists then, ghosts, devices that let you talk to the dead?" James continued.

"I've had experiences which make me think some paranormal phenomena are real."

"I reckon spirits and ghosts could exist," said Sharon. "I've not experienced anything myself, but there's got to be something after we die hasn't there?"

Chloe noted neither James or Nick made any sign of agreeing.

"Nick?" James smiled. "How about you? You reckon there are things that go bump in the night?"

Nick appeared reluctant to answer. When he did, Chloe got the impression he had chosen his words carefully.

"James and I, we've seen a lot of people die," he said. "It's an inescapable part of the job. And... while we do everything in our power to help someone reach the end of their life with as much comfort and dignity as possible, it's not always with as much comfort and dignity as we might like. Sometimes it can be peaceful, but quite often it can be tough, sad, unfair, distressing... There is one constant, though, when death arrives it *does* feel like the end. It *does* feel final. I can't speak for James, but I've never seen anything to suggest any essence, or spirit is released, that something, anything endures. What we each are, the sum total? I believe it's right here, tangible, flesh and bone." Nick looked at Chloe. "Did I just completely blow my chances of a second date?"

"Not at all." Chloe smiled. "Look, I appreciate what you're saying, but what if it's more complicated than that? What if there's an element of us which can't be seen under a microscope, or captured in an x-ray or any other gadget?"

"Isn't that's a bit of a get out?" said James.

"Cats can see in the dark, we can't," said Sharon.

"Yeah, but science can explain why a cat sees in the dark," Nick said.

"Haven't you been somewhere," Chloe said, "and felt something, I don't know... Sensed something *other* about it? Consider all the reported cases of hauntings, apparitions, poltergeists... In every country and culture in the world, throughout the whole of history, the notion of a spirit is recognised and understood. That has to mean something, doesn't it?"

"I'm really not sure it does," said Nick. "Just because people believe something that doesn't make it real. Take Hubert, he spent most of his life studying the occult, witchcraft, voodoo, and who knows what else, but just because superstitions, ideas or stories get passed down that doesn't mean they have any basis in fact, or that Hubert believed any of what he came across."

"You said it yourself, Nick," Chloe countered. "Hubert was intelligent and educated. If he thought it was nonsense would he really have devoted his life to studying it? He was obviously fascinated with the paranormal, witchcraft and the occult. Are you absolutely confident he never practised it too?"

"She's got a point. And it's true what they say, the quiet ones are always the ones to watch out for." James winked. "Talking of spirits and whatnot, I'm off to get another round in. Same again?"

-

The taxi slowed and stopped outside her flat. The clock on the dash said 01:35. She hadn't intended to get back so late, or drink so much, but it had been a good evening, one she wasn't eager to call time on.

The delectable Nick Spokes was just inches away.

"Just here thanks," Chloe said. The drink was making her words furry at the edges. In that way someone could grow either less, or in this case exponentially more, attractive by getting to know him better, Nick Spokes had definitely developed into something of a fox over the evening. The idea of simply seizing him by the pelt and dragging him inside was very tempting.

"I hope you didn't mind. James?" he said. "I swear I had no idea he was going to turn up. I think he meant well."

"He was fun, and his date, Sharon, was nice."

"Yeah… It's best not to get too attached to James' ladies. He's a good mate, but his Tinder profile picture should probably show a revolving door."

"And you?"

"I don't have a Tinder profile."

They were close. Nick leant in to kiss her.

And it was good, good enough that combined with the copious amount of alcohol slooshing around her body, decorum was being put under serious strain. She was drunk, and drunk decisions aren't always good decisions, so she broke away.

"I like you Nick Spokes." She finished the statement with a courteous nod, and opened the cab door. "You have my number." She climbed out, closed the cab door behind her. Waved a hand at the driver in a shoo motion. The vehicle pulled away, taking Nick Spokes with it.

Charles and Ray would approve, she was sure, even if the devil on her shoulder was incredulous.

Chapter Eleven

Ray had served three decades in the Metropolitan Police Force, the body responsible for law enforcement in the Greater London area, making it to Detective Chief Inspector before retiring to start his own private detective agency.

Being a private investigator in real life was very different from how it was portrayed in movies and books. It was less smouldering 'noir femme fatales' offering fascinating mysteries and more 'nah femme fatales', brain-numbing tedium and leaden buttocks from sitting around all hours trying to stave off sleep without consuming too many cans of Red Bull while waiting for the opportunity to seize some flashy twit's sports car with payments six months in arrears, or grab a picture of someone cheating on their partner.

It had taken just five years of RAY DARLING PI for Ray to convince himself that full retirement didn't look so bad. But he had scarcely finished winding the firm down when a call out of the blue set him on a new course. Life, as it sometimes did, served up a dish he hadn't even considered might be on the menu.

A former client had suggested him to Henry White, the co-owner of a new production company developing a television paranormal investigation show. White was looking for someone to fill the position of lead location researcher. At first, Ray had been dubious. To begin with he didn't believe in ghosts, and secondly, he had never once felt the urge to appear on television.

On the other hand, he had learnt never to ignore his gut instinct, and in this instance his gut was insistent he go meet with Henry White and his business partner, Kate Bennett, who would also be the show's principal presenter. Ray had liked the pair from the get-go. When they explained only a tiny part of the job would involve appearing on screen (not entirely true) and most would be spent researching the history of locations the show meant to investigate, the people most closely associated with it and the events they were famous or infamous for, the gig started to sound increasingly tempting. As far back as his school days, Ray had loved history. His profession had taught him how, and where, to look for information, and left him with plenty of contacts who could prove valuable too.

Right now, he was keen to know what the investigation into Len Arkin's suicide had determined, and who had headed it. He still knew plenty of coppers, lots who were still in active service, and a good many who trusted him enough to share information with him, confident it wouldn't come back to bite them in the bum. One was Richard Daley, ten years Ray's junior, once a member of his team, and now a DCI himself.

He called Richard at home. They exchanged the customary banter, until Rich eventually said, "Go on then, what can I do for you?"

"I need a small favour."

"Go on…"

"There's somewhere I'm looking into for the show, a place called Crow's Cottage, in Surrey. It was linked to a suicide in the eighties, a record producer called Len Arkin topped himself after attending at a party there, got in his car, drove to the coast and swam out far enough until he got tired and sank. A young woman is supposed to have gone missing around the same time, also last seen at the party. Could you maybe take a peek into it? See what the police angle was, who was in charge of the investigation?"

"Leave it with me, I'll see what I can do."

"Thanks, Rich. You're a star."

Chapter Twelve

Chloe wondered, pushing two painkillers from their bubble packs and washing them down with water from the office cooler, if being a TV presenter was showbiz enough to get away with wearing sunglasses indoors, and, if so, where could she get a pair?

The Brewdoo had certainly cast its voodoo on her, leaving a hangover that felt uncannily like a curse. Who knew shots and fancy craft beers were a bad mix? The half dozen halves and who knew how many shorts she had gone through socialising with the delicious Nick Spokes and his friends had packed a wallop. She had overslept, which meant getting ready became a stopwatch shower and a blast of dry shampoo. The train journey in had been an unpleasant mixture of thumping head, swaying carriage and rolling stomach.

Ray caught up with her in the office's tiny kitchen, pouring hot water onto three heaped spoonfuls of instant coffee and two spoons of sugar. After trying a few angles, he had managed to speak to Len Arkin's old songwriting partner, Dave Moore, and talked him into a brief meeting. He wanted her to come along. Moore lived in the Midlands. They could be there in a couple of hours if the traffic was light. Chloe prayed for the roads to be smoother than the rails had been.

Dave Moore's recording studio was nestled behind his amazing neo-art-deco style house, both of which were surrounded by a copse of beech trees in the Leicestershire countryside. Ray and Chloe were buzzed in at the gate and intercepted by a guy who introduced himself as one of Dave Moore's engineers.

He guided them to a studio control room where Moore was seated, poised Captain Kirk style in front of a large mixing desk full of buttons and sliders before a huge glass window. In the live studio room beyond, on the other side of the window, before a microphone, stood a handsome Indian guy in a trendy newsboy cap.

Moore spotted them outside the door and held a hand up, mouthing, "With you in five." He asked the singer to go again. The singer nodded his head, and repeated a couplet of lyrics, holding the last note for an impressively long duration, then finished by pulling a face which suggested he wasn't happy with his performance. It sounded pitch perfect to Chloe, just not all that welcome in the midst of a hangover. The paracetamol had eased her tender head some, but quite not enough to appreciate singing at volume.

Feeling further clarification might be required he said, "Sorry, Dave. That was bollocks."

"Nonsense, but I'm fine with taking another run at it. Why don't we grab a short break, Kammal, yeah? Attack it again in fifteen?"

Kammal nodded and slipped off his headphones. Moore waved Chloe and Ray in, the engineer held the door wide for them, then made himself scarce.

The music producer swivelled his chair around to face them and invited them to take a seat on the sofa which wrapped around half the back wall of the studio.

Chloe noted he sported a suspiciously dark head of hair for a man of his age, styled in a restrained faux-hawk, above a set of thick-framed glasses. Middle-aged spread had given way to late-middle-aged spill.

"Ray Darling?" Moore said. "And this is…?"

"Chloe Harker," said Ray. "Our new presenter."

"Pleased to meet you, Mr Moore. Thank you for agreeing to see us."

Moore leaned back, folded his arms. "How could I possibly say no? *Where the Dead Walk* investigating Crow's Cottage? Last place I saw Len? I'd have to be an incurious fellow indeed not to be interested, wouldn't I?"

"You were at the party that night too?" Ray asked.

"Yep."

Moore's tone was light, but his defensive body language conveyed mistrust. Chloe took a stab at steering around it.

"You're producing for Kammal Hanif?" she asked. She had recognised the singer through the glass, despite him having faded from the media's interest for a few years. Hanif had been a big deal for a small while. His debut album had been massive, but his second album hadn't been received with similar rapture. His third album was yet to materialise. While still a performer who had sold millions, he was a casualty of the fast-moving nature of the pop business. Once the hits stop coming, fans move on.

"Producing and writing material for him. He's a talented kid, very talented. Wants his new album to capture an eighties pop vibe, so he came to me." Moore smiled, but it was restrained, an outlook tempered by wisdom. After decades in the business, from hot to not, he was akin to the seasoned mariner who had traversed oceans both capricious and calm, clung to masts through wild storms and sliced through docile seas, and probably come to expect both.

"A lot of artists are trying to capture the eighties feel right now," he explained, "especially kids who weren't even around yet. Just when I got comfortable being viewed as a dinosaur it seems I'm in demand again. I imagine it's the old days you're interested in though, eh?"

"We'd appreciate it if could tell us about Len, and what you remember of Crow's Cottage," Ray admitted. "The party, Damien Faulks, Hubert Langley and Edward Needham?"

Moore nodded but said nothing. He appeared to be sizing them up.

"Okay," he said at last, "but once I have, maybe you'll be good enough to allow me to ask you for something in return. Not a demand, just something I'd like you to consider, okay?"

"Okay."

Moore nodded. Ray began.

"We've been invited to investigate Crow's Cottage by the current owner," Ray said. "Giles Langley, Hubert Langley's nephew. Hubert Langley passed away recently and left Giles the cottage in his will. There have been sightings of a figure, an apparition."

"A ghost, eh?" Moore looked mildly amused. "And you fancy it might be Len?"

"It was the last place he was seen alive."

"It was the last place he was seen at all. To my knowledge, his body was never recovered. Ended up as fish food, the daft beggar." Moore had stopped smiling. "What a waste."

"What was he like?"

Moore seemed to consider the question. "As a friend? One of the best I had. As a man? Reserved. Thoughtful. Not always the easiest person to be around. As a musician? A genius. Stick an instrument in his hands… He could play the guitar, keyboards, drums, practically anything you could throw at him. He had a decent voice too, not that he ever sang outside of a studio. If you know where to listen you can hear him on some of the backing vocals of our stuff, though. He had a rare ear for a tune. That was his real gift. You'd be jamming with him, just fooling around and the instant you stumbled on something even half good, he would seize on it and spin it into a tune you couldn't quit humming all day."

"How did you meet?"

"The way musicians often do. I was in a band. He was in a band. This was back in 84. I was writing the material for my mob, he for his. We were both East End boys, played a lot of the same venues, shared a few friends and acquaintances. Unfortunately, neither of our bands seemed to be going anywhere. Both had come close to getting deals, but for one reason or another, it never happened. Not uncommon in this business. Anyone could see he was the one with talent among his bunch, so I approached him about forming a new band.

"We started writing together. Neither of us were great front man material, but we reckoned we could find the right face with the right voice when the time came, same for the rest. Get the material right. Build the right band around it. We were confident in what we were coming up with, made a good team.

"I was moonlighting as a DJ at the time, working the odd gig here and there to help keep the lights and heating on and help pay for studio time. The whole Chicago House thing was just blowing up. I was mega into it. Len not so much. One afternoon he knocked up a track to show how rudimentary he thought the sound was. It was meant to mock it, only I thought it was bloody brilliant. I worked on the track a bit, then played it at a few of the clubs I was working over the next week. Everywhere went mental for it. Ones who were up on the house scene, the types who weres regularly importing the new stuff, the DJs like me, they all wanted to know what the track was called, so they could get it.

"Without telling Len I got a few thousand copies pressed up, paid for with a credit card which already had a pretty scary balance, and took them to a bunch of independent record store guys I knew would agree to carry it. A week or two later every single one was calling me begging for more stock.

"The track was 'Gotta Jack', our first hit.

"Around the same time the Soak Studio in Camberwell, which we had been using, hit financial trouble and went up for sale. I told Len we should buy it. He thought I was nuts, even back in 84 people were saying there was no money in the studio business. I could tell deep down he liked the idea though, and the timing just seemed too much like fate. We made them an offer, everything 'Gotta Jack' had brought in, and what we felt we could reasonably borrow from the bank on top. They said yeah. We kept rolling, writing material for the new project, and putting out a few more House style tracks. A few of them did decently, but nothing like 'Gotta Jack'. Len never changed his mind the track was fluff.

"We started to rethink the whole band idea. We were starting to realise we were perhaps more songwriters and producers at heart. We considered pitching our material to established artists but didn't fancy how that would position us. Anyone who was already having success would also end up getting the better half of the deal. So, we did something else, with the arrogance that only the young or the stupid truly can muster, we decided we wouldn't write *for* pop stars, we would *make* pop stars. The amazing thing was we did, time and time again. We scored a couple of top ten singles with Rich Farley, then a number one with the Hope Sisters, a couple of hits with Sharla, F-U-N, and later, of course, an amazing string of hits with Layla Foster, and Gary Swift."

"You said Len wasn't the easiest person to be around. Did the success help?"

"No," Moore said. "Don't get me wrong, I loved Len, but you have to understand how he was; not so much a glass half empty or a glass half full type, as much as an 'I don't like this glass' type. Even at the height of it all, when we had multiple singles in the top of the charts, he would still moan and groan. Part of it was perfectionism, creative and professional pride… but a bigger part of it was that was just Len."

"You found it frustrating?"

"Oh yeah. Drove me bloody nuts sometimes. I felt Len wanted us to be something we weren't. We had a talent for writing and producing pop songs, and we were selling millions of them, but he would always bring it around to how we should be writing *real* music. I didn't get it. I wasn't embarrassed by what we made. I love pop music, loved it then, love it now. People talk like making pop is easy, like crafting a song millions of people will buy is the simplest thing in the world, if you're simply crass enough to appeal to the lowest common denominator…" Moore pulled a face. "Bullshit. The cool set, be they indie-rock, rap, R&B, or EDM, they all secretly dream of breaking out and earning fame and fortune. Very few artists honestly thirst for a tiny audience of cool kids over millions of regular people.

"It's a brand of snobbery, and it baffles me. You know at the height of our success Radio One, the biggest mainstream radio station in Britain, wouldn't play our stuff? They had to on the UK chart countdown, of course, they couldn't snub us there, but on general daily rotation? They had an unspoken policy not to. We weren't seen as cool enough, even though the British public were buying our records in the millions. The nation's most popular radio station wouldn't play the nation's most popular songs. Ridiculous. And I believe it fed into Len's discontent. It wasn't enough for him that millions of kids liked our stuff, he wanted to be respected, taken seriously. I don't want to paint him as some miserable so and so. We did have fun. Those years? They were a good time."

"In general, you got along?"

"Yeah. We were still relatively young back then. We went clubbing, out on the town together, parties..."

"Like the one at Crow's Cottage?" Chloe asked.

Moore smiled, pulled an odd expression. "I'm not sure many parties were like the ones at Crow's Cottage."

"In what way?"

"A bit of a strange crowd all said. Damien Faulks was in the entertainment business, and as you'd expect that meant there were other people from the business at the party too, friends, actors, agents, producers and what have you, but there were clearly people who belonged to another social circle he moved in, folk from weirdo world, psychics, mediums, that type. I guess there was some overlap; Edward Needham was there that night, the medium. He was kind of showbiz too. He performed stage tours, and had a few television specials, I think.

"Damien's magic act leant into that stuff, the occult, pentangles and weird symbols, but I'd always assumed it was shtick. Apparently not. His interest in the occult, black magic, the paranormal or whatever may actually have been genuine. There seemed to be another group in the mix too, a small contingent of toffs. Not just upper class and monied, titles. Faulks had a close friend who was a baron or something."

"Hubert Langley?"

"Yeah, that's right, Langley." Moore nodded, "The party? Len, Gary Swift and I wound up there that night almost by accident. We were out celebrating. We had finished recording the material we needed from Gary for his third album late the same afternoon. We left the studio and bopped from one place to another before landing in the VIP room at Stringfellows, where I bumped into an agent who represented an artist I knew—the agent's name was Gerald Darcy? Gerard Darcy? Anyway, we got talking and he said he was waiting for a taxi to take him to some private party in Surrey, Damien Faulk's place. He'd attended a couple before and said they were always worth a visit. He insisted we join him. Apparently, Damien loved mixing with people in the biz. We must have thought why not? Len wanted to go light on the booze, he usually did, so was driving, so we ditched the taxi and all jumped in his Mercedes instead. Rocked up at the cottage uninvited.

"I spotted a couple of recognisable faces walking in, soap stars, and Gerald, or Gerard, or whatever his name was, found Damien Faulks and introduced us. We used to keep a low profile back then, so I'm not sure Faulks recognised our faces but he knew who we were, and he obviously recognised Gary. Either way, he told us to make ourselves at home and have a good time."

"The other guests you mentioned, the ones from 'weirdo world,'" Ray asked, "the mediums and whatever, did they mix well, with the showbiz set?"

"Seemed so. In my experience, creative types are usually more into that kind of stuff. Artists are a superstitious bunch."

"How about you?"

"Nah. Not really one for superstition or religion."

"What about Len?"

"Not especially."

"Did he get involved with anything along those lines that evening? The night he..."

"Topped himself?" Moore said. "Yeah, he sat in on a séance Edward Needham conducted in one of the rooms. I think about half a dozen guests did, not sure how he got roped in. I don't think it went well. Edward Needham left shortly after. He didn't quite storm off, but he definitely wasn't happy. I heard he and Damien had a bit of a disagreement. I asked Len what had happened and he said Faulks deliberately made him look stupid during the séance. Needham obviously didn't see the funny side.

"That was the last time I would ever talk to Len. Not for one moment... We'd been in the studio the whole day, and all at once the hours seemed to catch up on me. I needed to crash. I didn't want to torpedo Len or Gary's night, so I called a cab, said my farewells to both and split."

"You saw no indication Len was unhappy, vulnerable?"

"No. Like I said though, it was hard to tell with Len. He was often downbeat. It was just his way, or maybe I'm just trying to excuse myself? I knew him well enough, I should have noticed something was wrong. If I had been there longer, spent more time with him, I might have recognised something was up. I honestly had no idea he felt low enough to take his own life. I knew he wasn't always happy, but to go and kill himself?"

Ray nodded, let the moment breathe, then asked, "Do you think anything could have happened at the party to tip him over the edge?"

"Like what?"

"I don't know."

"I asked Gary later if he saw any warning signs. He said not. What Len did was as much of a shock to him as everyone else."

"This is Gary Swift?" said Ray.

"Yeah."

Chloe was familiar with Gary Swift. Not because she was a fan of cheesy eighties pop music, but because of the actor and singer's return to the world of celebrity in the 2000s. Almost forgotten, he had been propelled back into the public eye due to the miracle of reality television. Anyone who watched the show knew Swift's story. After all, reality TV was all about the story. Swift's was one of fame, hubris, self-inflicted ruin, recovery and by the show's conclusion, redemption.

Gary Swift had been a big noise in the eighties, for a time, very big. His role as tanned, beaming, surfing, blond-haired teen heartthrob Luke Campbell in the Australian soap opera *Matilda Bay*, popular with British school kids thanks to its Monday to Friday five o'clock slot in the schedule, made him a household name. When his love interest and co-star Layla Foster recorded a single with Moore & Arkin during a British publicity tour, becoming a million-seller overnight, Swift elected to try his hand at the pop game too. He did equally well, racking up half a dozen number one singles, and becoming a pop icon until the wheels on the Swift cart grew wobbly.

While squeaky clean in the public eye, Gary Swift developed a taste for the nightlife, and in private, drink and drugs. It was only a matter of time before a scandal ensued, and the tabloid press did what they delighted in doing, set about tearing down someone they had helped build up. Gary Swift started appearing in the papers for all the wrong reasons, and the impact on his career was immediate. The image that had made him famous was half the problem. He wasn't cool enough for his behaviour to be rock and roll bad, just bad enough for those who had bought into his boy next door image to feel betrayed.

Eventually, even the tabloids got bored of covering his diligent attempt at self-destruction. By the 90s Gary Swift was nothing more than a cautionary tale of fame and fortune and how fast a star could use up both.

Outside of the public eye, Gary Swift's descent continued unimpeded, until finally he hit his nadir, pulled up on the yoke, got help, got clean, fell in love, got married, and had children. No one appeared to notice or really care. Maybe that was what had made it possible.

In the mid-2000s, he accepted the offer to become a contestant in a new reality show, *Celebrity Mutineers*. In *Celebrity Mutineers*, a bunch of celebrities (a very generous definition of the term, as putting a name to half of them would have tested most pop culture fans) were put on an old galleon-style ship and tasked to sail the Caribbean for six weeks. They would endure the discomfort and labour of deck hands, hoisting sails, tying ropes, swabbing decks, sleeping on straw mattress bunks, eating dried salted meats and biscuits. Periodically, viewers voted to determine which celeb would be made to walk the plank until only three remained, and a final vote declared one Captain and winner of the show.

Gary Swift won *Mutineers*, and he won it through showing wit, grit, and a-who-gives-a-flying-fuck-through-a-rolling-ring-donut attitude, recapturing the affection of the British public and rehabilitating his career into the bargain. In the years since he had taken limited acting roles in several dramas, presented TV shows, performed in a few London musicals, and was currently a regular DJ on Awesome Radio's 80s station.

But thirty years ago, partying at Crow's Cottage, on the night Len Arkin went on to take his own life, all this lay in the future.

"Gary said he seemed his usual self. If there was any indication, he didn't catch it," Moore continued. "Although, to be fair he also freely admitted that by the time he left the party and tumbled into a cab his powers of observation weren't at their best."

"Was Len still there when he left?" Ray asked.

"He wasn't sure. He said he didn't think so."

"Did you hear anything about a woman going missing the same evening?"

Moore looked like this was news to him.

On the other side of the glass, Kammal Hanif sauntered back into the studio.

"Look," said Moore, "I'm not sure how much there is to say. Len went and killed himself. It was a bloody shame then and still is. For all our differences, and miserable beggar he could frequently be, I loved the guy. He was my partner, my friend, and I wish he were still around."

Chloe saw that these weren't just words. Moore obviously meant them.

"We do understand," said Chloe, "and we can see you're obviously busy and appreciate you making time to see us. It's been very helpful. Could I maybe just ask one more thing before we go?"

"Go ahead."

"If I said the Mephisto Arcane, would you know what I meant?"

Moore's face answered as surely as the words which followed. "No. What's that then?"

"A sort of fancy wooden box covered with symbols, a polished metal plate on the top?"

"Sorry. No idea. Should I?"

"No," Chloe said, "just thought it was worth asking."

They got up to leave.

"Aren't you forgetting something?" said Moore.

"Sorry?" Ray asked.

"We agreed once we were done you would let me ask you something?"

"Of course. Please, go ahead."

"You're making a television show, I get it. Entertainment is my business too, and I'm sure famous people, tragic deaths and ghosts make for a good story, but before digging too much of this up and sticking it on telly, maybe pause a moment and consider this: Len was a real person. Don't twist his death into a cheap mystery or reduce him to some ghostly presence unless you're sincere. Don't make a mockery out of someone who should be remembered for his talent and his achievements, eh?"

"I assure you," Ray said, "we're not looking to make a mockery of anyone, or cheapen their memory. If Len's death becomes something we touch on, I promise we'll treat it as sensitively as we can."

As far as Chloe could tell, Moore seemed satisfied.

They thanked him again and made their way out, accompanied by Moore's engineer who guided them back through the studio's corridors to the world outside.

As they slipped back into Ray's Range Rover, Ray repeated Moore's appeal: "Don't make a mockery out of someone who should be remembered for his talent and his achievements, eh?"

"Mm," Chloe responded, "or maybe don't go digging up the past and screw things up for me when my career is finally on the up again?"

Chapter Thirteen

Charles parked up, retrieved the Mephisto Arcane from the passenger side footwell, and approached Samantha Carrington's three-story house in Wimbledon with it tucked under one arm. The occult artist's home occupied a corner plot, as though keeping a sentinel-like watch on the crossroad before it.

Securing a meeting with Carrington had required Charles to bite the bullet and make a call to his old flame, the art collector. Fortunately, despite the relationship expiring, the spilt had been largely amicable. A call to Carrington, conveying Charles had a matter he wished to talk to her about regarding the Longwood Society, along with Charles' personal number, had resulted in a call back from Samantha Carrington a day later.

If she was aware of his work or not, Charles felt sure she had spoken to people she still knew in spiritualist and paranormal psychology circles first. It was gratifying to find his reputation apparently remained in reasonable shape. There was also, of course, the slim chance she recalled their past meeting at the exhibition.

He had explained during the call how an incident he was investigating was tangentially connected to the Longwood Occult Society, supplied the bare details of Giles inheriting Crow's Cottage, the item discovered there, and the connection to Faulks, Langley and Needham: the trio who had briefly attempted to resurrect the group she and the Bartleholms had first created.

Carrington had a reputation for valuing her privacy and a preference for solitude. He had anticipated resistance, and so was somewhat surprised when she suggested he visit her in person the following afternoon.

She suggested he bring along the Mephisto Arcane.

-

"The Longwood Society wasn't what people thought it was," Carrington said, "or if it was, then not in the vein they imagined. It wasn't a secret club, a cult, a coven, or a sect. It was just the occasional gathering of like-minded souls. Yes, we had members who would happily identify themselves as occultists, daemon worshipers, witches, warlocks and mediums, and sensitives of many types, but those things meant something different to us than they do most people."

Samantha Carrington sipped her lemon water. Charles had chosen tea. The artist was a striking woman. The short silky bob he recalled from their long-ago meeting, cut razor sharp at chin level, canted so it was almost under her ear on one side and to her shoulder on the other, was still in evidence. Then it had been dyed jet black, reminiscent of a twenties Berlin film star. Today it was white, fading to a subtle blue-grey at the tips, less canted and slightly longer. The boyish frame was still present too, currently draped in a pale blue sweater and jeans. Carrington struck a stylish and tasteful figure who seemed at ease approaching her seventies.

"There were demon worshipers?"

"There were some who believed in daemons, made efforts to commune with them. The distinction is important, though. I refer to daemons, d-a-e. Demons, d-e-m, are evil non-human spirits, the former are commonly seen as good.

"Worship is something of a loaded term, though. Many ancient civilisations and religions acknowledged spirits not derived from man, and sought their aid. Jinn, asura, angels, call them what you will, such elemental spirits were viewed as part of the fabric of nature, and inclined towards benevolence rather than malice."

Charles had been candid with Carrington. He saw no point not being so. He suspected she would be at least as familiar with the story about the Mephisto Arcane as he was. When he had arrived at her door holding the device he had watched carefully when she took it in. Unless she had a poker face to beat all poker faces, she didn't appear to recognise it. She appeared merely curious. It presently sat on the table between them. She nodded toward it.

"You're wondering if Hubert Langley, Edward Needham or Damien Faulks were daemon worshipers?" she said, not quite smiling. "Did they craft something more potent than they bargained for when they made this? A device capable of summoning something dark and dangerous, alien, an entity with the power to reduce a man to madness and pluck a woman from existence?"

"The wildest stories aren't always untrue."

"Perhaps not, but in this instance, to my knowledge, neither Hubert Langley nor Edward Needham struck me as especially concerned with daemons or demons. Granted, I only met them personally a handful of times. Damien Faulks, I never met at all. He must have joined their version of the Society a little later on."

"What was your impression of Langley and Needham?"

Carrington considered the question. "They presented as earnest, respectful… Idealistic? John was flattered by their desire to reinvigorate the Longwood Society, told them he had no objection to the venture. Of course, they didn't really require his blessing anyway. They could have set up any group they liked and called it whatever they liked. It didn't have to be the Longwood Society, save for the fact they romanticised what it had been, and what they perhaps believed they had missed out on. 'The Longwood Society' wasn't even a name John chose. It came about because he held the gatherings at his and Eleanor's home at the time, Longwood House. The Society was never as formalised or active as people seem to think. John hosted as few as four or five gatherings a year, over the course of seven or eight years.

"We invited people we personally knew who were gifted or knowledgeable in the supernatural, and let those people know they were free to extend an invitation to anyone they knew who also fitted the group. The result? The Longwood Society expanded and shrank in number, but existed in that ill-defined form for many years, full of extraordinary people who knew extraordinary things. We would debate, share stories, knowledge, techniques, offer support or advice, or simply enjoy being in the company of kindred spirits, free to speak openly without being viewed as a lunatic or a charlatan.

"Then John was diagnosed with Parkinson's. The symptoms grew from easy to brush off to impossible to ignore. As the condition progressed and his health suffered, the gatherings at Longwood grew less frequent and then eventually ceased altogether. There was some talk of other members taking the reins, but it never happened.

"So, when an enthusiastic young medium with a respectable reputation by the name of Edward Needham stepped forward years later, keen to resurrect the group, the notion appealed to John. The purpose of the group was one he still believed in."

"What did he see that as being?"

"To encourage a sense of community, of belonging, to offer support. It can be difficult to be woken to or aware of forces many cannot see, or perhaps refuse to. It can inflict feelings of isolation, shame, confusion. As a younger man, John struggled with his gift, to reach a point where he was able to be open about it. It's not an uncommon story. He feared sharing the things he saw and felt, so for a long time said nothing rather than risk facing ridicule and judgement. Meeting Eleanor was a turning point. She made him see he wasn't alone."

Charles nodded. Eleanor Bartleholm's gift had been psychometry. She was able to sense things or receive impressions from objects or people through touch.

"As a girl," continued Carrington, "Eleanor had also felt the pressure to keep her sensitivities hidden. She and John wished to see a world where that wasn't necessary."

Charles understood. It was a world he would welcome too. Carrington was right. The story was sadly not uncommon. He had no doubt the world was full of people who chose to live a lie, pretending they didn't possess a sixth sense or worse. How many, too afraid to share, feared for their sanity? Charles had been fortunate. His grandmother had been gifted too. She had seen it in him and stepped in to guide him, especially as his gift had flared brightly in adolescence. She assured him the strange things he saw, felt and heard were not the result of delusion or madness.

"John choosing to practice his mediumship openly was his first step towards seeking to effect change," Carrington continued, "and play his part in making people acknowledge a dimension to existence that many seem blind to. The Longwood Society was the next, an organ to bring the gifted together, learn from one another, share experiences and knowledge, somewhere one could feel normal.

"This is what the Society, John and Eleanor, delivered for me. I had always known there were facets to existence the majority of people around me did not see, spent my whole life glimpsing a hidden world. I never even attempted to explain what I saw to my peers; I had already earned the reputation of being 'that strange girl', but I tried with my family. They never understood. Words literally failed me, so I tried something else.

"My art grew out of an increasingly desperate attempt to articulate these glimpses, the extraordinary hidden in plain sight, something suggested in an arrangement of objects or conjunction of one thing and another."

It was a good description of Carrington's work. The most common attribute of her paintings was how they often left the viewer feeling like they were on the cusp of discovering a secret. The impression was exemplified most keenly in her most famous piece, entitled *The Third Animal*, which had formed the centrepiece of the exhibition Charles had attended all those years ago. The piece contained her trademark use of stark geometry and unsettling composition. It was always a challenge to identify the focal point in Carrington's work. In many ways, it was at the heart of what made them so compelling.

Depicted in an almost mediaeval style, *The Third Animal* features a background made up of a snaking wall that flouts any rule of perspective, against which stands a robed figure, which one feels should be the main figure, as it represents the largest single element present.

The robe the figure wears is unremarkable save for a diamond-shaped hole cut from the cloth which exposes its left breast, small and pale. The figure's face is covered in hair, but the effect is not simian; the eyes are wide and human and the lips are full. In the lower far right-hand corner of the composition lies a large, bulbous glass vase. Inside it hovers the shadow of a creature whose gauzy shape is as tantalising to ascertain as it is impossible.

The most frequent comment observers made was of something feeling conspicuously absent from the picture. Carrington freely agreed that for most observers there was: the painting's true subject, the third animal of the title. She also insisted, like a piece plucked from a complete jigsaw puzzle, one could gain clues to its form from what surrounded it. Carrington described her body of work as an invitation to view the hidden, almost a series of tutorials. John and Eleanor Bartleholm had been early patrons. Their relationship had not ended there.

At the exhibition Charles had attended, his date had explained more fully after Charles commented upon how intimate Carrington and John Bartleholm appeared. Samantha Carrington had not just been John Bartleholm's friend for many years, but his lover. When Charles had asked how Eleanor Bartleholm felt about this, his date had replied with a wry smile, "Comfortable enough, I imagine, given she's her lover too."

Carrington sighed, bringing Charles' train of thought back to the present. "Unfortunately, Needham and Langley's revival of the Longwood Society was to be short-lived. That business with that fellow who killed himself, he killed the venture dead too. Needham, Langley and Faulks had other concerns and didn't emerge on the other side on good terms as I understand.

"The public had their story for a while, one which revolved around fame and ran its course the way such stories do, but the people in our little world, who knew more about Needham, Langley and Faulks and the attempt to resurrect the Longwood Society latched onto a different tale, one which got passed around for far longer."

"Do you think there could be any truth to that story?" mused Charles. "The Mephisto Arcane having something to do with the man's suicide, the woman who supposedly vanished?"

"I'll be sixty-eight this December, Mr McBride. If I've learnt anything over the years, it's that it's unwise to believe all that is sworn to be fact, or discount all that sounds incredible." She stared at the ornate wooden box on the table between them, with its strange symbols and polished metal disc.

Charles was aware of what he saw, but he was also aware Samantha Carrington was gifted in a manner he was not.

"Miss Carrington, may I ask a favour?"

"You may ask. Although I may not oblige," Carrington replied, although not unkindly.

"Would you tell me what you see when you look at that device?"

Carrington reached out and adjusted the Mephisto Arcane so her artist's eye could assess each of its faces in turn, and considered the question.

"I warned you words are not my forte, Mr McBride, but if pushed, I'd say I see something that resembles a lock more than a key."

Chapter Fourteen

Ray was in the Red Lion on Parliament Street in Westminster.

The pub was certainly distinctive, all oak panelling and olive leather, with portraits of politicians adorning the walls, inspired, one imagined, by the close proximity of the Houses of Parliament. The effect somehow managed to graft the feel of a private old boys' club onto the architectural bones of an old-school cockney boozer. An impressive feat in Ray's book.

His mate, DCI Richard Daley, had called back, said he had some stuff on the Arkin investigation. Ray could have got it over the phone but knew Richard would feel more comfortable sharing what he had in person. Ray suggested a pint and a pub lunch. As Rich was based in the new Met Police HQ on the Victoria Embankment, he suggested, in turn, the Red Lion, located nearby.

"Bob Vickers is your man," Richard said, setting his pint of Thatcher's down. "He headed the Len Arkin investigation, such as it was. It looked like suicide, and that's what was determined. No body, but the supporting evidence, the abandoned car and clothes, were enough for the coroner to declare Len Arkin legally dead *in absentia*. I doubt there was any resistance. There was nothing especially suspicious about the circumstances, no unusual withdrawals of cash to suggest a manufactured disappearance. There were the usual efforts to locate the body; the coast guard and local cops told to watch the waters and beaches, but he never washed up. Bodies often don't, I'm told. Turns out the ocean is quite roomy, and filled with plenty of stuff happy to munch on a dead record producer."

"And the girl who went missing?"

"Couldn't find any mention of one."

"This Bob Vickers still a copper?"

"Nope. Left the force ages ago. Sitting pretty at a big private security outfit now. I gave him a call, introduced myself and enquired about the case. Said a friend of mine, also an ex-copper, was looking into the history of this Crow's Cottage and the Arkin suicide. I told him why too, no point in lying. Figured it's unlikely he'd talk to you without looking you up anyway, and being a television celebrity you're not hard to find."

"I'm not a celebrity."

"Just because you don't want to be doesn't mean you're not."

Ray rolled his eyes.

"I said you were just looking for a bit of colour on the place." Richard said, "Asked if he might spare a few minutes for a quick chat. Discuss what he could remember of the case. Nothing that isn't public record, *obviously*." He pulled out his phone and tapped the screen a few times. An instant later Ray's phone buzzed and the text with Vickers' number appeared. "He's expecting your call."

-

KSHF SECURITY was located in Canary Wharf. The headquarters looked the part for somewhere providing executive, exclusive, expensive personal security services to VIPs or people who were under the illusion they were.

Ray was shown from an impressive glass and steel reception to Bob Vickers' office, a similarly swish affair with windows the size of barn doors and a spectacular view of the city.

In his early thirties around the time Len Arkin skinny dipped his way to oblivion, Vickers was pushing mid-sixties these days, but physically in robust shape. Good build, straight-backed, his shoulders were square as a man half his age. Put a bag over his head to cover the steel in his hair and his wrinkles and Ray might have pegged what remained in view as belonging to an active man in his early forties. Vickers knew it, of course. He hadn't stayed in such shape approaching his seventh decade without putting the work in.

Vickers was what Ray always thought of as white-collar-corporate-fit. High pressure desk job where the heaviest thing likely to get lifted was a platinum-plated ballpoint pen compensated for by hours curling weights in the gym and training for the next marathon at mornings and weekends, battling to stay strong and youthful enough to fend off career climbers with their ambitious eyes on that sought-after corner office with the spectacular view.

Ray had finished his pint and called Vickers. He reiterated what Richard had said about his invitation to investigate Crow's Cottage, which would possibly encompass touching upon some of the notable events to have occurred there. Of which, in more recent times, Len Arkin's death was one. Vickers seemed amiable enough, and open to talking, although Ray knew better than to take someone with his background at face value. If a person wanted to develop an impassive and a calm demeanour, regardless of how rattled, baffled or irritated he really felt, dealing with criminals for a couple of decades offered no better test. Vickers said he was in the office until four and was happy to spare him a short window. Ray had said he'd be there within the hour, jumped on the Underground's Jubilee line and was there in forty.

"I've no problem telling you what I can," Vickers said, "but I'm not sure it's going to amount to much. It was a long time ago, and despite the media interest, in truth, there really wasn't much of a case to investigate. If Len Arkin had been a regular guy, if the party he had attended was full of nobodies rather than a few other celebrities, some kooks and a few wealthy socialites, I'm sure the investigation would have been over in half the time, but with the press sniffing a front-page story it was important to confirm what happened was as straightforward as it appeared. Not the sort of story which sold papers."

"I see. So, what did happen?"

"For reasons of his own, Len Arkin decided to leave the party at Crow's Cottage, drive his car to the coast, abandon it at a small short stay car park, keys in the ignition, doors unlocked, the driver's side wide open, and walk down to the beach. He got undressed, left his clothes right there on the shingle and sand, walked into the sea and swam out far enough for the freezing water, exhaustion and uncaring currents to make it impossible for him to change his mind. His wallet was in his jacket pocket, cash and cards still present. Hard to believe he had a casual swim in mind."

Ray agreed.

"I'll be honest," Vickers said, "I didn't know much about him prior to being assigned the case. I'd heard some of his songs. Moore and Arkin? You couldn't escape them back then. A quiet man was how most people described him, bit of an introvert. His partner, Dave Moore? He was a bit more of a personality, but Arkin? Preferred to stay in the background."

"I get the impression success hadn't brought him happiness," Ray said.

"Apparently not. If the spotlight wasn't something he craved, maybe the money didn't make much of a difference either? He was worth millions. He and Moore were selling records by the lorry load. Somehow. That stuff was terrible if you ask me. Different singers, different lyrics, but the same mind-numbing tunes. The eighties: the decade that tried to kill music: Synths, samples, drum machines… Musicians were musicians when I was a kid, they played instruments not programmed them, guitars and drums… Bowie, Bolan, Pink Floyd, Led Zeppelin… Proper bloody music." Vickers paused, smiled wearily, shook his head, "Good grief, listen to me, I've become my old man circa 1970."

Ray smiled. "Don't we all think music was better in our day?"

"Yeah, back when Britain was great, and you could have a night out, a bag of chips and a bus home for under five quid?"

"Something like that," Ray agreed. "The people you interviewed who were there the night Len Arkin killed himself, attending the party at Crow's Cottage, did any of them mention something which could have contributed to him choosing to do it that particular night?"

"That night? No. His partner, David Moore, said he hadn't been himself lately. He admitted there had been a little friction between them, creative differences. He said Arkin had been unhappy. Apparently, he was always something of a malcontent, though. For him to be quiet and downbeat was the norm. Moore said he had no idea he may have been contemplating suicide. I believed him. He struck me as being genuinely shocked at what had happened.

"We spoke to Damien Faulks who threw the party, and as many of the guests as we could," Vickers said, "but we had no cause to get heavy-handed and every reason to be delicate. Damien Faulks' social circle included a few famous faces, entertainment industry types, and a few upper-class types too, folk mindful of their image, wary of scandal. Both sets were wise enough they probably wouldn't tell the police how many sugars they took in their tea without a lawyer present as a matter of course. We did enough though, got a thorough picture to confirm there wasn't much to discover. It was as obvious a case of suicide as you could find. The lack of a body complicated matters, but the surrounding evidence ended up being enough for the coroner.

"Everyone who remembered seeing or speaking to Arkin said the same thing: they hardly recalled him being there. He did nothing to raise concern. He wasn't sitting in a corner weeping or anything, didn't have a breakdown or a bust-up with anyone. He just quietly left at some point late in the evening without a fuss. We weren't able to pinpoint the exact time, only sometime after midnight and before two when the last of the stragglers departed. If he was intent on killing himself, in the way those who really mean to do it are, it fits that he wouldn't have called attention to himself once he decided he was leaving."

Ray couldn't help but agree. If the party had provided a trigger perhaps it was not the obvious kind. What was the saying? Loneliness is a crowded room? If Arkin were already in a fragile frame of mind, feeling depressed, a few drinks, or given the showbiz contingent, maybe some drugs, downers... Cue the early hours of the morning and a maudlin soul might feel even bleaker. What or who was he leaving behind? Fame didn't seem to appeal to him, and, if you believe the maxim, money supposedly doesn't guarantee happiness.

"I understand Arkin wasn't married, no partner, no children," said Ray.

"No. All he had in the way of family was a brother I think, who lived halfway across the country."

"I heard something about a young woman who was at the party too going missing. Ring any bells?"

Vickers looked blank. "Not to my knowledge. What did you hear?"

"Just that."

"A name?"

"No."

Vickers shrugged.

"Did anyone you spoke to mention guests getting involved in any strange or unusual stuff at the party?"

"Unusual how?"

"Occult stuff, tarot cards, Ouija boards…"

"Sorry, I worked vice for a few years, so maybe my definition of strange and unusual stuff is different from most people's. Given Damien Faulks' friends and acquaintances made for an eclectic bunch, they might well have been up to all sorts of daft crap. Although I expect the majority kept to the usual: drinking, socialising. Who knows, maybe a line or two of something illicit given the showbiz bent of a few of the guests."

"Anyone mention something called the Mephisto Arcane?"

Vickers shook his head, looked puzzled, clearly wondering at the turn the conversation had taken. Ray had deliberately left these questions until last. It was always the danger when broaching the subject of anything supernatural, ghosts and such, with people who saw that stuff as utter nonsense. He could easily imagine Vickers being that way. Ray remembered a time when he had.

"What would that be then?"

"It's a device, a sort of wooden box, something Damien Faulks made for Hubert Langley, with Edward Needham's help. It was discovered hidden in the property a few days ago."

"What relation would it have to Len Arkin's suicide?"

Ray wasn't about to say, 'Because it was a box designed to talk to and look at spirits? Or maybe accidentally summon a demon?' Instead, he smiled and shrugged.

"It most likely doesn't."

If the ghost of Len Arkin was bothering Crow's Cottage, the odds of Bob Vickers holding the answers as to why were beginning to look increasingly slim. Ray decided to thank him for his time and bid him farewell before he wore out his welcome.

Vickers showed him to the door. They shook hands. Thanks for sparing the time, no problem, and so forth, except when Ray went to let go, Vickers held on a little longer.

"Look," Vickers said, "I know this whole business happened ages ago, but don't think that means I don't care. I investigated Len Arkin's suicide as well as I was able to. I can also imagine what making a television show might be like, how tempting it must be to amp things up, but if you were to suggest the case was in some way ineptly handled, I would take that personally. I would be offended, and unhappy, because I still have a reputation to maintain."

Ray looked into the fancy office he was about to exit, considered the work for wealthy and prestigious clients who paid for it.

"I assure you, we take our investigations seriously too."

On the journey back, he found himself wondering. Vickers had been remarkably accommodating in agreeing to see him, at very short notice. Even so, without that odd handshake and what felt like a gentle warning on the end of it, he might have walked away without a second thought, but now?

He was left wondering if the investigation into Arkin's death had been all it should have been.

Chapter Fifteen

They crossed the Thames at Tower Bridge.

Dusk was busy painting a shadow city on the shifting canvas of the river, a jagged line of inky black forts and towers. Chloe was a city girl, and Leeds was hardly a backwater, but London *was* different. The scale was different, height, width and breadth. The modern felt more modern, the old older, and the grand grander.

Across the water on the far bank, they had left the Tower of London behind them, a solid, stolid bastion of a former age deep-rooted in the metropolis which had sprawled and risen up around it, one of the countless reminders of the city's age and importance. The financial district to the left was another, a stark contrast of glass and steel. In just one evening they had strolled through Hyde Park, past Buckingham Palace, Westminster Abbey, the Houses of Parliament and Big Ben, Trafalgar Square…

Nick had called her at lunchtime, asked if he could take her out again, an evening in the Big Smoke. He wasn't a native of the city either, but had clearly grown to love it. Chloe had visited London precisely twice before moving south to work on *Where the Dead Walk*, once on a school trip and once with her mum and sister when they were kids.

She and Nick had spent the evening just walking and talking, talking and walking, swapping stories and engaging in some mutual, gentle interrogation.

They discussed what movies they liked, what music, which books, TV series, favourite foods… In between, Nick commented on the places they passed. His affection for the capital was obvious and infectious. He singled out this and that as they went, like the hulking grey battleship ahead, "The HMS Belfast, a floating part of the Imperial War Museum."

They took a pit stop at a bar, grabbed a table outside, enjoying a drink and the clement evening. The hum of the city. Maybe being a London girl was something she could get used to. Yorkshire, home, felt distant, enough to if not forget then more easily ignore. Nick Spokes might be something she could imagine getting used to too.

He was a Brighton boy, born and raised. His mum still lived there, he told her, with his aunt and uncle. They had lost his dad in his teens, and financially things hadn't been easy. He was an only child, he said, and had asked innocently enough, how about her? Did she have brothers or sisters?"

"A sister," she had replied, leaving a deliberately awkward pause, lengthy enough, she hoped, to convey it was a topic she would rather move past, and then adding, "It's complicated," for good measure.

Nick Spokes was not a fool. With scarcely a beat he said, "I watched a couple of old episodes."

"Of?"

"*Where the Dead Walk.* You're the new presenter of the next series?"

"Co-presenter, if they don't decide they've made a terrible mistake, hopefully going forward."

"They won't."

They strolled on, coming up on the recreated Globe theatre, a big, white Tudor-beamed drum, "built on the site of the original theatre," Nick explained, slipping back into tour guide mode, "where Shakespeare's own playing company performed. The original building burnt down." Tourists clumped outside. There were posters of shows on the wall outside, *A Midsummer Night's Dream*, *Hamlet*…

Someone called out to them as they passed.

"A poem for your fair companion, sir?"

The voice belonged to a street artist, dressed in full Elizabethan garb. He was sitting behind a small fold-up table with a pile of paper weighted down with a large ink pot, quill poking out. His sign before him said, *Poems! Choose your topic! £3!*

Nick paused. Threw Chloe a sideways grin. "What say you to a poem, my fair companion?"

"Yeah, why not? Go on then."

The poet picked up his quill. "Would you care to offer fuel to my muse, my lady? A topic?"

Chloe smiled. "How about we let sir choose. Nick?"

Nick fished three pounds from his pocket and dropped the coins in the bowl beside the ink pot, pulled a thinking face, smiled and said, "Ghosts."

The poet nodded, plucked a sheet of parchment style paper from under the pot and ostentatiously dipped his quill in the ink pot. "A moment please."

Chloe and Nick waited in respectful silence. After half a minute the poet began scribbling furiously. With an equally theatrical flourish, he stopped dead, laid down his quill and offered the sheet of parchment to Chloe.

She accepted it, Nick leant in and they read it together.

I am ethereal material,
Spun from purest gone,
Shorn the flesh that held the person,
Whose allotted span was done.
I am eternal and infernal,
The least who wants the most,
I am the essence and the absence,
I am what lingers.
I am your ghost.

"That's very good," said Chloe. "Thank you."

The poet doffed his floppy hat.

She folded the poem carefully into four and slid it into her jacket pocket. The poet was already engaged in snaring his next patron. They moved on. The Tate Modern loomed, pointing a brutal brick stack finger into the darkening sky. Once an old power station, it was now filled with pictures, sculptures and installations.

"How's your appetite for some art?" Nick asked.

"At the risk of sounding like a philistine, right now running a distant second to my appetite for pizza."

-

They crossed the Thames again. A hop over the Millennium Bridge and a short walk brought them to St Paul's, where they slipped into a pizza joint, securing a window table with a stunning view of the cathedral, "built in the wake of the Great Fire of

London," said Nick, "and designed by Sir Christopher Wren."

The sky was growing dark, the city slipping from its daytime duds into a showy spangle of late eveningwear illumination. If St Paul's looked grand in daylight, it looked even grander washed in spotlights, transformed into a palace of luminous columns and carved stone, figures, reliefs, and of course the spectacular dome towering above. They ate and talked, desserts were arrived at and demolished.

Nick visited the men's room, returning to find Chloe studying the poem.

"Sorry, it was the first thing that came to mind," he said. "Ghosts."

"I like it."

"You really, really do believe they exist? Ghosts?" he asked.

"Yes. I really, really do."

Nick smiled, went to speak and obviously thought better of it.

"What? It's okay, say what you were about to."

"I just can't see how it's all supposed to work. Let's say for a moment ghosts do exist. One day I die and find I am one. Am I here, or somewhere else, or somewhere in between? And since I don't have a body with a brain anymore, what am I using to reflect upon my new state of being?"

"Charles says spirits, ghost especially, are emotional entities. They feel more than think. Expecting them to behave like the living, talk like we're talking now, that's not how it works, or how communicating with them works. He says it's not so much the words you use, as what's going on in your head when you choose those words. The intent, the images, memories you call upon, the feelings…"

"Do we all become ghosts?"

Chloe shook her head. "No. We all become spirits, but ghosts are different."

"What? As in the 'souls who have unfinished business here' thing?"

"More spirits who retain some strong enough connection to our world to remain a part of it. Maybe that means they're spirits who got lost or can't let go, or maybe there isn't a *there* or a *here*. Maybe we coexist, but in most cases are completely unaware of each other?"

"But if there are billions of people alive right now, and billions upon billions who've died in the past, even if a tiny fraction meet the criteria, become not just spirits but ghosts, shouldn't there be ghosts everywhere you turn? Shouldn't we be up to our chins in evidence they exist? Especially now. I can see how it might have been tricky to document evidence once, but today when almost everyone carries a smartphone with a camera and video recorder?"

"The absence of evidence isn't evidence of absence, isn't that how it goes for you staunchly scientific types? And even when you do have proof, with digital editing being increasingly simple, how many people accept without question something seen in a digital picture or video? It's also possible ghosts can't be captured on those media."

"Sounds like a wonderful get out, and a bit convenient."

"Not if you're in the business of trying to do it. You're arguing from the standpoint of logic and science, but what if those things *can't* explain the supernatural world? What if the rules are fundamentally different? What if it's like trying to capture a smell on camera, or take a picture of a noise? What if all our various facsimiles of human senses, microphones, cameras, can't perceive a spirit? What if to see or hear a spirit you need to be a being with a spirit yourself?"

Nick said nothing. Chloe doubted very much it was because he had been convinced. She took out her phone, brought up the map app and did a quick search.

"I want to take you somewhere."

-

Chloe told the driver to pull in and settled the fare. Less than a minute later the beetle-black taxi cab was off, took a left and vanished into the night like it was never there, leaving them alone on a quiet Kensington street.

"Now are you going to tell me where we're going?"

"All in good time. Come on."

Chloe checked her phone again, thumbing the map around, walked them up the street until they came to the front gate of a children's playground. She entered and Nick dutifully followed. A concrete football pitch lay behind the playground. Behind this stood a wall, maybe ten feet tall. Above and behind was a collection of trees. Chloe walked forward to size the wall up.

"You'll need to give me a boost."

"What?"

"Then I can reach down and help you up too."

"What's behind the wall?"

"You'll see."

"You know this looks a lot like trespassing. Y'know as in illegal?"

Chloe pretended to consider his point, and then to remember something. "Oh shit!"

"What?"

"The cab we just got out of, do you think it's gone far?"

"Yeah, probably miles away by now."

"Did you catch the registration?"

"No, why?"

"I'm afraid you might have left your balls in it."

Nick made a face at her. "Funny."

"I'm trying to stretch your horizons here, Spokes. Trust me, I've done this before. As long as we're quiet no one will even know we were here. Ready?"

"No."

"Good. Come on."

He came though, clasped his hands, into which Chloe planted a size seven boot. One good lift launched her high enough to grasp the lip of the wall. She scrambled and threw up a knee, climbed atop, stretched a hand down for Nick.

"It's okay," he said, "I think I got this."

He backpedalled to the far side of the concrete pitch and then broke into a sprint, met the wall, planted a foot and vaulted up to grab the top. In a moment or two, he had hoisted himself up and was sitting astride the wall too.

Chloe smiled. "Nice." Before he could get comfortable, she swung her legs over the far side and dropped to the grass below. It was already dewy and damp. She wiped her hands dry on her jeans as Nick landed next to her. She took his hand and led him forward, and soon they emerged from the cowl of trees and came upon a path.

Brompton Cemetery was dark, silent and utterly spectacular. It didn't take Nick long to work out where they were.

"You brought me to a graveyard?" he said.

"Yep. Come on, let's walk."

The path was lined with headstones on both sides, jostling shoulder to shoulder, from grand to humble. There were huge chest tombs, monuments and mausoleums, stone cut into crosses, into angels, into crypts with vaulted roofs and Greco-Roman pillars. Friendly moss and lichen clung to the weathered words carved into them. Proper nouns and dates, names to remind the world a human being had once existed for a time, unique, momentary, the product of two other human beings, perhaps the mother or father of more, a human being who had perhaps been loved, admired, despised, envied, missed, but was now gone, from this world at least.

"So… why are we here?"

"We're here, Mr Spokes, because this is where the dead live."

"The dead don't *live* anywhere, Miss Harker."

She ignored him. "I want you to do something for me."

"Will it increase or decrease my odds of criminal prosecution?"

"Neither."

"Okay. What would you like me to do?"

"Close your eyes, and just… feel."

"Close my eyes and just… feel?"

"Yes."

"Why?"

"Just do it. Please?"

Nick sighed but obeyed. He straightened up, had a little shake to loosen up, and closed his eyes.

"What now?"

"Shush. Be quiet."

Chloe waited until she saw him relax.

"I want you to take a while and then ask yourself, not with your head, but with the whole of you. Do we feel alone here? Honestly."

After perhaps a minute Nick said, "Can I answer now?"

"Yes."

"You want me to be honest?"

"Of course."

"No. We don't feel like we're alone, but then… What you just did was extremely suggestive. Like when you're told not think of a blue elephant, and of course you can't think of anything but a blue elephant, and besides even that, our senses are unreliable."

"But feelings are real. The universe is still full of mystery and wonder. There's no mathematical formula to existence yet, and in practically every culture which exists, or has existed, the notion of a spirit is instinctively understood." She moved closer. "Sure, you can choose to measure reality in centimetres or kilograms, decibels or degrees Celsius, reduce us all to fancy meat machines, guided by biological computers, make it all about chemical reactions, enzymes and hormones squirted this place and that, causing us to feel happiness, sadness, anger, hate, desire, longing, love…" She moved

126

closer still, put a hand on his chest. "Sure, you can stand there and tell yourself you don't have a spirit because you can't find one with an x-ray or an MRI scan, but damn it, Spokes, fuck logic. Can't you *feel* you have one?"

She tried to read his face, see if she had made even a tiny impact, but saw no evidence to suggest she had.

"Have you ever seen one?" he asked. "A ghost?"

She stared into his eyes and decided the question had been asked in earnest. "My nan," she said. "I was sixteen. She had passed away the week before. I was devastated, absolutely devastated, and then she came to me."

"How?"

"In the middle of the night. I was in bed, and something woke me. Someone was in my room, and before I had time to freak out, I smelt her perfume. She always wore the same scent, lily of the valley. I wanted to turn to look, but I was afraid. Not that she would be there, but that she wouldn't. I felt her sit beside me on the bed. I made myself turn and look, and just for a second I saw her."

"And?"

"Then she was gone, but her scent wasn't. I woke my mum, told her what had happened. We went straight back to my room. She could smell it too."

He nodded. But she could already see it, the dry wheels turning in his head, the lab coat logic filter, the dull rationalising, the soulless sifting for an alternative explanation. How she was far more likely to have been dreaming, or half asleep, and having so recently lost her nan, well, of course, she would be at the forefront of Chloe's mind. She could have imagined the smell, scent memory could be quite powerful, and just the suggestion of the familiar scent could be enough to lead her mother into convincing herself she detected it too.

Picture a blue elephant.

The difference was Chloe had actually been there in that moment, and her nan had been too.

She felt the chafe of annoyance. She had hoped for more. She had certainly not intended to tell him about the other ghost she had seen a good deal more recently. Before she knew it though, the words were out.

"I saw another in Hubert Langley's cottage a few days ago. And this time I wasn't alone. I was with Charles. We both saw it, right ahead of us, as real as you are now."

"You saw a ghost in Hubert's old place?"

She nodded, satisfied to have dented his composure. She could tell by his face this instance hit closer to home. He had known Hubert, cared for him.

"What did it look like?"

"Dark, like a shadow, standing at the end of the hallway. It was right there, bold as brass, and then it stepped out of sight. We went after it, but it had vanished. When we film there, who knows, maybe we'll get it on video, something good enough to give even sticklers like you food for thought?"

-

It was the other side of midnight when the cab drew up outside Chloe's flat. She had suggested coffee. Nick had said yes, that would be very nice.

They watched the cab go off in search of its next fare.

Chloe turned to find Nick staring at her. He was good-looking, and tall, how she preferred a guy, but she already knew these things were not at the heart of what made him attractive to her. It was something far more dangerous.

There was sadness in Nick Spokes. It wasn't obvious, you had to watch and listen carefully to glimpse it. He joked a lot. He smiled a lot. But then, so did she. That didn't change the fact it was there.

The street was dark and empty. They were alone.

She had decided she was about to kiss him when he beat her to it. He put a hand to her neck. She snaked an arm under his, seized a fistful of his shirt, surprised at the impact the connection had on her. She tugged sharply the back of his shirt and broke off the kiss for a moment.

"Okay, Spokes," she said, not quite breathlessly, but damn near, "here are the ground rules: pre-approved for upper torso exploration, approval still pending for below hips shenanigans. Got it?"

He smiled. "Got it."

She took his hand and they headed across the road to her flat. As they neared, a polite cough caught them short. Someone was waiting in the doorway.

"Hello, sweetie."

The voice was unmistakeable, and a moment later the sight confirmed it. Chloe's mum was standing in front of her, a small case at her feet.

-

Chloe walked Nick downstairs and to the waiting cab and said she would call him tomorrow. She was too exasperated for kissing.

Then she walked the four flights back upstairs to her top floor flat, where her mum was waiting, her overnight case sitting just inside the front door. Chloe told herself she wasn't angry, because she was dimly aware that being angry might be unjustified, but she wasn't happy, and she forced herself to downgrade to Very Irritated. Before she could get a word in, her mum said, "I wanted to see you."

"So naturally you thought why not simply turn up unannounced, wait on my doorstep in the dark? Why ever might it be inconvenient to just rock up without warning? Why bother to call once you set out? How long were you waiting outside?"

"Not too long. I wasn't expecting you to be back so late. I got a coffee and a bite to eat down the road." Her mum was trying to sound bright and breezy, trying to pretend her daughter wasn't clearly aggravated, which aggravated Chloe further. "I thought I'd surprise you, that we could spend tomorrow together, and then a lazy Sunday. I'll cook lunch. A short visit. I'm booked on the train out of King's Cross Monday morning at nine."

"Well, it's definitely a surprise, Mum. Good job I haven't got the slightest thing planned, eh?" The sarcasm sounded more acidic coming out her mouth than it had in her head.

Her mum's cheery mask slipped.

"Chloe. I've seen you twice in what? Six months? I just wanted to catch up, talk."

"We talked only a few days ago."

"We talked for about half a minute a few days ago, and the time before that, and before that."

"What do you want me to say, Mum? I'm busy. This job's a big deal for me. Who knows, maybe even the start of a career, but it's a lot of work, a lot to learn, a lot to get to grips with. I don't want to screw it up. I still need to prove they didn't make a huge mistake offering me a shot. It's all I've really had on my mind, pretty much all I've really had time for."

Her mum nodded, but then her eyes flicked back to the door, the one Chloe had just re-entered after seeing Nick to his cab. Mind reading was not required. The inference wasn't subtle. *Busy, but not too busy to squeeze in a date.*

"I get it, I do, but I'm your mum. I can't help worrying about you."

"You don't need to. I'm fine."

"You're halfway across the country."

"Yeah, this is where the job is."

"I know, and I'm really pleased for you. I am, but—"

"What?"

"It would be nice to feel I still have one daughter in my life."

Aaaand there it was. Chloe knew it wouldn't take long to arrive. Wooooh-Wooooh! All aboard for the guilt trip! Could all passengers please take a seat. We wish you a grim and interminable journey! Passengers, could you please keep your emotional baggage with you at all times…

Chloe couldn't help herself. She snorted.

Her mum frowned. "What's that supposed to mean?"

"It means I don't want to do this shit anymore. Even for you. Kara, Kara, Kara... Good grief, Mum, change the record."

"Your sister is missing. That doesn't mean anything to you?"

"Of course it does. It just doesn't mean *everything* to me. I don't allow it to."

"I see."

"You think it's easy for me?"

"Honestly, I'm not sure."

"What? I don't care because I refuse to put my life on hold or expect the world to grind to a halt? Because I'm trying to come to terms with the possibility she might never come back, that I might never find out where she went? Because I won't start every day praying this might be the one where she gets in touch? Because I won't allow half my mind to be somewhere else, waiting for the phone to ring because someone claims to have spotted her, or the police have found a body fitting her description? Because I won't invent scenarios to torture myself? Because I refuse to think about her all the fucking time? I will not do those things, Mum, because I think I matter too."

"You don't understand. It's different for me."

"Why, because to me she's just a sister, but to you she's a favourite daughter?"

"You know that's not true."

Chloe was about to open her mouth to bark back, but stopped herself, because she knew whatever came out was something she would regret, and because... well, she wasn't a total fucking monster.

Ultimately, they both knew she wasn't about to send her mum packing either. Far from happy about being pushed into a corner by a surprise arrival, this mum and daughter weekend thing was happening whether she liked it or not. Two days. Just a Saturday, a Sunday and then a nine o'clock train out of Kings Cross to Leeds and it was over.

She sighed. "Come on, Mum. You know where I am, and why I'm here. It's not even close to being the same, at all. I do want to see you. Maybe I should find more time to, and I do want to talk. But not about her."

"If that's what you want."

"It is. You can have my room. I'll take the sofa."

"I couldn't do that—"

"Mum. Just take my room. Okay?"

"Okay, thank you. It'll be nice, I promise. You can just relax. I'll cook dinner, and make your favourite dessert too. Bread and butter pudding, only made with chocolate chips instead of raisins?"

Chloe bit her tongue.

What was to be gained by pointing out bread and butter pudding made with chocolate chips was Kara's favourite?

Chapter Sixteen

She hadn't pestered, and she knew damn well she hadn't begged, and of course that hadn't stopped Kara acting like she had, but then Kara struggled to do anything without lengthy sighing followed by weary, eye-rolling surrender. Kara insisted on being both the centre of attention, and to be left alone, seemingly often minutes apart, or occasionally at the same time.

She always got her own way, usually because it was easier than having the fight, where all tools would be employed, from playing the victim or the one who supposedly always gave way and rarely asked for anything, to full-on harassment or what amounted to a screaming tantrum to shame most toddlers. In any dispute, you were either wrong, mistaken or paranoid. If cornered in the act of being vile it was always somehow a reasonable response, justified by someone else's behaviour beforehand. In short, Kara was always blameless.

Chloe would never be sure as youngest whether she was easy-going by nature, or in response to the way Kara was, or just in comparison. Kara's moods had always seemed to operate at the extremes. As difficult as she could be, she could also be dazzling and ridiculously charming, funny and generous. If she wanted to be.

Ultimately, Kara had agreed to Chloe's request, and so she had gone ahead and made a makeshift board, drawn out the letters and numbers with a fat marker pen and chosen a glass tumbler from the kitchen. They had the house to themselves. Mum was working an evening shift and wouldn't be back until the early hours. Just a couple of months shy of turning eighteen Kara had been judged old enough to babysit, which made Chloe sound like she was five rather than fifteen, and painted Kara as someone who was responsible. In truth, though Kara might pass for twenty-five in make-up, Chloe was the more sensible.

She arranged everything on the floor of her room, and they had dimmed the lights. Chloe at one bottom corner of the board, Kara the other.

Chloe asked the question again, "Nan, it's Chloe and Kara. Are you there?"

Nothing happened. The same nothing that had happened the dozen or so times before. Hardly five minutes in and Kara was beginning to fidget and lose interest. Chloe's confession that Nan had visited her from beyond the grave was a good example of Harker family dynamics. Her mum had taken her seriously. Whether she believed her was another question, but the disclosure had been treated with respect. Kara had immediately poked fun at her.

When the spirit board idea had taken hold and refused to let go, she knew asking her mum to help was a no go. Even if Mum had gone along with it, and Chloe doubted she would, just talking about Nan still got Mum upset. To be fair, Nan's death had upset Kara too, but Kara had a knack for forward motion. While Nan's death lay in the past for all of them, in the weeks and months since they lost her, somehow Kara seemed to have travelled further away from it than Chloe and their mum.

Chloe knew Kara wasn't a great choice for the spirit board experiment. She didn't really believe in ghosts, wasn't a fan of the ghost hunting shows Chloe watched, although that didn't mean she didn't watch them too. She occasionally did, to offer snarky comments and poke fun at them, and by association Chloe for being daft enough to eat up their 'crap'.

Were it possible to use the board alone, Chloe would have, but it wasn't. Not really. To be confident you weren't moving the glass subconsciously because you wanted it to move, you needed at least one other person to provide a check. She had one or two friends she considered asking, but it had felt wrong. It felt like it should be someone who had loved Nan too, which made for a short list of candidates. If it couldn't be Mum, it had to be Kara.

Chloe tried again. "Nan, are you there?"

They each had a single finger resting on the upended and stubbornly stationary tumbler. Kara cracked an ostentatious yawn. The message was clear: Bored! Chloe knew if nothing happened soon, she would bail—but then it did.

The glass moved.

Kara's mouth suddenly snapped closed. All of a sudden, she was sitting straight. Her narrowed eyes shot to Chloe.

"Did you—"

"No."

"I swear if you're—"

The glass lurched again, only this time it continued moving. For a moment it drifted in a loose and lazy figure of eight, before rounding in on a letter. Kara scrambled with her free hand, grabbed the pen next to the board and clawed the note pad over. The glass was already on the move again as she jotted the first letter down.

L.

The glass kept going, pausing a beat on each letter. Kara recorded each one on the pad.

"Nan?" said Kara. The glass picked up speed again. More letters. Kara quickly scratched them down. Then, as suddenly as it had gained life, the glass fell still.

They waited.

Chloe found her voice again.

"Nan."

Nothing.

Kara looked at the pad. Chloe saw her eyes flit over the letters, reading. She seemed to digest what was there then swallowed…

"Oh, shi…"

"What?"

"Read it."

Kara passed Chloe the pad. She read the message.

LINE BUSY PLEASE TRY AGAIN LATER.

Chloe looked up to find Kara smirking.

"That's not funny."

"Come on, it's a little bit funny."

"You're a fucking cow."

Kara's smile vanished. "And you need to fucking grow up. You're getting too old for this shit. Ghosts don't exist, Chlo. When you die, you die, that's it. Done. Over. The end. Simple as. Nan's gone, and she didn't come back from the grave to say howdy to you."

Then the shouting really started, deteriorating into insults, slammed doors and finally silence. Chloe had ripped up the board, furious with her sister, and with herself. She should have known better. Sleep was impossible.

It was very late when Kara eventually sneaked into Chloe's room. It seemed she wasn't the only one awake. Chloe resolved to ignore her, even when her sister climbed into the bed next to her, curled an arm around her and gave her rigid body a hug, and said sorry. Sorry was a big deal for Kara.

"I miss her too, you know?" she said. "I really do, but she's gone. Me, you and Mum? We'll be okay if we stick together, look after each other. That's what Nan would have wanted, right? I know I can be a cow sometimes. Maybe with Nan gone, I'll try harder not to be, yeah?"

Chapter Seventeen

It should have felt like a nice gesture, the toast, the tea, the scrambled eggs.

Her mum had been up with the birds and taken it upon herself to tidy around. Then she made them both breakfast, freely exploring the kitchen cupboards and drawers in order to gather the ingredients, locate the plates and necessary utensils.

When Chloe lived at home, her mum had sometimes cleaned her room, even when expressly asked not to, even after arguments. The task involved touching her stuff and moving her things. It had felt like an intrusion then, but one childhood had conditioned her to tolerate.

"It might be your room," was the refrain, "but it's still my house, and I refuse to let it become a pigsty." It was a tough argument to counter when Chloe had lived back home. What it wasn't was an argument which held water here in London. The flat was Chloe's, and if it occasionally veered towards untidy now and again that was her choice.

Perhaps if she hadn't slept on the sofa and hadn't woken to a stiff neck and cold feet the invasion might not have raised her hackles quite as much, or if the thing to wake her had not been an irritatingly chirpy, "Are you awake?" at least an hour too early. Whatever the circumstances, she was feeling quite salty before having even brushed her teeth.

They ate at the small kitchen table, Chloe unenthusiastically consuming her scrambled eggs and chewing her toast, making no attempt to hide her mood. Raising two teenage daughters, one of them Kara, developed certain skills. Her mum, no stranger to sulks, countered by pretending to not notice.

They got dressed and went into the city. They did some stuff, ate some stuff, maintained enough momentum that not talking about who was really on their minds didn't become too awkward. In the early evening, they took in a movie, affording them over two hours of legitimate, nay mandatory, silence, and afterwards enough additional conversational fuel to fill at least another half an hour of idle chat.

Chloe imagined that to any fly on the wall they would have looked like just another mother and daughter on a day out. They would be unaware of the spectre trailing a pace behind them. Chloe and her mum could sense it, though. She had been foolish enough to hope they might get through the day without inviting it any closer, pretend it was just the two of them. She should have known better.

It was Sunday, and they were talking about how things were going with the show, how great the crew were, how much she was learning. She had started to relax. Her mum seemed to be really listening, hearing her, and then she had reached out, squeezed her hand and said, "She'd be proud you know. Kara."

Chloe forced herself to take a long slow breath before answering.

"Would she?"

"Landing a job on the telly, of course, she would."

When Chloe didn't answer, her mum added, "She wasn't all bad."

"I never said she was."

"I know, I just meant—"

"Didn't we agree not to do this?"

Her mum opened her mouth, maybe to appeal, protest even, but thankfully, in the end, she simply nodded and shut up. Kara was not mentioned or alluded to again, not for the whole rest of the day, not when they went out for lunch, nor returned to the flat, not when they ate her mum's homemade lasagne, or the bread and butter pudding made with chunks of chocolate instead of raisins, or washed and dried the dishes together, not when Chloe accompanied her mum to King's Cross the next morning and watched her board the train back to Leeds.

That didn't stop the damage being done. Chloe realised too late she had been stupid; she should have gone home to visit her mum, just for a day or two, no matter how unappealing the prospect. By avoiding it she had invited her mum's visit, and even as she watched her board her train, she knew not all of Kara had gone with her.

It made her wonder how people like Nick struggled to accept the existence of ghosts, how they could ever think people aren't too big to be contained by a body, by flesh, blood and bone. It's their spirit which intrudes into the fabric of others' lives and the places they inhabit, like greedy weeds, squeezing into the gaps and winding around the foundations, present even when the person is absent.

Even if you could rip them out, the space they inhabited would feel wrong.

Chloe had no trouble accepting the existence of ghosts.

Kara proved you didn't even have to be dead to be one.

Chapter Eighteen

Chloe was still walking into the Bennett White Production offices when Charles intercepted her like a quality-tailored heat-seeking missile.

"Keep your coat on. I just spoke to Edward Needham. He's agreed to see us."

Charles caught her up on the way. If his summary of their conversation was anything to go by, Needham hadn't sounded especially eager to discuss Crow's Cottage, his efforts to resurrect the Longwood Occult Society or his relationship with Hubert Langley and Damien Faulks. It was around this point Charles had mentioned Giles Langley inheriting Crow's Cottage, the discovery of the Mephisto Arcane and manifold reported sightings of an apparition, and that he and Chloe were among those to witness it.

Charles had other reasons for wanting Chloe along beyond another set of eyes and ears. When meeting another medium, he explained, there was inevitably some degree of tension. In a field where the astonishingly gifted and appallingly fraudulent often practised in similar circles, sadly to equal success, the foremost question in any first encounter with a peer was which side of this divide did they fall? Needham had a fair reputation, but this was not always a faithful guide. Since skilful frauds could often convince unwitting audiences, and sceptics viewed all sensitives as fakes and consequently condemned them as charlatans, most mediums were at some point both lauded and condemned as fakes. Charles included.

Chloe had spent enough time in Charles' company now, seen him work up close at first hand to believe he was the real deal. While it was true much of what he picked up on could be described as vague or impossible to corroborate, on a number of occasions he had supplied details during an investigation which had proven to be surprisingly accurate following additional research. More than this, he didn't feel like a cheat, and he had earned the crew's trust.

What she had learnt, and long suspected, was intuition played a significant role in the process. Perfectly natural conclusions any observant individuals could make were mixed with supernatural insights they could not. At times she expected there were instances where even the sensitive himself wasn't sure which talent he was employing.

There was no doubt that sometimes Charles was reaching, perhaps even being a little creative, but there were also times where she knew he was experiencing something she wasn't. This was a conclusion based on spending time in his company and watching him work, and not something arrived at in a single meeting.

Yet a single meeting with Edward Needham might be all they got.

Edward Needham's home lay around an hour and a half's drive away, a converted barn on the outskirts of Salisbury.

A tall black woman, model-slim and beautiful, answered the door. She introduced herself as Maxine, Needham's wife, and welcomed them in. Chloe found herself attempting to guess her age.

Something told her she was older than she looked, perhaps even late fifties, but wearing extremely well. Either way, she was stunning.

The lower floor of the barn was mostly one large undivided space, a lounge which morphed into a kitchen diner at the far end. An elderly man was seated in an armchair and beginning the difficult process of climbing from it. This was Edward Needham. Chloe had, of course, googled him, but it took a moment or two to reconcile this version with one in the pictures she had found online. Taken at the height of his success in the mid-eighties, the youthful Edward Needham cut a jaunty figure, dark-suited, with a helmet of chocolate brown hair cut in a style that looked like it still wasn't yet quite ready to relinquish the seventies.

The elderly Needham's hair was pure white, on a frame that was currently struggling to stand. There was a distinctly yellowish cast to his skin. He didn't look well. The changes didn't end here, though. In place of the cool grey-blue eyes from the pictures, he stared from dim unfocused marbles. From the way he didn't bother to look directly at them as they entered Chloe felt almost certain Needham was now blind.

"Edward," Maxine said, "Charles McBride and…"

Charles supplied the missing information. "Chloe Harker."

Maxine smiled. "Please have a seat. Would either of you like a drink?"

Charles asked if he might have a cup of tea, Chloe black coffee.

Needham had returned to his armchair.

"I appreciate you agreeing to talk to us, Edward," Charles said.

"Someone found that stupid wooden box then?" Edward Needham said, his voice retaining a strength the rest of him surely envied.

Chloe looked to Charles, who shot her a look back. It appeared Needham was the direct sort.

"The Mephisto Arcane you created with Hubert Langley and Damien Faulks?"

"A ridiculously over-embellished thing? Covered in fancy symbols, with a big shiny metal plate screwed on top?" Charles shot Chloe a second look. She saw he, too, had not expected this, but Needham wasn't done. "And you're investigating Crow's Cottage? Lovely building as I recall, charming, doubtless laden with centuries of rich history, although I suspect you're hoping to unearth something a little more recent. Stories of dark magic and demonic rites? If that's the case, I'm afraid you're going to be disappointed."

Chloe couldn't help herself. "We are?"

"Yes, because Damien's parties were just parties and that object was never an earnest attempt to recreate the Mephisto Arcane, if the original itself indeed ever truly existed. It was Damien's way to keep Hubert pliant."

Maxine returned, and set their drinks on the small rustic lounge table, Charles' tea in a china cup and saucer and Chloe's a mug of black coffee. She took a seat in the armchair near her husband's.

"I understood you, Damien and Hubert were all close friends?" asked Charles.

"Hubert and I were, for a time. Damien less so," Needham said, although Chloe caught a distinctly sour emphasis hanging on Needham's 'were'.

"How did you come to know Hubert Langley?"

"A mutual acquaintance. I performed sittings for a fellow he attended Oxford with. He introduced us to one another. I found Hubert fascinating from the first. He was perhaps the most dedicated scholar of the occult I ever met. Whenever he was in the country we would make efforts to catch up."

"And when you were seeking to resurrect the Longwood Occult Society…?"

"I knew Hubert would be interested. His knowledge of the occult, specifically of folk magic, sorcery, witchcraft, deserved to be shared with others, particularly those who were gifted, but perhaps lacked a broader, historical lens through which to view their gifts."

"I spoke to Samantha Carrington a few days ago. She talked about your desire to resurrect the group."

"I had long viewed John Bartleholm as a role model, a true pioneer advancing the mainstream acceptance of mediumship. The more I learnt about him, read about his work, talked to people he knew, the more I admired what he had tried to do, and wondered what the Longwood Society might have achieved if his poor health hadn't led to its premature demise.

"By the early 1980s, I had earned a modest reputation as a medium, sufficient to feel emboldened enough to contact John directly. He agreed to see me. They say you shouldn't meet your heroes, but John Bartleholm was no disappointment to me. He was very generous with his time, gracious, especially given the toll his illness inflicted upon him.

"I told him of my ambition to start a similar group, asked if he might consider lending his blessing to such an effort. There's so much we don't know about the paranormal, so many of us have different experiences of how we interact with it, how it touches us. Like John, I saw the potential in sharing our experiences, by inviting those with gifts or simply an honest curiosity and a thirst to study the unknown to come together. John was very supportive. He made it clear he couldn't contribute, but wished me well. He said he would contact a few people he felt might be sympathetic, make them aware of the venture. A few got in touch."

"How did Damien Faulks come to be involved?"

"He contacted me. Someone he knew heard about the group, mentioned it to him. I was aware of who he was, but assumed the occult flavour he applied to his conjuring act was pure theatrical affectation. He insisted it was inspired by a genuine curiosity in the paranormal."

"You invited him to join the group?"

"The group was open to anyone, and his interest felt earnest. Damien was good company, very personable, and quickly became one of the more active participants in those early days.

"It was during one of the group's early meetings, I can't remember which precisely, Hubert, Damien and I were discussing Anglo Saxon witchcraft, and the Mephisto Arcane came up. Hubert was telling me how he had finally persuaded a collector of occult artefacts he knew to allow him to photograph a set of illustrations the man held in his collection, purporting to show the device in great detail. The provenance of the drawings was murky, but the age of the material and the style of the illustrations was credible, and they depicted the device over four illustrations, one for each of its four sides.

"I was familiar with the Mephisto Arcane, but Damien was not, so Hubert told him the legend. He explained how it was a device crafted to glimpse and talk to the dead, the life's work of a seventeenth-century traveller who found himself in East Anglia, in the midst of England's rising hysteria regarding the practice of witchcraft and the ardent campaign to stamp it out.

"The traveller was a worldly and educated man, a former seafaring merchant who had documented his journeys, specifically the stranger practices and beliefs he encountered. In short, the supernatural. He did not hold the view they were in the main wicked. He was appalled to see men and women he viewed as innocent being persecuted, and was moved to intervene.

"Seeking to discover whatever acts of witchcraft the accused were alleged to have committed, he ingratiated himself with those conducting the trials. Perhaps he even believed he might find a way to spare some of those who faced the threat of torture and death. Might find a way to temper the zeal of the men pursuing them. As he grew to know them, underlying motives and perhaps the real truth of the situation soon became apparent.

"Once accused, a suspected witch was seized, imprisoned, and made responsible for the financial burden of conducting their trial. During interrogation there was always the insinuation naming fellow practitioners would lead to their own crimes being looked upon more favourably. If their lives could not be saved, they might at least be spared the worst of what could befall them, and enjoy a swift death. This naturally led to more accusations, more victims, further trials, and further financial charges levied to conduct them. Given the witch hunters routinely positioned themselves or close allies as judges and executioners too, most were growing quite wealthy as a result.

"The traveller was incensed and tried to expose the racket, only to seal his own fate. He was arrested, and his belongings seized and searched. They discovered the Mephisto Arcane and held up as irrefutable evidence he practised witchcraft. The trial was short. The traveller was roasted at the stake with the Mephisto Arcane at his feet, both man and device reduced to ashes."

"It's a quite a story," said Charles.

Edward Needham might look frail, and physically he undoubtedly was, but there was nothing weak yet about his spirit. The soul of the man who had commanded huge theatre audiences was still in evidence. His speech was even and his mind seemed sharp.

"It is." Needham agreed, "Damien certainly seemed to enjoy it, but it didn't end there. He asked Hubert if he wasn't tempted to use the illustrations to recreate the Mephisto Arcane. Hubert smiled and said he had not even considered the possibility, but it was obvious once he began to, he was taken with the idea. Without doubt, Damien saw it too because he was soon petitioning Hubert for the task. He was a skilled carpenter and cabinetmaker. He had designed and built all his own stage apparatus since he was a youth. A recreation of the Mephisto Arcane could be a joint project. He suggested I act as a consultant and once the device was completed, conduct an attempt to test the device. I agreed I would be happy to assist in any way I could, in truth not really expecting anything to come of it.

"I was wrong about that. Damien followed through.

"In the event, I was never as involved as Damien or Hubert were. Damien was crafting the device, and Hubert was there to guide him. Very occasionally, one or the other would seek my advice on some aspect or another.

"Hubert was invested, though?"

"Very much so. He frequently met with Damien, and after a short while Damien took up residence in Crow's Cottage, one of Hubert's properties. He claimed to have been searching for somewhere closer to the city. Hubert owned many properties, and while the Mephisto Arcane was an ongoing project, he was perhaps motivated to help and keep Damien happy. A few Longwood gatherings were subsequently held at the property, but Damien was fond of throwing parties too. To which I and other members of the Society were always invited and made welcome.

"I enjoyed Hubert's company and Damien could be entertaining. For Hubert and me, the parties were a peek into an unfamiliar world, a somewhat glamorous and exciting one. Damien maintained a lively network of friends, including other celebrities, and Crow's Cottage was far enough from prying eyes, and the press, for them to feel comfortable and let their hair down. I won't lie, Damien's parties were fun, for a time. They were where Maxine and I met, and I suppose I shall always be thankful to him for that."

Maxine Needham reached over and took her husband's hand.

"And Damien Faulks was constructing the Mephisto Arcane during this period?" Charles asked.

"Yes. Hubert would mention how it was progressing, occasionally encourage me to join him in a visit to see Damien and take a look at how it was coming along."

"When did Damien Faulks complete it?"

"I wasn't aware he had. The party where that fellow had killed himself… Well, it brought things to a head, and then shook them apart. The press were eager to find something salacious, and if muck was to be raked, real or manufactured, no one wanted the stink near them. Everyone distanced themselves. The Longwood Society was a casualty, as was my relationship with Hubert, and Damien. The former was a genuine loss, the latter not so much. I'll freely admit, Damien's company had begun to wear on me."

"How so?"

"Just that the more I saw of the real Damien, the less I liked him."

"You said before that the Arcane was just his way to keep Hubert pliant. What do you mean?"

"Hubert was wealthy, and very well-connected. Damien was ambitious, only moderately successful compared to his ambitions, and manipulative. I greatly suspected he was occupying Crow's Cottage rent free. Hubert was decent and too trusting.

Everyone knew Damien wanted his own television show, without doubt Hubert probably had friends, or friends of friends, who could make it a reality."

"You feel Damien was taking advantage of him, exploiting his appetite to recreate the Arcane?"

Needham nodded.

"How close to completion was it, the last time you did see it?"

"Reasonably. Whole, but bare, unvarnished."

"You never actually went as far as experimenting with it in an incomplete state? You, Damien, Hubert, or anyone else?"

"I did not. I can't speak for Hubert or Damien."

"Could someone have after it was finished?"

Needham steadied his glazed stare in the direction of Charles' voice. Chloe fought a shiver. Silly. The sightless gaze was unnerving but hardly sinister. Too many spooky movies.

"By accident you mean?" he said, his words fair dripping with derision. "Are we referring to a silly story where two bumbling party guests, a record producer and a young woman happen upon a room containing an occult device, fool around with a dangerous tool they cannot possibly comprehend, resulting in one being clawed from our world to some broiling black belly of sin, and the other shaken free of his sanity? Driven to madness and suicide? Isn't that how it goes?"

Charles said nothing. Like Chloe, he sensed Needham wasn't finished.

"Do you believe in demons, Mr McBride? Because in all my years of mediating between the living and the dead I've yet to definitively encounter one. Angry spirits, yes, disturbed spirits, yes, deceitful and malicious spirits, yes, but a demon, a non-human spirit? I don't believe so. Have you?"

"No. But, I've been mistaken over other things I would not have believed possible."

"May I be candid?"

"Please."

"I don't think there's any call to seek a paranormal explanation for that poor man's suicide, or for Maxine's friend Jessica's disappearance."

Chloe knew Charles must have felt the same jolt of excitement she just had. So there was a woman who vanished, and her name was Jessica.

"In my experience," Needham continued, "the rich, the famous, the wealthy, they are rarely more content than the rest of us, often much less so in fact. There are any number of perfectly reasonable, although sad, dull, and altogether unexciting reasons why a man might take his life, and as for Jessica? I believe she came to London looking for work from somewhere, and from somewhere else before that, and who knows where before. Maxine?"

Needham's wife, who had until now sat quietly at his side, lent her confirmation. "I wasn't surprised when she took off. I liked Jess, but it wasn't hard to see she had issues. She avoided talking about her past, but I got the impression she'd made mistakes, was possibly still running from a few of them. I think the press interest resulting from Len Arkin's suicide spooked her. So she just moved on, again."

Chloe couldn't help interjecting, "But you don't know for sure what became of her?"

"No, but there was really no reason to assume anything untoward. As Edward said, everyone could see the press wanted to paint a scandalous picture of what had happened, find some reason that man killed himself, something that would sell papers, something more exciting than he was plain unhappy."

"This Jessica, do you remember her surname?"

Maxine Needham looked like she did, but wasn't keen to share. Fortunately, her husband, possibly because he couldn't see the micro expressions Chloe saw, was more forthcoming.

"Simm I think. That was it wasn't it Maxine? Jessica Simm?"

"Yes."

"May I ask how you came to know Jessica, Maxine?" Charles asked, to Chloe's mind pushing his luck.

"I did a little modelling for a time, and also public relations work through an agency, car shows, exhibitions, that type of thing. Jess was with the same agency. She was very attractive. We would sometimes end up working together and became friendly. We sometimes went out clubbing. When I met Damien through another friend and got invited to one of his parties, he suggested I bring a girlfriend, so I asked Jess. That was how she got to know Damien."

Needham turned his sightless gaze toward his wife. "She and Damien were a couple for a while, weren't they?"

Maxine hesitated before answering. "I think it was a bit more informal than that. Damien never struck me as the type to settle down, and Jess even less so."

Needham suddenly asked, "May I ask where you found the Mephisto Arcane?"

"A tradesman carrying out some work on the property found it behind a panel under a bath. Do you have any idea why it would have been put there?"

"None at all. I'd no idea what became of it, and, to be frank, nor did I much care. As I said, my conviction is that it was a prop, a means to an end. A beguiling one, granted, like all Damien's illusions. He clearly applied his skills and no small degree of effort into its construction, I'll give him that, but who even knew if the illustrations it was based upon were of the real Mephisto Arcane, or if there even had even been a real Mephisto Arcane in the first place?"

"Did you know the collector who agreed to let Hubert photograph the illustrations?"

"No. Hubert wouldn't say, and I would never have pressed him to do so. There are many such collectors and they are commonly secretive about what they acquire. Often such items are not the sort of thing one flaunts in polite society."

"Yes, I can imagine," Charles said. "Hubert was meant to keep the device once Damien Faulks had finished it?"

"That was my understanding."

"We spoke to Dave Moore, Len Arkin's partner. He mentioned you and Damien had… words, the night of the party?"

Needham didn't respond straight away. He didn't appear keen to, but then he said, "Yes, that's true. Damien felt it would be amusing to interfere with a séance I was conducting. I didn't agree."

"It was deliberate?"

"Very much so. I expressed my irritation, and Maxine and I left the party soon after. Even if the whole business with that fellow killing himself hadn't drawn something of a definitive end to Damien's parties, I believe my relationship with him was fast reaching a natural end. Not only mine perhaps. After the incident, one of the first things Hubert did was request Damien vacate Crow's Cottage, so maybe I wasn't alone in having had my fill of him."

"You didn't maintain contact with Hubert?"

"No. He took to travelling again."

"Later, though?"

"I expected to. I wrote to him, but he chose never to reply. In truth, I was left with mixed feelings about the whole period. My attempt to resurrect the Longwood Society hadn't proven especially successful, and then the business with the party... A man dead, the papers looking for dirt... I suppose in the end it seemed easier to draw a line under most of it and move on. As you might have gathered by now, it's an episode of my life I'm happy to leave in the past."

Chloe sensed they were close to getting all they were likely to out of the Needhams, and evidently Charles felt the same way, keeping to the wisdom it was better to leave before they were shown the door. Charles and Chloe thanked the couple, said their goodbyes, and commenced the journey back to Guildford.

"So," Chloe asked, as Charles pulled off the Needhams driveway. "What are we to make of all that?"

"I'm not sure yet," Charles said, "but I'd very much like to see if I can find out where this Jessica Simm went to, and get to speak to Damien Faulks, wouldn't you?"

157

Chapter Nineteen

The crew were filming at the Edwardian boys' school, which would have been the final location of the series until Crow's Cottage had dropped in their lap. The building was slated for demolition, awaiting unfriendly wrecking balls and men with sledgehammers to reduce it to rubble, but not until next year. After this, the site would be redeveloped, most likely populated with houses and flats.

The school had a storied history and looked fantastic, in the abandoned-and-deserted sense. It was creepy as hell, four forlorn floors of dusty, dark, vanishing point hallways connecting a warren of classrooms.

The building's age was evident wherever the crew looked, in the height of the ceilings, the style of the windows and doors, the original parquet wooden floors, polished and buffed and scuffed and varnished and polished and buffed and scuffed, to the huge timber framed windows with their multitude of small square panes segmented into a grid. A bygone age was evoked, rigid and austere, where boys wore suits and caps and teachers were free to cane them if they dared step out of line. Naughty boys, idle boys, disrespectful boys, disobedient boys, indolent boys and, all too often, completely blameless boys too. All at some authority figure's personal discretion and impunity.

The ghost which was alleged to haunt the school was said to be the spirit of a former headmaster, infamous for his brutality. Stories passed down through alumni, and to Ray by the school's final caretaker, claimed he would not cease caning an offending boy until rewarded with blood, be it on an outstretched hand or bare buttock. So energetic was he in executing his beatings, went the stories, that this was how he met his end, suffering a fatal heart attack in the middle of vigorously disciplining one unfortunate student.

In recognition of his service to the school, the sitting board commissioned a portrait, which hung posthumously in the school's entrance hall. Chloe was willing to bet the boys had found their own, less sombre way to mark his passing.

Was the headmaster story true?

Hard to say.

Ray had carried out the appropriate extensive research, never having done anything less, but some things were hard to confirm. While ugly stories had a way of surviving, being passed down from one generation to the next, documented evidence, if it ever existed, had an unfortunate habit of getting lost.

There was no doubt the use of corporal punishment was once widespread, viewed as a legitimate means to maintain discipline, and the school they were in was old enough to have practised it, but they were unable to specifically confirm if the headmaster was really as brutal as the tales about him claimed. Ray had managed to track down an old photograph from the 1930s of the entrance hall featuring the headmaster's famous portrait, though, and Chloe had to say, he did have the look of a miserable old bastard. The idea of his incorporeal spirit roaming the halls hunting for palms and arses on which to inflict corporal punishment was certainly arresting, and the school offered plenty of space for him to stretch his legs.

The edifice was sprawling and cold as a penguin's pantry. The heating had been condemned when the building was closed, and the abundance of stone, brick, plaster and tiled floors retained little of what heat daytime provided, which today hadn't been much. It was grey and grim out. The wind and drizzle had picked up as the day progressed, leaving the crew thankful they had chosen to dress appropriately. Chloe had her favourite new parka on. Its hood, complete with fake fur, was almost a third the size of the rest of the coat. Plumes of condensed breath puffed from everyone's mouths testified to the single digit temperatures. The effect would look great on camera at least.

They followed the usual structure. Chloe and Mark found somewhere appropriately atmospheric for her to deliver the opening monologue to Mark's camera, in this case, the head of one of the school's long, gloomy corridors. She introduced the location and mentioned some of the alleged activity reported there, the famed whispers, the sudden icy chill many visitors claimed to experience, and the sensation of an invisible figure walking at their heels.

After this Charles and Ray went through their to-camera bits, Ray delivering a potted history of the school which touched upon some of the notable figures connected with it, Charles expanding upon alleged sightings and unexplained phenomena in greater detail.

A brief interview with the school's last caretaker was already done and edited; this would probably be slotted in before the daytime walkaround segment, which they moved onto next. Chloe accompanied Charles as he roved the building, isolating areas where the spiritual energy was strongest, and visiting spots where previous activity had been reported.

On schedule and with some good material, they quit for lunch and then prepped the equipment for the night time vigil. Outside the grey day was growing dark and the wind was continuing to pick up, shaking the heads of nearby trees like pom-poms.

The school, bereft as it was of soft coverings on floors or anything else, was a network of echo chambers. Noise sometimes carried through its corridors and stairwells for remarkable distances. At one point, Keith and Claire even radioed Chloe and Charles to inform them they were able to clearly make out their conversation from their position two floors above. The whispered voices commonly reported might be reasonably chalked up to nothing more than hard surfaces and some freaky acoustics resulting from early twentieth-century architecture.

Keith had a series of audio devices set up to capture any instances of EVP, electronic voice phenomena. Every hour he fed the recordings into a piece of software which searched for spikes and patterns redolent of speech. They got a few good instances. In one recording, if the volume was sufficiently cranked up, the phrase 'I will punish you' could be heard, or maybe 'I will push you'. If one were stringent? Maybe, 'Hywlllphhhhhoooo'. If one were really, really stringent? Possibly just a bunch of garbled white noise. Truth be told, Chloe wasn't really convinced on the EVP front. She suspected

Keith wasn't much either, but it played well on the show, and she couldn't totally rule out there being something in it.

All said and done, they got some decent material, if nothing extraordinary. They decided to close out the vigil with a séance in what had been the headmaster's office, home to every master since the school's opening. They didn't end every episode with a séance, but if a haunting suggested the presence of a single dominant entity, as in this case, it usually made for a good closer.

Mark was filming as usual, which left Claire, Keith, Ray, Chloe and Charles to comprise the circle formed around the abandoned table they had found dumped in a nearby hallway. Everyone's hands were rested flat on the table, its scarred surface the victim of decades of stationery set compasses. The circle formed an unbroken ring, with everyone's pinkie finger touching the person's next to them.

At the centre of the table, Charles had arranged his customary quartet of candles, their flames providing an oasis of light in the darkness of the office.

He begged for silence and lowered his head. Chloe watched his chest rise and fall as he took a series of low, meditative, deep breaths. Then, he spoke.

"Spirit, I call upon you. Join us. Do not be afraid. Cleave to the flame's light and warmth. Find us at this table. Enter into our company. Make your presence known to us in whichever manner you can..." Charles straightened a touch, stared into the candlelight. "You've nothing to fear. Come closer..."

162

A soft thump from somewhere outside. They all heard it.

Charles cast his gaze around the room. "Spirit?"

The sound repeated: a thump, and if Chloe listened carefully, an intermittent tap in its wake.

Keith asked in a hushed voice, "Where's that coming from?"

Chloe listened hard. It was definitely coming from somewhere in the depths of the school. She looked around the table.

"Should we go look? Perhaps it wants us to?"

The sound repeated. How could they not go look? In seconds the decision was made and the séance abandoned. Soon they were creeping in a group down the hallway lined with classroom doors, Mark on their heels with the camera.

The sound repeated and repeated, drifted toward them, something menacing in its uneven rhythm. Chloe let Charles take the lead, aware it would look better. Deferring to him to steer them to its source. The sound was growing more distinct now, stronger, enough for subtleties to emerge from the thump and ensuing tap, a spooky sssssssushhhh, sssssssusshh, sssssssusssh now discernible in the mix.

An image sprang into Chloe's mind: The old headmaster advancing down one of the interminable pitch-black hallways, his footsteps creating the soft thump, the cane held in his furious knotty grip, its tip kissing the ground as he went producing the tap, the hem of his raven black gown trailing behind him, dragging on the dusty well-trodden varnished floors, whispering an eerie sssssssusssssh…

They continued, turning to advance down another hallway lined with classroom doors, homing in on the sound's origin, until at last, they reached the door from which it was coming. Chloe strained her eyes to look inside, but the classroom's window was thick with grime and dust, and the interior pitch black. From outside, the night vision camera was rendered useless too.

Again, Chloe's mind conjured the image of the old headmaster at the head of the room before a huge chalkboard, striding back and forth, his face a cold, stoic mask covering a sadist's hunger, a cane clutched in his bony grip, itching to swing, thirsting to strike, to draw blood like the stories said. He wouldn't stop until rewarded with blood…

Charles put his hand to the door handle, turned to meet the crew's collective gaze.

"Ready?"

They all nodded. Mark got behind Charles and Chloe, camera poised, at the ready.

Charles threw the door wide. Mark swung the camera in the direction of the sound.

They all saw it.

In the window on the far side of room a pane was broken. A piece of board, a makeshift repair, tacked into place, was dangling now by a solitary nail. The wind whistled through the breach, agitating the half-broken blind over the window. The blind swelled outwards as the wind drove through, only to return with a strike and a tap as the movement travelled the length of the slats which had become bent and splayed. They dragged as they settled, producing an eerie sssssssushhhh, ssssssssusshh.

-

Had the location been more distant they might have booked into a local hotel, but with a two-hour drive home on empty early morning roads between the crew and their own comfy beds, they had voted to head home post-shoot. They distributed themselves among the transit van carrying the equipment, the motor home which doubled as a mobile production office, and Charles' car. Chloe had claimed shotgun with Charles. Halfway through the journey Charles and Chloe were discussing the old school's impending demolition.

"If it was up to me, I might knock them all down," Chloe said. "Bring in the wrecking balls. Run, children! Run free!"

"Am I to infer you didn't enjoy school then?"

"Not so much. Aren't all schools just zoos? You take all these different animals and confine them in one place, try to retain some semblance of order with endless rules. Get the whole thing behind gates, impose strict feeding times, open the enclosure a couple of times a day so the beasts can feel the sun on their hides... I knew where I was kept: the geeks and freaks enclosure. Want a tip? If you have an interest in the paranormal, at school it's best to keep it to yourself. Unless you want constant jibes from dickheads."

"It may not have helped even if you had. Unless they've changed significantly in the years since I attended school, children seem to have no trouble identifying those who are different." Charles glanced away from the road for a moment to catch Chloe's eye. He was half smiling. "No, I wasn't very fond of school either. Eventually, I learnt to try and conceal the things I heard and felt from other children, but it wasn't always easy, and I wasn't always successful. I too spent most of my school years in the, what did you just call it?"

"The geeks and freaks enclosure."

"Yes, that," he said. "I imagine some children must enjoy the experience."

"Oh yeah, my sister loved school. If you're one of the top lionesses in the big cat enclosure I've no doubt it's a blast."

"I didn't know you had a sister."

"I... prefer not to talk about her."

"Then I wouldn't dream of asking you to."

Chloe appreciated Charles giving her an out, permission to switch conversational lanes, but the very fact he had granted her this meant he deserved better. After all, she had brought Kara up. Why had she brought her up? Because since her mum had left, Kara had been on her mind far too frequently.

"She went missing around a year and a half ago. We don't know where she is."

"I see," Charles said. "That... must be hard."

"It's all my mum thinks about. All the time."

"You don't think about it?"

"I try my best not to. It doesn't do any good. Thinking about it doesn't help, doesn't change anything. Thinking about it won't tell my mum any of the stuff she wants to know. Where Kara is or if she's—" Chloe stopped, begun to wish she had taken Charles' offer to change the subject. "I don't want to be rude, but can we talk about something else?"

"Of course."

Charles deftly made a comment about the wind, and they were soon discussing the recent turn in the weather, and then other topics entirely, as far removed from absent sisters as Chloe could hope for, but inwardly her sibling stuck around.

Not for the first time, Chloe wondered, if she and her mum were told Kara wasn't just missing but dead, was never ever coming back, would that be better than the way things were now? People expected to deal with death, seemed adept at idealising the dead, ignoring the crappy things they did in life, repackaging them into a saintlier figure. Unsavoury portions were tossed away, leaving the living free to embrace what was good, or at least less rotten.

If a policeman were to knock on the door, carrying blunt news and sympathy in uniform, an end to all the questions on his tongue, would that allow her to relinquish the lingering resentment and hurt, love her sister in an uncomplicated way, arrange the warmer memories of her in a gilded frame, jettison the ugly moments, forget that they had ever happened? She honestly didn't know.

But grieving for the dead had to be simpler, didn't it?

Not like the missing.

The missing were awkward bastards.

Chapter Twenty

Ray won a phone conversation with Gary Swift via a call to his agent and a teeny half-truth. As a producer of a reasonably popular television show, he easily obtained the number for Swift's agent, called and was put straight through. Whereupon he hinted at the vague possibility of work. *Where the Dead Walk* hadn't featured guest celebrity investigators yet, and in all honesty hopefully would never need to pull such a cheap ratings trick, but plenty of other ghost hunting shows had. Ray threw out a line, simply enquiring if Gary Swift might be open to such an offer in their next series, nothing was decided yet, but they were canvassing a few names who they felt would be a good fit. He had deliberately avoided going into further detail. The agent said he would speak to Swift and see.

Swift had called back later the same day. At this point, there wasn't much to be gained with pretence. Ray explained they were investigating Crow's Cottage and had already spoken to Dave Moore and would like to speak to him too. Swift listened, seemed to think about it for a spell, then said why not? If Ray was an early riser and fancied a morning trip into the city, they could grab a coffee before he went to prep for his afternoon show at Awesome Radio. He confirmed a Starbucks near the radio station's headquarters on London's Golden Square in Soho, a media company hotspot.

Awesome Radio was an independent concern. It broadcast on FM out of London and digital to the rest of the country. It owned a bunch of stations, each designed to impale a different wedge of the demographic dartboard. There was Awesome Rock, Awesome Dance, Awesome 60s... and so on. Gary Swift was a jock on Awesome 80s. He frequented the Starbucks to jot down notes for that day's show. Ray said that would be perfect.

Chloe and Ray arrived early, but Gary Swift had beat them to it. They spotted him from outside, sipping from a bucket-sized beverage a few tables in. They entered and introduced themselves.

Swift was relaxed and appeared happy to talk. Ray told him some of what Dave Moore had shared with them. Swift listened, nodding occasionally. Ray asked him what his memories of the night were.

"Sketchy? Eighty-eight was a long time ago, a lifetime ago it feels like." Swift smiled. "Far enough back I hadn't got around to fucking things up yet."

Chloe had trawled through a bunch of Gary Swift interviews and spotted a common thread. It was admirable how Swift had rebuilt a life for himself after skirting so close to destruction, but he did rather like reminding people of it. The impression she came away with was that he secretly enjoyed his former bad-boy reputation, maybe as much as his clean and reformed one.

"We were out to celebrate a bit, blow off steam. Same as my first album, the second one had to be recorded on a hellishly tight schedule. I was still filming *Matilda Bay* back home, and could only negotiate a couple of weeks away from the show. So, I would fly in, Dave, Len and I would spend practically the whole time in the studio until it was done, and I'd fly straight back out. I was still recording vocals for the first album minutes before the cab came to take me to the airport. The second went better. We got the vocals for the final track done a whole day before I had to fly home. Len and Dave were confident they had enough to complete the rest without me, so we celebrated by hitting the town, somehow ending up at Damien Faulks' party."

Chloe tried to picture the Gary Swift who had hit the town in 1988 and wound up at Crow's Cottage, the boy with a highlighted blond mullet and dazzling grin, who danced and sang in music videos in stonewashed double denim.

The Gary Swift before her now was a stringy, weathered man a notch past fifty. The night Len Arkin killed himself, Swift was around the same age Chloe was now. As he had felt the need to point out, screwing it all up, snorting and drinking his way onto the front pages of the tabloids, condemned, lampooned, shamed and vilified until the story got boring.

The denim-fitted heartthrob might have died, but Swift had survived, and maybe he deserved to remind people how lucky he had been. Maybe it wasn't about ego, Chloe thought, and more his way of pinching himself to check he wasn't dreaming. A lot of celebrities who veered off the track were less fortunate. The live fast, die young club wasn't short of members. Swift beat the odds and eventually, through the vehicle of reality television and *Celebrity Mutineers*, found a path back into the public's good graces.

The show had allowed him to confess his sins, admit to bingeing at the hedonistic trough of fame and fortune, and repent. He had behaved badly, but to his credit, he had never tried to make excuses or ask for forgiveness. He had had it all, and pissed it all away, very nearly his life into the bargain.

There was a moment in *Celebrity Mutineers* where Swift had something of a late-night heart-to-heart with a former heavyweight boxer, and recounted waking up after a seizure in a hotel room. Swift didn't recognise the woman in his bed, and couldn't work out why his shirt was stuck to his chest with dried blood. Stumbling to the bathroom it became evident his poor abused nostrils had haemorrhaged during the lost small hours of the previous night. From the way he described the scene to the boxer, lazily steering the ship, his hands on the galleon's huge wheel, staring not at his companion but into a watery horizon dissolving a setting sun, one assumed this had been his rock bottom moment.

The point of the tale was that it was not. The point was he probably wouldn't have recognised rock bottom if it sailed past on a neon-lit barge with dancing girls and flags and loudspeakers blasting "La Cucaracha".

What did eventually save him was an accident, and love. Stumbling into the road outside a London nightclub and getting clipped by a passing black cab some months after the hotel incident put him in the hospital with a fractured femur, broken ribs, and a shattered jaw. It also brought him into contact with a doctor who had zero time for his bullshit, but a lot of time for him as it turned out. The doctor got him help and made sure he kept getting it. She was also the woman he would marry three years later.

Gary Swift raised his eyebrows. "So you think that Damien's old place, Crow's Cottage, is haunted? And it may be... Len?"

"Technically, the place belonged to Hubert Langley," Ray corrected. "Damien was merely renting it or borrowing it at the time of Lens' death. It was Hubert's nephew who contacted us, hoping we might investigate. Len Arkin left there and took his own life. Ghosts are often considered troubled and unhappy spirits..."

"Yeah, I see what you mean."

"Dave Moore mentioned you stayed a while longer at the party after he left?"

Swift shook his head. "I did, although my powers of observation probably weren't at their sharpest. I'll be honest, at that time I was under a lot of stress, handling a heavy filming schedule on *Matilda Bay* back home, promoting and recording the music, all while having to maintain a squeaky-clean image. I think the night of that party I was just ready to cut loose a bit, and it felt like somewhere I safely could, somewhere to enjoy a few drinks out of the gaze of the public and the press. There were a few other famous faces, a couple of Brit soap stars. Damien introduced me to one. I think he played the landlord of the pub on *Winchester Gardens*?

"I'd spent time with Len earlier in the evening, but he must have been somewhere else in the house later because I don't really remember seeing him. When Dave came to find me to let me know he was off, I'd had more than a few drinks."

"Dave Moore mentioned Len sat in on a séance?" asked Ray. "There was some argument afterwards, between the medium conducting it, Edward Needham, and Damien Faulks. I'm just wondering if maybe that upset Len?"

"I recall a bit of an awkward scene. Damien and some other guy had words, but it didn't last long. They went outside, and the other guy must have left because only Damien came back in. He was all smiles like it hadn't been any big deal. Not sure Len was involved. I don't think so."

"Did you speak to Len after this happened?"

"I don't think so."

"There was a young woman at the party who went missing around the time Len's suicide was discovered. Jessica Simm? She might have been seeing Damien Faulks."

Swift started to shake his head and then stopped. "Hang on? Jess? The redhead? Actually, I do remember her. We only chatted for a short while, but yeah, she was the sort of girl who leaves an impression, you know? She was a firecracker, I reckon every straight bloke in the room snuck a good look at her. Maybe the ones who weren't straight too. She said she liked my music and my work on *Matilda Bay*. How do you mean she went missing?"

"We spoke to a friend of hers who seemed to think she just decided to take off. Do you remember if Len talked to her at all?"

"He might have. I got the feeling Damien had her and another couple of girls sort of operating as party hostesses, but I can't say I remember seeing Len and her together."

"Did anything strike you as strange that evening, unusual?"

"I remember thinking some of the guests were a bit strange and unusual. Some seemed really into the old spiritual stuff. One complimented me on my aura." Swift drained the last of his bucket of coffee. "You really think Len's ghost could be haunting that old cottage?"

"We'd like to find out," Chloe said.

Swift didn't look happy. "Man, I really hope not. He was a good guy. Quiet, but friendly. I remember hearing the news once I was back home. It didn't seem real. I didn't have time to catch up with Dave or Len the next morning. My flight was early and I slept through most of it. Dave called and let me know. Once the police located his car, his stuff on the beach… Tragic."

"Do you remember anything about the police investigation?"

"No. My agent got a call. I was told I might be contacted, but I never was. I guess the cops felt if there was nothing crucial to ask, why bother a guy halfway around the world?" Swift checked his watch. "Look, I hate to cut and run, but I'm due in the studio soon."

"Of course," Ray said. "Could I just ask one more thing?"

Chloe was fairly sure she knew what was coming next, and found herself preparing to study Gary Swift's face.

"An object was discovered at the cottage recently," Ray said. "It looked as though it had been hidden."

"What sort of object?" Swift's face revealed nothing but mild curiosity.

"A sort of fancy wooden case, allegedly a replica of an occult device called the Mephisto Arcane. Damien Faulks, Hubert Langley and Edward Needham made it."

Swift slowly shook his head. "Sorry. What might it have to do with Len?"

"Probably nothing at all."

Chapter Twenty-One

Chloe slipped out of bed, grabbed her knickers from amid the clothing littering the floor and slipped them on, moving quietly to the bathroom and leaving Nick Spokes in her bed. Sleeping beauty.

She peed and drank from the tap, the salty take-out pizza probably more responsible for her thirst than a mild hangover from the wine. She straightened up and the bathroom mirror threw back an unwanted portrait.

Kara's voice echoed from some crevasse deep in her head.

That's a nice-looking guy you got in your bed back there. Begs the question, what's he doing with you?

She resisted the urge to picture her absent sister, a big smirk plastered on her face. Failed. For Kara, boyfriends had always been a matter of selection. At school, she all but had a list to pick from. Chloe not so much. The contrast between Kara and herself had always been conspicuous, with the common response since childhood being, "Really? Sisters?"

Chloe's boyfriends during her secondary school days numbered exactly two, with the longest of these romances lasting three months. She had attended prom with a boy who was a friend, but not a boyfriend. She had dated a handful of guys since but had never been one of those women men cricked their necks to grab a look at in the street. Kara had been.

For sisters, even half-sisters, they didn't look much alike. Where Chloe was pale, wrapped in skin determined to burn on any sufficiently sunny day and promptly peel in as unattractive a fashion as it could manage afterwards, Kara's skin tone was warmer, almost Mediterranean, and obligingly tanned to an even mocha brown with scarcely a lick of limp sunshine.

The differences didn't end there.

Kara's hair was fair and obedient, agreeable to being cut and coloured into whichever style was most popular. Chloe's hair was an unruly mess of curls, fighting to stick up and out every which way, and outdoing itself in the present moment. Nick had run his hands through it in the throes of passion, which was admittedly hot as fuck in the moment, but in aftermath made her look like a cartoon character who had hung onto a stick of Acme dynamite that crucial second too long.

Kara's eyes were a sumptuous honey brown. Chloe's were dark and inclined to be surrounded by shadows even when feeling at her most refreshed.

Kara rocked curves that would have caused Cat Woman to consider stuffing her bra with tissues. Chloe wasn't totally flat chested, but more sparingly endowed in the tit and bum department than she would wish.

"I thought you'd disappeared?" Chloe said.

The imaginary Kara standing behind her in the bathroom mirror rolled her eyes, the message clear. *Jeez, Chloe, learn to take a joke for once.*

Chloe hadn't meant to speak aloud. She waited, ear cocked, half expecting Nick's voice to call, "What?" but it didn't.

Imaginary Kara merely raised an eyebrow, more amused than offended.

Chloe turned her back on her. The mirror she left behind. Kara not so much. Instead of returning to bed she diverted to the kitchen and poured herself a tall glass of juice. The evening was mild for the time of year. She took the juice with her, plucked a hoodie from the peg in the hall and pulled it on, walked to the sliding patio door which opened onto a small roof terrace. The roof terrace had swung the decision when she had been flat hunting. She had immediately pictured herself out there, drinking cappuccinos on summer evenings, chilling. It was perhaps a bit grandiose to call it a roof terrace. In reality, it was around seven square feet of flat roof that had been fitted with decking and a rail, but it offered what it had promised. She slipped out onto it now with her juice, set her elbows on the rail, and took in the neighbourhood at night.

It seemed Nick had heard her after all or sensed her absence. She heard him coming, the door slid open and he joined her. His arms looped around her, his warm chest against her back. The fit was snug and felt good.

"My sister is missing."

The words just came out. In the wake of her mum's visit things had changed, in precisely the way she feared they would. Despite the declaration being a total non sequitur, Nick said, "I see. Missing for how long?"

"About a year and a half now."

"You have no idea where she is?"

"None."

"The police?"

178

"Haven't been much use. She's over eighteen and had established a pattern of coming and going without telling us exactly where or why. She's on record as a missing person, but no one's knocking doors or wearing out shoe leather looking for her."

Once she started, she found she couldn't stop. To her surprise, she told him not just about Kara disappearing, but many of the sticky everythings and nothings that felt a part of it. The messy Harker family history.

Chloe's mum, Lucy Harker, nee Chalmers, had got pregnant with her sister Kara aged eighteen. Unlike a lot of younger couples, her mum and then-boyfriend, Stephen, had confounded expectations by failing to implode. Instead, they got married. Stephen worked two jobs, and they got a mortgage on a little two-bed house. They were happy. Even if her mum hadn't said so, Chloe had seen the photos, the beaming couple with their gorgeous baby. Stephen maintained his jobs, one in a factory, and one as a motorcycle courier. It was the second that killed him, aided and abetted by a busy junction and a Volvo.

Her mum met Chloe's dad, Phil, a year later. Even for Chloe, it remained an enduring and impenetrable mystery to identify what the fuck her mum had seen in Phil. Chloe could only conclude dizzying grief and the prospect of raising a child alone impeded her mother's judgement, because while Chloe loved her father to some extent, he was as close to useless as a human being could come.

By the time her mum belatedly caught on she was pregnant with Chloe things were already rocky. Her mother and Phil parted ways shortly after she was born. Chloe got the same surname her mum and Kara had: Harker, her mum's decision. The fact Phil hadn't bothered to protest she should have his said much. Chloe had the surname of a man who was not only not her father but had died before she was even conceived.

When Chloe was old enough to contemplate it all properly, she discovered she wasn't much bothered. She felt no urge to claim Phil's surname, and struggled to think of him as her father in anything but the most literal sense. He was around enough never to qualify as estranged, but never involved enough to be useful, and things like birthday and Christmas presents were always a genuine surprise, because some years he forgot them completely. At a stretch, Chloe could imagine how a birthday might slip someone's mind, but even Phil couldn't fail to notice the appearance of tinsel and baubles, fir trees, snowmen and Santas every December, Bing Crosby and Dave Bowie singing "Little Drummer Boy" on the pub jukebox. Parupapumpum...

To Chloe, family meant her mum, Kara and their nan, who lived about half a mile away. Chloe and Kara often ate dinner there after school or slept over when their mum worked late shifts as an auxiliary nurse at the local hospital.

So, while light on the dad front, Chloe and Kara still felt like they had two solid parents. Their nan was unwavering, in her support, her love, her patience and her determination that Chloe and Kara felt safe and secure. Chloe adored her, and when Nan died things were never the same.

Kara was always a handful. Strong-willed, and without their nan to put forward a united front, her mum struggled. Kara took advantage, more often did what she pleased, went where she pleased, with whoever she pleased. She looked older than her years and this included going clubbing at weekends with friends who were older. Her sights set on university, she was smart enough to keep on top of her studies. First though, she planned to take a gap year, earn some money, prepare.

A friend of a friend helped get her a job, lucrative but short term. The friend of a friend was the niece of a nightclub manager, who was always looking for table girls. If a girl could carry off the right attitude and her face and body fit, there was good money to be earned. Kara's friend swore tips could run into hundreds of pounds in a single day, and it was true. In Kara's first week, she made more than her mum made in a month.

Soon, not all the money Kara was earning was making it into her university savings account. When she wasn't working, she seemed to be partying. When Chloe and her mum did see her, she was irritable and quick to bite. Under the carefully applied make-up she looked tired, the air of someone burning the candle not just at both ends but blowtorching the middle too. A year came and went; university was kicked into the long grass.

Then out of nowhere, Kara lost the job. She never said why, but also didn't seem especially concerned. She had contacts, she insisted, when their mum dared ask what she planned to do next, finding something similar wouldn't be a problem. The partying continued, but the new job was always around the corner.

Arguments had become part of family life, but the friction was building, and then came a real megaton bust-up. Their mum demanded to know how she was paying for all the partying now she wasn't earning, Kara colourfully informed her it was none of her fucking business and, always most cutting when on the defensive, listed some of the many ways their mum had made a mess of her life and to stop and think about that before telling anyone else what to do. The same knives were drawn, but Kara had long since stopped using them to prick or jab, instead driving them home with abandon. Bad mother, uneducated, paranoid, dumb enough to be knocked up at eighteen, jealous she had never got to enjoy partying at the same age... Eventually, Kara made a call, and shortly after a guy in a huge SUV screeched up outside the house. She stormed out, jumped in the car and took off. The door had hardly closed before it sped away.

They didn't see her for two weeks.

Then she had rocked back up like nothing had happened, or certainly nothing she had to apologise for. She stayed a few days, during which they received passing glimpses of her cold shoulder, and time for yet one more bust-up, this time between Chloe and Kara, but overall she was out more than in. Then she vanished for a few more days, before returning briefly one afternoon, and that was the last time they saw her.

After a month passed without a word and trying to contact her proved impossible, Chloe's mum went to the police. They were professional, but also carefully explained that Kara was an adult. Unless they had a specific reason to assume she was at risk, they were limited in what help they were able to offer. She was reported as missing and some limited efforts were made, but essentially that was that. A year and a half later Kara was still missing.

If assured of her wellbeing, they might remember to dread her return a little too, but they weren't assured of her wellbeing. They didn't know if Kara was living it up or living rough, healthy or hanging on by her fingernails, giving someone else a dose of her poison or being abused, alive or dead.

Nick listened without comment, seeming to know she needed to get it out. Then, instead of offering stock sympathy, or pretending to understand, he did something which meant much more.

"You know I said I lost my dad in my teens?" he said.

Chloe nodded.

"What I didn't tell you is how I lost him. He killed himself, rented a lockup, blocked the doors up and left his car running. Carbon monoxide poisoning. My mum and me, we had no idea anything was wrong.

"They were an old-fashioned couple, my mum and dad. My mum worked a part-time job and pretty much kept what she earned. Dad was the breadwinner, paid the bills. Everything was in his name, his business, the house… His business ran into trouble, a client went under owing him a lot of money, being a smaller firm, it wasn't limited. My dad had always gambled a bit, for fun, never enough to view it as a problem, but maybe the stress made it worse, or maybe he thought he could fix everything with a few big wins.

"When the dust settled my mum discovered she wasn't just a widow, not even just flat broke, but in debt. The business folded. Our house had been re-mortgaged, up to the hilt, and had to be sold. We moved in with my aunt and uncle. Soon after, I left school and entered nursing.

"That day we first met? Getting news my offer had been accepted on the house, it was a big deal. It's taken a lot of saving, but I'm finally going to be able to get her a place of her own. I'm calling it an investment because that's the only way she will let me do it, but it's about setting things right. I've tried to forgive my dad, for abandoning us, for giving up, for robbing us of the chance to support him, for leaving us with nothing, and in the way he did, but I don't know if I'll ever be able to completely. My mum deserved better. I did. I hate the way all the years before are spoilt, how it's impossible to think back on them and enjoy the best of him." Nick fell silent. "I suppose what I'm trying to say is I know what it feels like to be angry with someone who's not around."

Chloe didn't know what to say. She thought he had finished, but then he added more.

"But I also don't want to spend the rest of my life holding onto that anger. It's too easy. It means I don't have to think about how unhappy he must have been to have left us."

Chapter Twenty-Two

Charles knew he would make the call, eventually. If anyone was equipped to discern whether the Mephisto Arcane was more than an elaborate prop it was Eamonn Lister.

What complicated matters was that, to a certain extent, Charles remained a good friend to Eamonn by leaving him alone.

Eamonn wasn't simply the most knowledgeable person he knew when it came to matters supernatural, he also happened to be the most gifted sensitive Charles had ever encountered. An accolade which was, depending on your perspective, and the degree of sensitivity on any given day, either a staggering gift or a debilitating curse.

Like a tinnitus sufferer plagued by incessant ringing or buzzing, Eamonn could not easily escape the impact of spiritual energy surrounding him. Distancing himself from places where it was most concentrated was one way of making existence more tolerable.

The worst places were most often where people lived or congregated. Living souls act as a magnet for dead ones. When Eamonn had lived in London, he had occupied the top floor of a tower block, and owned the floor below, leaving it vacant, employing it as a buffer. It was a modestly effective solution, and obviously expensive. Eamonn earned the extravagance by consulting for a small and very select group of special clients.

Ultimately though, living in the London sky had proven insufficient. Eamonn had since relocated one step further away from humanity, a spot remote enough it had scarcely been inhabited at all.

His new dwelling was a small cottage on a Welsh peninsula, a bland grey rectangle on Google Maps' satellite view. The closest neighbouring property was nearly a mile away. A disused lighthouse.

Charles' journey had taken most of the morning, the last leg of which required him to negotiate a string of twisting, skinny country roads with no markings, flanked by fields, trees and hedges. Eventually, even these narrow arteries devolved into ruts of rudimentary gravel-studded track. Finally, Eamonn's home swung into view, a single-story whitewashed block. It was a little utilitarian in appearance to be called a cottage, featuring none of the architectural charms of Crow's Cottage. It was flat-roofed and functional, conspicuous against the green hills, cliffs and band of sullen sea beyond.

As he neared, the red door fronting the property opened and Eamonn's slight figure appeared on the threshold. Were Eamonn anyone else, Charles would have assumed the sound of his car's engine had somehow carried over the stiff breeze whistling in off the sea. In this case, Eamonn had probably sensed him coming from miles down the track.

Charles parked and walked to meet his friend, and found himself taken aback by his appearance.

What struck him was how relaxed and well Eamonn looked. He was actually smiling. Short with sandy hair, Eamonn's taste for cardigans, corduroy trousers and slippers remained, but the fragile and frayed, wired, skittery man who inhabited them appeared altered. Eamonn looked rested and well-fed. His tick was still present but seemed greatly reduced. It fired off in a series of spasms through his neck and up his head as he issued a greeting.

"Good afternoon, Chur-Churr-Charles."

-

Eamonn flexed his hands and placed them on the table beside the object. There was the tiniest of pauses, Charles saw his friend brace himself and then he placed them on the Mephisto Arcane. Over the next few seconds, Eamonn's brow formed a deep V. He removed his hands and worked his fingers, clenching them and straightening them out, then once more set them back onto the device.

Charles occasionally received psychometric impressions from things he touched, a fleeting sensation of something, a mood, an image, a sound or smell, but it was rare. For Eamonn, it was the rule more than the exception.

Eamonn shifted his hands around the box, like a blind person might, assessing its shape and dimensions. At last, he said, "Suuuurr-ssss-strange…"

"Strange?"

"Only in that there's lur-little to report." Eamonn hesitated. "I think someone *was* afraid of this thurrr-thing. They hid it?" Eamonn tried again for a spell, walked his fingers over the polished wooden box. "Or something connected to it?" Frustration fluttered through his pinched face. "Sss-sorry Charles."

"Not at all. It's more than I received."

Charles had hoped Eamonn might get more but knew it was possible he wouldn't. While Eamonn was many times more sensitive than he was to residual energies, the process was mercurial, far from a science.

"If the story was true," Charles mused, "about what really happened to this record producer and the girl, you would expect more, wouldn't you?"

"I whurr-would, but there are no hard and fur-fast rules, even if the story rang true, even if this device does wuh-what the legend surrounding it claims.

"The thing is," Eamonn continued, "the story doesn't r-ring true. You know as well as I do a whur-working of any type depends as much on the practitioner as the process. The notion two individuals, unschooled and unwitting, churr-could, simply through f-fooling around with an object like this accidentally summon a demon? Doubtful. I remain unconvinced ssss-such entities even exist. Angry spurrr-spirits yes, confused spirits, wuh-wild and p-powerful spirits… but dur-demons? A non-human derived ssss-spirit? I've never knowingly encountered one. Which suggests they are either extremely ruh-rare or pure myth. Either instance suggests they are not casually summoned."

"A record producer and a model don't strike you as likely candidates?"

"Cuuur-quite."

Eamonn had removed his hands from the Mephisto Arcane, but not his eyes. "Could you lurr-lurrr-leave this thing with me for a bit? I'd like to examine it in greater detail, see if there is s-something to be teased out of it. I have an idea I might know the origin of these suuur-symbols, but

I'd like to check to make sure. I have a couple of books that will need digging out, and there's a khuuur-couple of people I can speak to."

Ray was keen to film at Crow's Cottage sooner rather than later, but if the Arcane was holding something back Charles was equally keen to give Eamonn the chance to unearth it.

"Would a day be long enough?"

-

Charles had just negotiated the bumpy track from Eamonn's cottage and was about to hit the narrow and unmarked roads leading back into civilisation when his phone rang.

He pulled over. It was Ray.

"Hi," Ray said, "you still out on the edge of nowhere?"

"Just about to cross the border to somewhere actually. Why?"

"Damien Faulks called. He's willing to see us, tonight. We've been invited to his magic club. Think you can make it back by eight?"

"I think so."

Ray gave him the address.

Chapter Twenty-Three

Chloe had been loitering with Ray near Faulks' club.

Charles had arrived in time, but only just. It had looked like they were in danger of having to meet Faulks without him, but then he had called, informing them he was parked in a multi-storey just a few streets away. He quickly caught them up on his visit with Eamonn as they approached Faulks' club.

The Effectary lay down a lean side street. The only frontage existed in the form of an unassuming black door with a brass knocker and a hand-painted sign, almost a plaque. The impression conveyed was of visiting some sort of exclusive secret hideaway or clandestine club, which Chloe supposed was very much the idea.

Ray gave the knocker a sharp rap. A moment later the door swung inwards and a man in a black tuxedo and with an imperious bearing looked them over. Ray explained they were guests of Damien Faulks. Tuxedo man consulted a list, presumably located their names and welcomed them in, instructing them to follow him through.

They trailed through a dimly lit anteroom, baroquely decorated in crimson and gold, before turning a corner to encounter a black velvet curtain. Tuxedo man stopped and turned on his heel, tipping his head.

"Please, enjoy your evening."

Then with a flourish, he whipped back the curtain, only to reveal a dead end.

The wall featured a large painting in an ornate gilded frame, depicting a room on the canvas with as much depth as the wall was flat: a modest spot-lit stage, surrounded by an audience of silhouettes seated at tables. The canvas's oils were so thickly applied Chloe could see brushstrokes licking from the surface like breaking waves. A palette of black and blue shadows contrasted sharply with yellows, oranges and reds. Taken as a whole they united to create a sumptuously moody scene.

Tuxedo man looked at first surprised, and then a little embarrassed. He coughed. "Sorry. Forgive me."

With a sharp tug, he pulled the velvet curtain back into place and clapped his hands. Suddenly he was holding a wand, the kind stage magicians in cartoons were rarely depicted without. Its glossy, ebony black body was capped at both ends with silver tips—a stereotype of a wand. Tuxedo man presented it to Chloe.

"A smart tap madam, and, of course, the magic word." He nodded toward the curtain as further clarification.

Chloe was game. She took the wand, and tapped the curtain with a suitable flourish, felt the wand's silver tip strike the wall through the heavy fabric and said the word, "Abracadabra!"

Tuxedo man smiled courteously and retrieved the wand. Another clap of his hands saw it vanish.

He grasped the black velvet curtain for a second time and whipped it back. Only this time both wall and painting were gone, replaced by a door. Tuxedo man twisted the handle and pushed it open. Chloe stepped through, smiling, Charles and Ray in tow. The room beyond matched the scene in the vanished painting exactly.

It didn't require a mastermind to work out how the trick had been done. A sliding panel doubled for the dead end, in the shape of a wall with a framed painting. The panel concealed the door. The second time the man drew back the curtain he drew back the panel with it. The illusion was as simple as it was effective, and solving the mechanics didn't spoil the fun. The magic survived in the staging and execution, the artistry in the way the picture matched the real view of the room, capturing the ambience perfectly.

In the painting the audience were vague silhouettes, in the room they were an eclectic bunch. A glance around revealed patrons ranging from twenty to eighty. It seemed fans of magic were alive and well, and came in all shapes and sizes. There were around two dozen tables in The Effectary, and almost all were full. Another tuxedoed member of staff, this one female and blonde, ushered them to one of the few which wasn't. It offered a prime view of the room's small stage. She removed the 'reserved' sign, let them get seated, took their drinks order and said she would inform Damien they had arrived.

Presently the stage was occupied by a magician beside a contraption which held a thick stack of banknotes, an ornate mechanical press. The device was fitted with a spout at one end, under which lay a large glass bowl, the sort a goldfish might swim in.

On the stage, the magician began to wind the handle on the press, screwing the stack of notes ever tighter. The audience watched the pile shrink, then, slowly at first but faster as he went, coins began to tumble out of the spout into the glass bowl. Soon the bills were gone and the bowl was full of coins. The magician bowed to much applause, and the spotlight faded as he departed the stage.

Chloe spied Damien Faulks approaching from across the room. He was older than in any of the pictures she had seen of him, several decades older, but she still recognised him immediately. Time had been kind. Save for a few wrinkles and his hair being styled less extravagantly and greyer, he looked, dressed in a tasteful black suit, black shirt and tie, remarkably similar to the black-clad conjurer from his '80s publicity shots. She noticed, as he walked towards them, that he still wore the distinctive double banded silver ring on his right hand.

Upon nearing their table, he flashed them a performer's smile and proceeded to introduce himself, "Damien Faulks. Welcome to The Effectary."

"Thank you for the invitation," Ray said. "And for being generous enough to see us. I'm Ray Darling. We spoke on the phone. This is Charles McBride and Chloe Harker."

Faulks made a point of shaking everyone's hand. He went in for the two-handed variety, where the free hand that isn't taking care of the shake gets acquainted with the other person's forearm. The clasp-shake, a common choice of politicians, was supposed to come across as warm and friendly. It always struck Chloe as an overly tactile greeting though, and paradoxically insincere, like a broad smile that doesn't reach the eyes. If you knew someone well enough to get grabby, what was wrong with a hug? If you didn't, then a straight handshake covered things just fine.

The tuxedoed blonde who had seated them returned with their drinks. Faulks placed an avuncular hand at the small of her back, in a way Chloe knew he certainly would not have with a male member of staff. She asked if they required anything else. They said they were fine and she left.

"So…" Faulks said, "*Where the Dead Walk* is set to investigate my erstwhile digs, Crow's Cottage, eh?"

"Giles Langley, the new owner invited us in. Hubert Langley's nephew."

"I see. Fantastic old place, isn't it? And… I assume someone thinks it's haunted now?" Faulks smiled, but the question was direct enough to demonstrate he wasn't averse to cutting to the chase.

"That's what we'd like to find out."

At some point, Faulks had produced a deck of cards. Chloe missed the precise moment when they appeared, but they were in his hands now. Her attention was drawn to them when he began to shuffle the deck. He fanned them and held them out.

"I wonder," Faulks said, "how often do people return to haunt a place where they once lived, and how often does a place haunt them first?" Chloe found the cards proffered in her direction. "Indulge me." Faulks smiled. "Pick a card, any card. Don't let me see it."

She drew a card from a third of the way into the deck, scooped it up before her so only she could see it. The card was the Jack of Diamonds.

"Now, if you'd care to sign it, and return it to the deck," Faulks said, averting his gaze. Chloe saw a pen had somehow appeared on the table too. She scribbled her name on the front and pushed it back into the pile. Faulks shuffled the deck again and moved to Charles and then Ray, who chose their own cards and signed them. With the stage temporarily empty, several performers had emerged to work the tables and practice close magic around the room.

"The truth?" Faulks said, knocking the deck of cards back into a tidy block in one deft movement. "I wasn't sure I wanted to meet with you. I haven't thought about Crow's Cottage for a very long time. Maybe because I prefer not to. It was a place I grew fond of, before my memories became tarnished by how things ended there." Faulks set the deck of cards down in front of Chloe. "Young lady, would you care to shuffle these and then cut them into equal piles, one placed in front of each of you?"

Chloe took the cards and carried out Faulks' instructions, setting three neat stacks in a row, one before Charles, Ray and herself.

"And exactly how did things end?" Ray asked.

"The whole Len Arkin business? It seemed to poison everything. I've nothing but sympathy for the man, no one who's happy chooses to take his own life, but the reverberations? The press loves a scandal. When they spied something that looked like it might be spun into a big fat juicy one, they set to work. When they discovered there wasn't actually a scandal after all, they simply massaged what was available to fit the bill. A lot of damage through insinuation. Throw the word 'parties', 'celebrities', 'occult' and 'suicide' into a tabloid headline and it almost doesn't matter what the real story was."

195

"What was the real story?"

"That my parties were just parties. A bunch of friends and acquaintances socialising. No more, no less. Only one guest decided he would take his own life after leaving rather than go home. I expect he would have done so wherever he spent the evening. To my knowledge, nothing occurred at the party to contribute to his decision. The police investigation concluded as much, but that didn't stop the gutter press from speculating, filling pages with unsubstantiated, salacious garbage about what *could* have been going on. Everyone knows Len Arkin's swim cost him his life, far fewer know it cost me a number of friendships and damaged my career just when it was about to take off. I'm not looking for sympathy, just stating a fact."

"Maybe, even all these years later, we could help set the record straight?"

Faulks didn't look convinced. "I'm sorry, but I can't see how raking it all up is likely to change anything." Faulks shrugged, managed a tepid smile, and turned to Chloe. "Madam, if you would turn over the topmost card on the stack before you?"

Chloe obliged.

It was the Jack of Diamonds, bearing her signature.

"All publicity is not good publicity," Faulks said. "Offers of TV work which had been growing steadily more frequent suddenly dried up. That, in turn, impacted my live show bookings. Beyond work? It injured my friendship with Hubert Langley. He was mortified by the press attention and misguidedly blamed me for it. He wanted the whole business to go away and evidently believed having no further contact with me would somehow help. I'd been informally renting Crow's Cottage from him for over a year. Weeks after Len Arkin's suicide I received a letter from Hubert's lawyer telling me I was to vacate the property forthwith."

"That was when work on the Mephisto Arcane stopped?"

Faulks made an ahhhh face. "The Mephisto Arcane. No, it, was complete. In the days prior to the party, I had applied the last few finishing touches. Hubert was going to collect it the night of the party. I assumed he had, because the following morning it was gone. The discovery the next day of Len Arkin's car and clothes, his suicide, created more immediate concerns. The police wanting to question me and my guests for a start, and then the story appearing in the press. Not just that Arkin had committed suicide, but where he had been before he chose to do it."

"You never confirmed Hubert had taken it later?"

"Honestly? By the time it seemed of any importance, I didn't care much whether he had or not. If a guest had stolen it for some reason it wouldn't have made much difference to me. It wasn't a memento I was eager to have around."

"Hubert had effectively commissioned you to craft the Mephisto Arcane, though?"

"It was nothing that formal. After hearing the story of the original, and that Hubert had illustrations supposedly depicting the device in detail, I just asked what felt like the obvious question. Had he considered attempting to recreate it? I felt I had the skills. I've always enjoyed building things, making things, crafting things. Seeing Hubert was clearly excited by the prospect, I offered to take up the challenge, suggesting, purely off the cuff, that Edward Needham could even attempt to operate it when it was complete.

"That Hubert would have the device was implicit, I felt. I had no real use for it. The idea of crafting it was attractive, but once it was done? I knew Hubert would value it far more than I ever would. The product of any art is not really for the artist. The pleasure lies in the sharing." Faulks nodded the deck of cards nearest to Ray.

"Would you?"

Ray flipped the topmost card of his pile.

It was the King of Clubs. Ray's erratic signature across it.

"It also seemed a perfect vehicle for expressing my gratitude," Faulks continued. "Hubert had graciously loaned me the use of Crow's Cottage while my theatre run at the time kept me near London. Hubert didn't really need money, so a meticulously recreated Mephisto Arcane struck me as an ideal alternative."

Faulks flipped the card back over and set Ray's stack on top of Chloe's, leaving Charles' stack the only one remaining. "I expect you're going to ask me about the stories now? I'm aware of them, of course. Bumbling party guests, a dangerous occult device… Sorcery and demons… Mr McBride?" Faulks nodded to the final pile of cards in front of Charles. "Would you?"

Charles flipped the topmost card over.

It was the Ace of Hearts, and unmarked.

Faulks seemed momentarily thrown, but did a good job of hiding it. The frown that flickered across his brow was gone in a blink.

Without comment, he flipped the card back over and collected the stack, set it on top of the other two-thirds of the deck, and resumed talking as if the trick hadn't just gone sideways.

"The story about Arkin and Jessica," he said, "finding the Mephisto Arcane and summoning a demon? It might even be funny—if Arkin hadn't actually taken his own life. Since he did, it feels in poor taste. Trust me. There was no demon, no girl dragged to hell."

"Jessica Simm did vanish, though?" Ray said.

"That she did," Faulks said. "Although 'vanished' makes it sound like a mystery, when it really wasn't. I believe her things were gone, from her flat. She skipped town, as she had many towns before, and no doubt would again in the future. I wasn't surprised. No one who knew Jess was. Like Hubert, I assumed she didn't want to be involved in any fallout, the press looking for dirt, and the law. I liked Jess, partly because that was the sort of girl she was, impulsive, unpredictable. I had even started to consider if she might make a good stage assistant. I had been thinking about adding one to my act."

"You just said she was impulsive, unpredictable... Those don't strike me as great traits for a magician's assistant," Ray said.

Faulks smiled. "No, but she had assets to compensate. She was street smart, a quick study and very attractive. In these days of political correctness, the illusionist's traditional glamorous assistant has fallen out of favour, but there's a very good reason they existed and worked so well."

"There is?" said Chloe.

"Magic, or illusion, is a blend of skill, creativity and misdirection. The greater the misdirection the more latitude the illusionist has to exercise those first elements. A cracking set of legs in a sparkly one-piece makes for a wonderful bit of misdirection. The male half of the audience is apt to be watching you with only one eye from the get-go. In that respect, Jess would have been perfect."

"Do you know where Jess went after she skipped town?" asked Ray.

"I don't. Nor would I ever have expected her to tell me. I think she had just come from Manchester when I first met her, or that's what she told me, but Manchester wasn't her home town. She was obviously familiar with a lot of cities. She talked about spending time in Birmingham, Glasgow, and Liverpool. I think she grew up in Wales. She hid the accent, but you could detect the odd lilt it if you listened closely, especially when she drank. A few rums and Cokes and Welsh Jessica began to leak out. I loved it. I liked her. She was good company, but she also had issues. Not everyone would have noticed, but I did. I was still working through a few of my own back then."

"You were?"

"She had the same drive, compulsion to escape from where she had come from, who she used to be. Like me, but I diverted all of that energy into my work. I'm not sure Jess had a similar outlet. She never spoke about escaping, she didn't have to. I saw it in the way she looked at life, in the choices she made. Like me, Jess was a kid who had got used to looking after herself, who'd long since stopped expecting anyone else to. Takes one to know one, right? Same as not everyone can tell the difference between cigarette burn scars and having 'a few moles removed'. Not all families are happy families.

"I ran away from home when I was fifteen. Hitchhiked to London with nothing but change in my pocket. Performing card tricks on the street was the only thing that prevented me from going hungry some days. Fifteen years later I was performing in front of packed theatres. Magic saved me. I hope eventually Jess found something to save her."

Faulks was being remarkably candid with them, and what they were hearing didn't have the ring of Gary Swift style self-mythologising. These felt like personal details, bald and genuine, and Chloe reckoned she knew why he was sharing them. Behind the hearty handshakes, the performer's smile and deft moves, Faulks was afraid. Len Arkin's suicide had once cost him dearly. What they were hearing was a plea to leave it in the past, lest it reach out thirty years and wound him again.

While there was no TV show, not even a single episode, he had still succeeded in making a fair living doing what he enjoyed. Chloe was willing to bet The Effectary was far more than most magicians managed; a day job and part time bookings at children's parties was closer to the mark. Faulks was happy with how things were, and wasn't looking for renewed notoriety.

"You never heard from Jess again," Ray asked, "found out where she went?"

Faulks shook his head.

Charles asked, "In your time at Crow's Cottage did you ever witness anything unusual?"

"You mean did I see any ghosts? No, and Hubert never mentioned anything about the place being haunted. If it was, I'd have expected him to, given our mutual interest in the paranormal."

"Did you ever try to contact Hubert," said Charles, "rekindle your friendship?"

"No. As I said, it's not a time I'm eager to look back on. It's hard to have to think of what might have been. I dreamed of my own TV show, and I don't think I was wrong in feeling I was very close to getting there. What performer doesn't dream of a larger stage? Speaking of which, I'm expected to perform on that one there shortly." Faulks collected his stack of cards. "Was there anything else you were specifically hoping to find out?"

Charles looked to Ray and then Chloe. It seemed not. "No. I think we covered most of it. Thank you, you've been most accommodating."

Faulks simply nodded and went to leave, only to stop short. He turned and looked toward Charles. "Do you perhaps have a business card I might have? Something might come to me later. I can contact you."

"Of course. One moment."

Charles put a hand into his jacket and removed his wallet. He opened it and was about to reach inside for a business card when he paused. Poking out of the first pocket in his wallet was a playing card. Even from the half on display, Chloe could see it was a joker, signed with a signature she knew belonged to Charles.

Chapter Twenty-Four

Charles had set off early to repeat his trip halfway across the country from London to a sparse and craggy elbow of Wales. He was eager to hear what Eamonn had to say after studying the Mephisto Arcane more extensively.

The device sat on Eamonn's kitchen table, next to a couple of weathered books. Eamonn had tabs marking a number of pages. He opened one at a tab and angled it so Charles could see the page of symbols laid out there in a grid. Many of the symbols looked familiar. They matched the ones worked into the Arcane.

"The ssss-symbols are of Renaissance occult origin," Eamonn said. He reached out and turned the Arcane to display each of its four sides. "They're most closely associated whur-with a Renaissance-era philosopher and magician nur-named Andrea Fiorentino. Fiorentino studied under Heinrich Cornelius Agrippa. It's not known if he devised these symbols himself, or learned of them sss-somewhere, but they appear frequently in his work. If you were to lur-look for someone who fits the profile of the traveller from the Mephisto Arcane legend, Fiorentino fuur-fits the bill."

"So the legend is true?"

"Mmmm-maybe, and maybe not. Given the d-device was based on illustrations acquired by a collector of occult pieces, we have to cur-cuur-consider the possibility the pictures could have been faked. I suspect a great many pieces are. The b-b-biggest and wealthiest collectors tend to be incredibly secretive; the items they own aren't always procured through legal means, and oftentimes they're not thuur-thuuur-things the general public would find palatable. This leaves collectors vulnerable to forgeries. Were a fuur-forger setting out to make a fake set of illustrations depicting the Mephisto Arcane, he may well have chosen to use these symbols precisely b-b-because Fiorentino offers a plausible fit for 'the traveller' burnt at the stake in the Mephisto Arcane story."

"Do you know what the symbols mean?"

"They seek to describe all the d-different elements of the incorporeal world, their ver-various states, the fur-forces capable of being applied to them, and the consequence of each. There are thirty-two symbols in total. All are ruh-represented here, eight on each face."

"Do you think the story is based on a real event, that there was a traveller, an original Mephisto Arcane, destroyed along with its owner?"

"I've always felt there was a rur-ring of truth to it. I've heard versions where the Mephisto Arcane was not destroyed. If it survived into mm-modern times it is exactly the sort of item to wind up in the hands of a private cur-cuur-collector. If it duh-did then the illustrations this device was based upon could have been produced any time during last the five hundred years or so."

"You haven't got anything from handling the device itself?"

"Nothing I feel c-confident about. Very weak residual echoes, the sort any object carries, too vague to trust. I'm sss-sorry Charles. I wish I could tell you m-more."

"Do you think there could be a specific ritual required to make use of it?"

"Possibly. If it operates purely as a conduit, it's shown no sign of it for me, and I've given it plenty of opportunity to. Although, if it was designed simply to amplify energies I might m-make a poor choice of operator. In my experience, energies will always take the most direct route, and I am not a difficult man to reach. It's the entire reason I live all the way out here. On the other hand, I sss-struggle to believe the device would be effective for a complete novice."

"Like Len Arkin, or Jessica Simm?"

"Indeed. Unless one possessed ssss-some latent sensitivity or was versed in performing some form of engagement with spiritual energies."

"What if Faulks was versed?" Charles was thinking out loud. "He mixed with people who were gifted, schooled in aspects of spirituality and the occult. What if he tutored the girl, Jessica?"

"To whuh-what end?"

"I haven't a clue. Just thinking aloud. Something about Faulks doesn't sit right with me," Charles said. "We met with him yesterday, at his magic club. On the surface he seemed open to discussing what had happened at the party, and what happened afterwards, the impact of it, the detrimental effect it had on his career and friendship with Edward Needham and Hubert Langley. On the surface he was remarkably candid, and helpful..."

"But?"

"I also feel he wasn't telling us the whole story, perhaps even messing with us. He performed a card trick while we were talking, appeared to mess it up. But the real trick turned out to be the card in my wallet, the card I'd randomly pulled out of the deck." Charles reached for his wallet and took out the card. He held it up, showed Eamonn the face. His signature looped across a clownish dancing figure.

"A joker," Eamonn said.

"I don't know if Damien Faulks' knowledge of magic extends beyond fancy card tricks, making rabbits appear from hats or appearing to saw pretty girls in two, but I do know I can't quite swallow the picture he's painted of himself as the victim in this whole Len Arkin mess."

-

Charles arrived home later than he had anticipated. An accident on the M4 had reduced his return leg to a slow crawl.

It was early evening by the time he opened his front door to experience a tremor of unease. Through the hall, he saw his study door was open. He never left it open, not unless he was working in there. It had been closed when he went out. He was sure of it. Well, almost sure.

He took a few steps into the hallway, and knowing it was crazy but unable to help himself, he called out, "Hello?"

He wasn't surprised when he received no response.

He moved further in, peeked into the lounge, saw nothing out of place, and advanced into the kitchen.

Likewise, everything appeared perfectly normal. He progressed to the French doors at the head of the dining room which opened out onto his garden, gave the handles a rattle. They were still locked. He checked the windows too. Also locked.

Slowly, he began to relax a touch

Exactly how sure was he about having closed the study door this morning?

He knew he had gone in to collect the Arcane, and thought he had shut it behind him on his way out.

But had he?

The problem with habits was performing them without thinking. When he recalled closing his study door this morning, was it really this morning, or one of the hundreds of times he had in the past? He could have neglected to close it. It was possible. He removed his courier bag containing his iPad and the Arcane, hooked the strap over the back of a dining chair.

He was about to turn and go check upstairs when he clearly heard a thud come from what sounded like his bedroom. Before he even had chance to consider the wisdom of investigating, a figure dropped past the window onto the patio outside the French doors. He was wearing a navy-blue hoodie, and he wasn't hanging around.

The man sprinted down the garden and clambered over the back fence. For a moment Charles was so shocked, he couldn't actually move.

When he could, he fumbled out his phone and dialled 999.

Charles waited near the front door until the police officers arrived. Together they searched the upstairs of the house. The window in the spare room was still gaping wide open from where his would-be burglar had made a hasty escape. As far as Charles could determine, nothing had been taken. Fortuitously, he looked to have arrived home not long after the intruder had gained entry, although how he had gained entry was a mystery. One of the officers, who to Charles looked young enough to qualify for a child's ticket at the cinema, but addressed Charles as if he had just wandered out of an old folks' home in his pyjamas, clearly suspected a window had been left open.

Charles knew otherwise.

He was certain the windows had been closed, and equally certain, now, that the study door had been shut. When he insisted this was the case, the other officer had conceded it was possible that, if skilled, the intruder may have been able to gain entry without causing damage. They had searched for signs of some but found nothing.

Charles got the impression the officers were growing bored with him. Nothing had been stolen, and the intruder had chosen to take flight instead of getting violent. He had been lucky, they said, although strongly advised he get a security system fitted. It was a shame, but invariably true, baby face said, that most people only got around to installing one once they had been burgled.

Charles accepted the pubescent constable had a point, and resolved to call a local home security firm the next morning.

Chapter Twenty-Five

Chloe had wanted to see Nick but resisted the urge to call and invite him over. It was still early days and she was wary of coming across as too eager, but then he had called her, asked if she wanted to grab something to eat. Splitting the difference, she had suggested he come over to hers. They could order in.

Nick hadn't had the best of days. He looked tired and wired, coming off a long shift which unexpectedly ran into the early morning. He didn't say, but she guessed it was with a patient who wasn't doing well, had perhaps even passed away.

A Chinese takeout. A little conversation. Some very good sex.

They were in bed, and it was late.

Chloe knew what was happening. There was no point kidding herself. That powerfully heady, magnetic, visceral force of attraction was at work. She had felt it before of course, first experienced in her teens, texting her first boyfriend and colossal crush, Jamie Parker, late into the night. She had been careful to keep her door shut so her mum wouldn't see the light spilling from her room and investigate, realise why she found it such an effort to get up in the mornings. Swapping jokes and school gossip, flirting. Jamie was beautiful. He went to the boys' school up the road. Going to a girls' school and not having any brothers rendered him a wonderfully mysterious creature to Chloe, like a unicorn, albeit with acne and bum fluff.

She and Jamie Parker had dated for a whole six weeks before he dumped her for Hannah Kenny, who was apparently more liberal in the putting out department. When the news came it was in text form. Blunt and heart-breaking.

DON'T WANT TO GO OUT WITH YOU ANYMORE. SORRY

It came as some consolation to see Hannah Kenny didn't last much longer than she had. She learned school romances could be a fast-paced, ruthless business, and to subsequently approach boys with more caution.

That feeling of heady, intoxicating attraction, though? She doubted wisdom diminished the impact whether she be fourteen or forty.

She was falling for Nick Spokes.

She liked the way his body was lean but felt solid. She liked how it felt to be tucked up close to him, to talk about everything and nothing. She had told him about filming at the Edwardian boys' school. The broken window and flapping blind which had not turned out to be the skulking spirit of a headmaster. There was just Crow's Cottage to go and filming for the series would be complete.

"So, when are you spending the night at Hubert's old place?" he asked.

"A week or so? It will have to be soon, we're cutting it fine as it stands. If I'm honest, I'm itching to go back. The more we find out, the more interesting the place and the whole business with Len Arkin gets. What started with a few reported sightings of an apparition and an odd-looking box has turned into a huge, fascinating ball of wax. Occult societies, dead record producers, missing women, wild parties and recreating occult devices, there's a lot to unpack."

"You think the apparition is the ghost of this Len Arkin, the record producer who killed himself?"

"Maybe."

"What about the story about him and this woman who disappeared, them accidentally using this Mephisto Arcane thing to summon a demon?"

"Yeah. Still just a story, not a single thing to support it. Shame, because it's a great story. That's the lure of a good tale, isn't it? Of all urban myths and ghost stories, I suppose. They're seductive. Something in you wants to believe them."

"So, this Mephisto Arcane? Where's that now?"

"Charles picked it back up yesterday. He took it to some guy he knew to check it out, another medium. What I really wish is we could locate this Jessica Simm. The woman who disappeared? Two minutes with her would put a lot of questions to bed at a stroke. I know Ray has been trying, but I don't think he's having much luck."

"This all happened when?" Nick asked, "Eighty-seven? Eighty-eight?"

"Eighty-eight."

"Over thirty years ago. The world was a different place back then, right? No social networks, no mobile phones, no GPS, no digital footprints, hell, no digital really, no internet at all. Hardly any CCTV, and what there was would have been analogue, videotapes, probably only kept for a week or two? Police databases had to be in their infancy. We're talking about a world that still ran mostly on paper.

If someone suddenly moved across the country, you've got to imagine tracking them down could be a serious job."

Chloe knew only too well that even today the police didn't launch high-profile searches for grown women with a history of mobility without evidence they were at risk or might have come to harm. It was the first thing they asked: is the absence out of character?

What do you say when it isn't?

Sure, the person is still registered as missing, and there's supposed to be an investigation, but if the report gets graded medium to low risk, or even low risk, no one's calling to fire up the sirens or impose blanket overtime until the person is found.

Chloe was staggered to learn the statistics. Approximately three thousand people were reported missing every year, and while it was true over ninety percent eventually turned up, most in the first few days, that still left a few *hundred* every year who didn't. This was today.

Back in 1988, it had to be more.

"I just can't quite understand why everyone we've spoken to seems so unconcerned Jessica Simm just vanished. Perhaps they're right, and she didn't share more than a few words with Len Arkin that night, or maybe she did. Maybe more than a few words, and something did happen to them."

"Like what?"

"Damned if I know, but someone's got to, don't they?"

Chapter Twenty-Six

"Nineteen million viewers tuned in the night I was stabbed and left for dead in Danny Biggs' café, now I can't even get a half decent role in a bloody Christmas panto."

It would be fair to say Leslie Wilkinson was still sore his star had fallen. Once a key actor in popular British soap *Winchester Gardens*, he had never reached the same heights again, and the burly frame and good looks which had made his character, Terry Maguire, something of a heartthrob were long gone.

In the soap, Terry had got on the wrong side of a local East End gangster, and barely surviving a hitman's attack, had chosen to relocate to the Costa del Sol to open a bar in Marbella. One could imagine Terry Maguire running his bar there still, lean and tanned. Leslie Wilkinson had taken a different path. He had gone to seed. The bald head which had once made him look tough now just made him look old, and his once barrel-chested torso had since swollen to just plain barrel.

He clearly felt he had deserved more. He was written out of *Winchester Gardens* at his own request, to pursue bigger and better things. A brief spell in Los Angeles chasing dreams of a career in Hollywood followed his departure, but the dream never materialised. Eventually, he had come home, got a few bit parts, a few minor theatre roles, been a guest on a few daytime TV quiz shows, and rapidly faded into obscurity.

Ray contacted him and reminded him they had once met at a Children in Need charity event, and also reminded him he was the producer of a television show. Wilkinson had perked up at that. Ray explained about Crow's Cottage and told him that, if Wilkinson was willing, he would be interested to hear Wilkinson's recollections of the evening that had wound up being Len Arkin's last. Wilkinson was amenable.

Wilkinson's home was modest, a two-bed bungalow in suburbia. Ray would have expected a decade on one of the nation's favourite soaps to have left him more comfortable.

"The minute you hit seventy that's it, no one wants to cast you in anything," said Wilkinson.

Ray nodded sympathetically. "It's a ruthless business."

What Ray didn't say was being over seventy hadn't proved an obstacle for Wilkinson's co-star and screen wife on *Winchester Gardens*, Fiona Harris. She currently had a plum role in *Darlington House*, a period drama that was performing very well across the Atlantic. Ray steered Wilkinson back to the topic in hand.

"Did you recognise any other famous faces at Damien Faulks' party that night?"

"One or two. Fiona and I were there, I think that Aussie singer kid? Gary Swift? Obviously, the pop music producer you're interested in who topped himself, and his partner Dave Moore. And let's not forget Damien Faulks himself, who wasn't really *big*, big time, but was famous to some extent. Edward Needham was moderately famous too I suppose. I'm not sure if mediums consider themselves entertainers, but he managed to put more bums on seats in theatres than Faulks did."

"By Fiona, you mean Fiona Harris?"

"Yeah. We were a thing back then. The on-screen chemistry everyone banged on about was real, take it from me. Fair enough, it didn't work out in the long run, but credit where credit's due, Fiona was something else back then. If you think she looked amazing on television you should have seen her in the flesh. Stunning. Playing a dumpy old grandma these days." Wilkinson snorted. "The only size nine she's likely to fit into now is in a shoe."

Not that you're at all envious she's doing well, thought Ray.

"I'd been to one of Damien Faulks' parties a couple of months before," Wilkinson said, "and he'd given me an open invite to any others. His personal assistant, or I assume it was his personal assistant, used to call and let me know when there was one coming up. Faulks wasn't stupid. He wasn't just throwing those things to give people a good time. He was out to make friends and win favours.

"Create the right image, look like you're super successful and people will assume you are, right? The circles he moved in, the people he invited, I'm sure they all had something he wanted. The industry types and celebrity friends made for useful contacts and the right image. The oddball spiritualist, occult folk? I'm guessing they were there to lend his persona flavour. His act had that veneer, so maybe rubbing shoulders with those types offered inspiration? Or maybe a few had money and standing too? I remember his pal, one of that crowd, was a baron of somewhere and somewhere. That had to mean money and connections.

"It was obvious Faulks was angling for his own TV show, and the way things worked back then, probably more so than today, who you knew was the important thing. I bet the baron had a ton of public-school Oxbridge ties. The old boys' network and all that. The top brass of the BBC and the ITV was full of Hugos and Tarquins from what I saw.

"I skipped a couple of invites but when another came, I thought Fiona might be into it. She loved that spiritual mumbo jumbo stuff, astrology, crystals. I thought she might have some fun mixing with that side of Faulks' social circle. Get herself a tarot card reading or hear what colour her aura was, maybe get a reading with Faulks' friend, Edward Needham. Only I'm not entirely sure they were friends, or if they were, not after that night."

"I heard they had an argument, the night of the party?" Ray said.

"You heard right. Very awkward. Fiona and I got caught right in the middle of it. We ended up sitting in on a séance Needham conducted. Fiona heard he was going to do one and was keen to take part, dragged me into joining her. I suppose I was a bit curious. After all, Needham was selling out big theatres across the country back then. You can bet any of those punters would have killed to sit in on a private séance with him.

"Anyway, we all traipsed to some room away from the party and got ourselves comfy around a table, linking hands and all that malarkey. The first part of the séance was about what I'd expected. A lot of questions along the lines of does anyone here have a

John, or a Jim, or maybe a James who has passed? That sort of thing. Names common enough that even faced with a small table of people most of us would have been able to dredge up someone we knew who fitted the bill, but then around ten minutes in suddenly the table goes bump. We all felt it.

"A spirit is trying to make contact, Needham says. He asks who they are. A second later the table goes thump again. I'll admit it, it was unnerving. I'd had a few drinks, and there we were in this dimly lit room tucked away in some corner of this old cottage, surrounded by woods and fields.

"Needham asked the spirit more questions. Was it troubled? What did it want?

"Every time the table went bump.

"Then we all heard it, a muffled laugh. A moment later Faulks opens the door with this sort of clicker thing in his hand. He gives the button a press and the table goes bump again, then he holds it down so it's practically vibrating. It's clear he has a gadget under there. He holds his hands up, winks at Needham and says, 'Sorry Eddie, couldn't help myself. Only a bit of fun.' Only Needham wasn't laughing. He was mad, and you could see it. He tells Faulks to get intimately acquainted with himself, asks us to excuse him and storms out, shoving past Faulks who was doing his best to look surprised at Needham's reaction.

"He wasn't surprised. He set Needham up to look like a fraud and a tit, and we were there as witnesses. Faulks went after him, still apologising, but I don't think even then he was actually intent on appeasing him or making good. Quite the opposite, I think he wanted to ensure Needham didn't get to leave without a fuss. I think Faulks wanted people to be curious what was up, for the story about why Needham was pissed to get around.

"They ended up outside, Faulks, Needham and his girlfriend. After a few minutes Faulks comes back in, all smiles, and 'oh, dear, I think I appear to have upset Edward.'"

"Do you have any idea why he might have wanted to make Needham look bad?"

"Not the foggiest, but I'm sure he had his reason. I reckon somehow Edward Needham was in his way, and Faulks wanted him gone. I doubt Needham knew who he was dealing with."

"What do you mean?"

"I heard a story about Faulks later, long after his rising star had sputtered out, and he was back to working clubs and small theatres."

"Oh yes?"

"Yes, one which paints an interesting picture of Damien Faulks, and who he used to be. The Damien Faulks I met was the one the public saw. Slick and smooth, successful, apparently on the up, big house, nice car, stylish suits. Maybe the best illusion he ever performed.

"A couple of years after the business with that Arkin bloke's suicide, I became friends with someone who knew Faulks from old. In order to keep *Winchester Gardens*' Terry Maguire believable, I had a few places I drank in now and again, authentic, traditional East End pubs and clubs. I became good friends with one club owner, a bloke named Lee. He'd tell me stories about his experiences and people he knew, and I'd chat with him about people

I'd met in show business. Faulks' name came up one day. Lee didn't look impressed. He said he used to know Faulks, long before he was famous. He said Damien Faulks wasn't even his real name. When he knew him he was still a kid named Ronny Turpin."

Okay, thought Ray, this is new. Go on.

"Young Ronny Turpin, according to this Lee bloke, had a knack for getting into trouble. Came from a bad home. He landed himself in borstal, or a youth detention centre as they call them now, aged fifteen, for pickpocketing tourists on the London Underground. He met Lee in there. Lee was in for joyriding. They became mates. When not getting himself in hot water, Lee said Ronny could usually be found practising his other hobby: magic, card tricks, palming and the like. He was good at it.

"The lads in borstal were encouraged to acquire more practical skills though, ones which might enable them to get jobs once they got out, become law-abiding members of society. Skills like woodworking, which was fine by Ronny, because he found he could use them as another means to develop his magic tricks. He started to build things to help him perform his illusions, boxes with hidden compartments or mirrors, or ones that collapsed with the push of a catch, and began to have dreams of becoming a famous stage magician."

It was funny, but as Wilkinson talked, Ray could have sworn he could hear a pinch of cockney bleeding into his voice, the ghost of Terry Maguire.

"It was a nice dream," Wilkinson continued, "but a world a million miles away from the one Ronny inhabited. When he and Lee were let out of borstal, they were both technically adults, but still teenagers, and suddenly left to fend for themselves. Lee got a flat above a fish 'n' chip shop, and Ronny crashed and helped with the rent.

"Lee made ends meet by gambling in card games, which he had a talent for, and Ronny made decent tips performing card tricks on the street. Both were just about profitable enough to avoid manual labour but neither was going to see them living the high life. Ronny kept arguing how simple it would be for him to cheat in Lee's card games. They were private affairs. New players had to be vouched for by one who was already trusted; Lee should vouch for him so he could play in a few. It was dangerous, Lee warned, but eventually one month they were both broke enough he went along with it

"And sure enough, Lee said, they quickly started to make some serious money, too much and too quickly maybe. Enough for word to get around, for people to suspect they were being had. Someone decided to mark a deck to find out, and Ronny got caught red handed. These were men who didn't appreciate being taken for mugs and demonstrated it by administering black eyes, busted noses, and broken ribs.

"All those tricks, that clever sleight-of-hand he does, it looks good, but it's even better if you know about that beating. They stamped on his fingers. Smashed them up. If you watch carefully you can still see one pinkie is all but useless. That double ring he wears? The one that goes across his last two fingers? He had that made specially to keep his useless pinkie from straying and ruining his tricks."

Ray had noted the distinctive ring during their meeting at The Effectary. It had struck him as an unusual piece of jewellery, but he would never have guessed it served a practical purpose.

"Before the beating, he tried to save his skin, though, by throwing someone else under the bus. He told the men about to teach him a lesson it wasn't his idea to cheat them, but Lee's. They still gave him a good kicking, but made sure to save enough energy to give Lee one too. Their friendship didn't last long after that.

"Years later," Wilkinson finished, "it seems Ronny got his break, and apparently decided it was time to cut little Ronny Turpin loose, shed his skin to become the altogether suaver sounding Damien Faulks."

"You have to admit," Ray said, "it does have a better ring to it."

"True," Wilkinson agreed. "Want my opinion?"

"Of course," said Ray.

"I'd be surprised if Damien Faulks shook off all of that kid named Ronny Turpin who picked pockets and cheated at card games."

Chapter Twenty-Seven

"This is brilliant."

James Barlow was leaning out over the guard rail surrounding Chloe's roof terrace, looking out on the neighbourhood. Nick was inside fetching a beer from the fridge.

Chloe agreed. The terrace might just be a section of flat roof someone had knocked a hole in the lounge wall to access, installed French doors, laid decking and fixed a guard rail around. It might have room enough for a small table and a few garden chairs and nothing more, it might have cost no more than a few hundred quid, but all that meant nothing to Chloe. The bohemian feel it lent the flat was priceless. Sipping coffee at the table in the morning as the sun rose, or a glass of wine in the evening as it set, made her feel like someone from a lifestyle advert.

"It is... although I have a suspicion it's a DIY job, and a planning officer might have kittens if they saw it. To be safe, I might not lean on that rail if I were on the hulky side. I wouldn't fancy tumbling five floors to the paving down there."

James checked her face to see if she was kidding, saw she wasn't and lifted his elbows off the guard rail, resting his hands on it instead.

Nick had said James had asked if they fancied another double date, a planned one this time. Chloe had said sure. It would be nice to see Sharon again. Nick had agreed it would, if she'd not been replaced by another pretty face by the evening the date rolled around. Sharon, it seemed, had not and was presently in a cab on the way to join them for some pre-drink drinks before they hit the town.

"He likes you," James said, apropos of nothing, after casting a glance back through the French doors, to check Nick was still inside and not in earshot.

"I like him," Chloe said.

James smiled. "That's good, because he might just be the most decent person I've ever met, and he deserves a win."

-

It was a fun evening. James Barlow was a force of nature. For all that his personality and ego bulged as much as his biceps, Nick clearly meant a lot to him. They had been workmates first, then flatmates when Nick became James' lodger, and then just plain mates. They talked about London, talked about work, talked about food and drink and movies and music and TV and a whole bunch of nonsense besides as the night wore on and the drink tally stacked up. It was a good time.

Being with Nick Spokes was a good time.

Nick stayed until morning. They made plans to see each other later. He wasn't due back into work until the following day. When he called and apologised, explaining he would have to cancel because he was needed back in early to cover a shift, Chloe was surprised by just how cheated she felt.

Nick Spokes was a good time.

She liked him.

Something that scared her more than any abandoned building or midnight graveyard ever could.

Chapter Twenty-Eight

They were in the hall again. Arguing again. Her mum was blocking the door.

Kara had come back just long enough to change her clothes and grab a few things. She looked terrible. Their mum tried to tackle her before she could leave again, and, of course, it took all of ten seconds for something to light her sister's fuse.

If Chloe closed her eyes, just allowed the words to become mush and listen to the tone, it was the same argument she had engaged in with Kara days before, just a bigger, meaner evolution of all those arguments they'd fought since childhood. Kara's verbal venom mixed with her mum's battle to cajole and reason with her. Chloe hovered at the top of the stairs, torn between entering the fray, and the knowledge that it would be futile. She was no better at handling Kara than her mum or anyone else was; worse, if anything. Kara always knew which buttons to press to reduce things to a shouting match, where the point of the argument, which made her look bad under cold light, got lost in the heat.

Kara could sucker Chloe every time.

Kara wasn't interested in a reasoned debate. Same as always, she wanted to do what she wanted to do, and anything in the way was an obstacle to be charmed, ducked, manipulated or bullied into submission.

"You have to see that you're pathetic, right?" Chloe heard her sister say to her mum. "That if you had a life, you wouldn't be fixated on mine?"

"I'm worried," her mum answered.

"Bit late in the day to try for 'world's greatest mum' now, isn't it? Let's face it, Nan did more to raise me and Chloe than you. Probably for the best. When haven't you been useless? You should be grateful me and Chloe aren't a total mess. Knocked up at eighteen by a guy too stupid not to get himself killed on a motorbike. Then knocked up again five seconds later by, let's face it, the world biggest fucking loser. If you hadn't got dumpy and lost your looks, who knows how many other wasters might have impregnated you?"

"This isn't about me—"

"Why, because it's too easy to prove you're a joke? Stay out of my business. If you've got time on your hands, pry into Chloe's shit instead. She's the one spending nights in derelict buildings and graveyards with her weirdo mates. Me? I can manage without your advice."

"Chloe tells me what she's doing and where she is, and you know full well she's filming her YouTube things—"

"Oh yeah, I forgot, very normal. Not fucking weird or screwed up at all."

"Kara—"

"I'm going. Get out of my way."

"No, I'm not going to let you—"

"GET OUT OF MY FUCKING WAY!"

It was the sound of a struggle which finally got Chloe to her feet, but by the time she reached the hallway Kara was out the door and her mum was climbing back onto her feet, looking like a prizefighter who had gone the distance, but lost badly on points. Outside a huge SUV was peeling away down the street. Her mum was crying.

And Chloe?

She felt nothing but relief. For a while their home could return to the steady low hum of anxiety which had become its resting state, and was at least preferable to the outright battleground it often turned into when Kara was around, short-fused, dismissive, secretive and vile as ever. Chloe was happy to enjoy the respite until she returned.

Only Kara didn't return. It would be the last time they saw her.

Chapter Twenty-Nine

Chloe was woken early, by a phone call. It was Ray, and he sounded strange. She got the impression she wasn't his first call of the day.

"A fire?" she said, wondering if she weren't still asleep and in the middle of some particularly vivid dream.

"The whole office is a ruin. The fire service eventually got it under control but there's no point heading there today. What hasn't been destroyed is drenched in water. Luckily, almost everything we have on the video asset front is automatically backed up to our off-site data centre. I should give Keith a raise for getting that set up. He and Mark prefer to edit at home, so most of their work is safe too. Did you have anything valuable or personal at Bennett White?"

"Nothing I can't live without. Any idea how the fire started?"

"The alarms went off, which suggests a break in, or a window was smashed, so arson? Kids up to no good? It could be worse. No one got hurt, and we only have Crow's Cottage left to shoot. I reckon we can hire or buy what we need for that. Once we're done, we can see about getting back on our feet properly."

"Anything I can do?"

"I'm hoping to find us a temporary working space. Let me get that sorted and I'll let you know."

"Nothing in the meantime?"

"Actually." Ray seemed to remember something. "On the topic of Crow's Cottage, I got a bit of info from a friend in the force. He called me yesterday. He checked missing persons for me. It was a long shot, but it seems the database was partially updated from old paper records. He found something on Jessica Simm. Apparently, her flatmate reported her missing, around a month or so after Arkin's death? I looked into the address, made a few enquires. The flatmate had long since sold the place and moved on, but she had a pretty rare surname. I checked the electoral roll for the year in question. Got a few more details, found her on a census from a few years later... Long story short? I have an address for someone I think stands a very good chance of being her. Name's Lisa Gastrell."

"Reported her missing?" said Chloe, "Sounds like this Lisa Gastrell wasn't quite as unsurprised as everyone else when Jessica Simm vanished."

"Want to take a trip up to Bristol to see her?" Ray said. "See if you can get her to talk to you, quiz her about Jessica Simm? Given you don't have the disadvantage of having appeared on TV for several years like the rest of us, I thought you might be able to pose as a straightforward investigator, maybe someone hired by Jessica's family to attempt to locate her?"

Chloe was already rolling out of bed. "Consider me Bristol bound. Details?"

Chapter Thirty

Lisa Gastrell lived in an attractive apartment block in Southwell, near the harbour. Chloe located her name on the intercom panel by the front entrance and buzzed her flat. A woman's voice answered, "Hello?"

"Hi, my name is Chloe... Smith. You're Lisa Gastrell?"

"Yes. What can I help you with?"

"I'd like to ask you about Jessica Simm."

There was a pause.

"Why?"

"A relative has hired me to see if I can find her. She went missing, around thirty years ago?"

"And she never turned up?"

"No."

There was another pause.

"I'm supposed to be leaving for work in a quarter of an hour."

"Just a few questions. It needn't take long."

Chloe heard the intercom buzz and the door to the apartment block unlock.

-

"I reported her missing half because I was sort of concerned, if something had happened to her, and half to piss her off if it hadn't. She left owing me money. Not a huge sum, but enough given my situation at the time."

230

Lisa Gastrell was a big, brassy woman, and going by the uniform and name badge on her lapel, a shop floor manager at M&S. Chloe had caught her ready to leave for work. She looked a little harassed, but the mention of Jessica Simm had made her curious enough to call a colleague and inform her she would be in a half hour late.

"It wasn't uncommon for her to be gone for a couple of days," Gastrell said. "She would stay at that magician's place, in Surrey? When she didn't show her face for over a week, I started to wonder what was up." Gastrell pulled out a boxy vape pen. "Do you mind?"

Soon a cloud of blackcurrant scented vapour was wafting between them.

"You were worried about her?" Chloe asked.

"Not especially, but she owed me rent and I could have done with it. She was lodging with me. A flat in Notting Hill. I'd bought it the year before, when interest rates were starting to settle down, then the next year they leapt up again, and my mortgage payment, which had looked manageable, shot up by over a third.

"Letting the spare room helped cover the difference. Jess was the perfect lodger in some ways. She was gone many weekends entirely, and she was nice, or charming at least. The cat thing used to irritate me."

"The cat thing?" Chloe asked.

"She would feed strays, or maybe the neighbourhood cats were just getting extras. It got so I expected some flea-bitten creature to be lurking near our front door, wondering when the cat food fairy would make an appearance. It was a sure-fire way of knowing she was around, a couple of bowls of tuna or pilchards by the step. I could never prove it, but when it was really cold at night, I'm sure she let one or two into her room through the window." Gastrell sucked on her vape pen and blew out another fruity plume of mist.

"She was never timely with the rent, but when she did pay up, to be fair, she always added a bit on top as compensation for it being late. Only it kept getting later and later. She hadn't paid me for ten weeks by the time I reported her missing to the police. I'd tackled her about it the week before, told her I needed the money. She said she would sort it out over the weekend, but Monday came and went and she was nowhere to be seen. Then the rest of the week went by and still no sign of her. As the days rolled on, I started to get more and more annoyed, but also a bit concerned too. If she had just taken off that was one thing…but if she was in trouble of course I cared.

"In the end, I went through her room. Most of her stuff seemed to be there. She wasn't the tidiest person, clothes were as often on the floor as in the wardrobe, but I couldn't find any of her ID at all, no bank books, passport, driving licence… not a shred of paperwork, just clothes, and a bit of cheap jewellery that looked the part but wasn't actually worth much. No cash. So, either she never kept that stuff at the flat, or she'd run into trouble, grabbed the essentials and done a bunk. Leaving me in the lurch.

"There's no nice way of putting it, a lot of things about the girl felt sketchy. She always paid me in cash, and always waved off having anything formal about our arrangement. When she took the room, she paid three months up front, the first and last time she was ever ahead with her rent, and then there was how she went about making a living."

"She did model work, exhibitions and public relations?"

"Ha!" Gastrell scoffed. "Public relations? Relations maybe. I'm sure that's what she told people, but I heard her calls to work. Jess worked for an escort agency. Even if I hadn't overheard it would have become obvious eventually. She worked evenings, dolled up to the nines."

Chloe was beginning to find the vape pen's sickly sweet scent of blackcurrant nauseating.

"I suspect the magician she got friendly with was a client," Gastrell continued, "or started as a client. He was a bit of a celebrity, on the up apparently. I suppose for someone like that, making dating a business transaction keeps things simple, and let's face it, what's a date? Anyone who thinks escorting means dinner, clubbing, a polite wave goodbye and a cab home at the end of the evening has to be born yesterday. Jess looked angelic, but trust me, she was no babe in the woods. Reporting her missing to the law seemed fair if she had somehow got herself into trouble, and just as fair if she'd decided to stiff me for two and a half months of rent. My conscience felt clear on both counts."

"Did you ever hear what became of her?"

"No. By the following year interest rates had climbed even higher. The clothing boutique I was a buyer for went bust, I struggled to find something that paid as well, and failed. Things became impossible. I sold the flat in Notting Hill, walked away, a few grand in debt, and moved back home to live with my mum and dad for a year or two, ended up settling down here. My dreams of living in London and working in the fashion trade hadn't worked out as I'd hoped. I try not to think about what that flat is worth today."

"Which do you think is more likely?" Chloe asked. "Did she get herself into trouble, or did she skip town to avoid some?"

"I think she skipped town."

Chapter Thirty-One

On the way back from Bristol, Chloe got to thinking and decided to take a diversion to Salisbury for an unannounced visit before heading home.

When she knocked, Maxine Needham answered the door. "Hello, you're—"

"Chloe, Chloe Harker. We spoke a little a while back?"

"I'm afraid Edward isn't here. He has an engagement, won't be back until tomorrow."

"Actually, it was you I was hoping to speak to. The investigation into Crow's Cottage, there are a few things which have come up I was hoping you might be able to help clarify? I promise not to take up too much of your time."

Maxine Needham's face suggested time wasn't the issue, so much as the topic. Despite this, she stepped aside and invited Chloe in.

-

Chloe had no problem believing Maxine used to be a model. She still could be. Any cosmetics company looking to target women aged over fifty was missing a trick. She was gorgeous, and Chloe could only imagine what she looked like back in the day, but if Lisa Gastrell wasn't mistaken, maybe Maxine hadn't really made her living modelling at all. If Jessica Simm had been an escort, and Jessica and Maxine were close friends…

Maxine had invited Chloe to take a seat in the lounge area of the barn's huge central space.

"So, what exactly were you hoping I might be able to help you with?"

"Am I correct in recalling you said Jessica Simm worked in modelling and PR?"

"Yes. That's right."

Chloe wanted to tread carefully, but there was no easy way to ask what she wanted to ask. "I spoke to Jessica's former flatmate. She seems to think Jessica made her living another way."

"Go on."

"Yeah… She said she worked as an escort?"

Maxine said nothing.

"Mrs Needham, trust me, I'm not looking to dig up dirt. I'm just trying to get a picture of what Jessica Simm's life looked like, why she may have felt it necessary to leave suddenly without telling anyone where she was going. Her former flatmate claims she left owing her money. Rent arrears. Could she have had other debts perhaps? Ones she was already running from?"

"Miss…"

"Harker. Chloe."

"Miss Harker. Why? What difference does it make why she took off? Debts or no debts, escort work or not? I fail to see what bearing it has on some alleged apparition at Crow's Cottage."

"I'm just curious."

"Well, I think I'd like you to leave now." Maxine started to get up.

"Please, let me explain."

Maxine stopped, but didn't sit down.

"I have a sister. She's missing. Almost a year and a half now. She's around the same age Jessica was when she vanished. I can't help the one causing me to think about the other. One day my sister decided to take off too, or at least I hope she chose to. Eighteen months on and my mum and I still know nothing. We haven't had a call, not a word. The police aren't bothered. Like Jessica, they have no reason to pour valuable resources into finding someone who might not want to be found and has every right not to be. But I'd like to know. Didn't you worry about what happened to her? Didn't you even once, as her friend, wonder if she might be in trouble?"

"Of course, I did. But I also knew her. I meant what I told you last time. I wasn't surprised when she took off. No one who knew her was." Maxine sat back down. "I'm sorry about your sister. It must be very difficult for you."

"I try not to think about it, although that seems to be getting harder."

Maxine sighed. "Yes. Jess did escort work. It was how she first met Damien Faulks, but she did also earn a living modelling and doing PR at events, that wasn't a lie. It's how we met."

Chloe nodded.

"Damien used Jess's escort agency," Maxine said. "He liked the company of attractive women, and it didn't hurt to be seen with one on his arm. The lack of strings suited him too. He took a shine to Jess. They became friends."

"And when he started throwing parties and needed a couple of hostesses, he went to Jess, and… Jess asked you?"

"Something like that. I want to make it clear, though, in case you already have the wrong idea. 'Escort' is not synonymous with 'prostitute'. Jess told me some of the girls at the agency she worked for occasionally flirted with where the line was drawn, but the agency didn't condone it, they didn't encourage it, and they didn't profit from it. Jess told me it wasn't something she chose to do."

"Do you think she was telling the truth?"

"She had no reason to lie to me. We were friends. I wouldn't have judged her even if she had."

"If she was in some sort of trouble, would she have come to you?"

"No, I don't think so. Jess knew how to take care of herself, and I don't think she was used to asking for help. She was a good person, kind, and thoughtful. She could tell if someone was upset, but wasn't as easy to read herself. We were friends, but she only let people get as close as she wanted them to. Maybe she had learnt to be wary."

"When we spoke to Damien Faulks, he seemed to feel Jess may have had a tough time growing up, possibly come from an abusive home?"

"I wouldn't have been surprised to discover it. It was pretty clear she had issues. She had obviously moved around a lot. Maybe she was searching for somewhere that felt right, starting over again, and again, hoping the next place would be it?"

"Were she and Damien a couple?"

"On and off. I don't think either of them viewed it as serious."

"I've been told she was very beautiful."

Maxine smiled. "Oh, she was."

"In my head, she looks like my sister."

"Does your sister have red hair?"

"No. Blonde. Do you have one? A sister?"

Maxine shook her head.

"I can't speak for anyone else, but living with mine was like living with someone you frequently feel like strangling, possibly even hate sometimes, but at the same time you love them too. It's part of you, woven into your DNA, or your soul or something. Impossible to cut out even if you wanted to." Chloe stopped herself. "Sorry, I'm talking bollocks aren't I?"

"Not at all. I think you explained yourself very well. I have a picture."

"A picture?"

"Of Jess. If you would like to see what she actually looked like?"

-

Maxine set a biscuit tin on the coffee table. It looked old, a bit scuffed and dented at the corners. She prised off the lid and began to sift through the contents.

Chloe had a tin like this. It was filled with ticket stubs from gigs and movies, old photographs of her mum's, a notebook her school friends had all signed on their last day of school, her old mobile phones... Did everyone have a tin like this? Filled with artefacts from a life. Beloved detritus. A place to keep items with zero value to anyone else, but irreplaceable to you.

Maxine finally located what she was looking for. She pulled out a few square, yellowing photographs. Polaroids. Chloe's nan had had similar ones in her old photo albums. Instant pictures before digital ones existed.

Maxine passed her one of the Polaroids. It showed two young women, not much older than Chloe was, dressed to impress eighties style. Vibrant cocktail dresses and outrageously huge hair. Both women were jaw-droppingly gorgeous, a genuine peril to men walking near lampposts. One of the women was Maxine. The other had ruby red hair, huge green eyes, and a smile that made Chloe wish she could have been her friend too.

"Wow," Chloe exhaled. "You were mother fudging gorgeous, Maxine. Not that you aren't now, but... holy moly. And this is Jessica?"

"That's us. A million years ago." Maxine sighed, with a wan smile.

"Could I?" Chloe pointed to the other photos, and for a moment Maxine seemed reluctant. Maybe seeing Jessica's face again had raised old ghosts, brought back feelings she hadn't anticipated. After a beat, Maxine nodded. "Help yourself."

Chloe plucked out the other pictures. There were three more.

One was a selfie, sort of. The Polaroid camera that had taken it wouldn't have had a screen to check the composition. As a result, Maxine and Jess's faces were blurry and just within the frame. They were in what looked like the back seat of a car, faces pressed close together, heads tilted inwards and upwards, adopting almost comedically sultry expressions.

The second snap was of just Maxine in casual clothes, drastically less makeup, but somehow even more beautiful for it.

The final Polaroid was of them both again, tanned, in shorts and bikini tops, in front of a rugged, whitewashed wall in the sun, outside what looked like a bar.

They looked like the best of friends, enjoying a time before everything got complicated, before Jess cut her ties for the umpteenth time and took off, relocating her red hair, green eyes and beguiling smile to some new town, far from the last town.

Chloe pulled out her phone and took a snap of the photos. It was only when she looked up, she realised she hadn't asked Maxine first.

"I'm sorry, do you mind?"

Maxine looked like she did, but just as Chloe considered offering to delete the snap she said, "No. It's fine."

Seeing the pictures instantly achieved two things. Jessica Simm had become a real person, and in Chloe's mind, she no longer looked like Kara with a head of red hair.

Chapter Thirty-Two

"Holy fudge." Chloe pinched the picture on Ray's iPad to zoom in on the blackened mess which had once been the Bennett White Production offices. They were a ruin, reduced to a gutted, black, mostly windowless box on a business estate. By the time the emergency services had arrived and dealt with the blaze, the damage had been done. They were unlikely to be returning there any time soon.

Ray was working on getting somewhere else sorted out, but until then they were all convened at his house. Hopefully a short-term measure. A firm date had been fixed to shoot at Crow's Cottage, in just three days. They had enough background material to suffice, and once Crow's Cottage was in the bag, they would have time to reorganise and regroup.

Giles Langley was excited, looking forward to his brief appearance welcoming them inside the property, which would appear before the walkaround portion of the show, and the potential of Charles offering him a ghost-free holiday home.

What they had to do now was make some tough decisions about the angle they were going to take. Ray had obviously given the subject a good deal of thought already.

The crew were sitting around his dining table, Ray's wife Julia had set them up with tea, coffee and a rapidly dwindling packet of chocolate Hobnob biscuits.

"I think we leave the whole urban myth around Len Arkin and Jess Simm alone," he said. "A tale about two guests accidentally summoning a demon with the Mephisto Arcane is intriguing, but in all honesty, we don't have a shred of evidence to support it. We can't even be certain Jessica Simm spoke to Len Arkin, let alone was in a room alone with him and the Mephisto Arcane, or that either of them was aware it existed, never mind set hands on it. We don't have anything concrete to suggest Jessica Simm didn't simply skip town either." He took one of the remaining few biscuits and dunked it in his tea. "If we were talking about something that happened a hundred years ago? Maybe I'd feel differently about tossing the story in, but we're not. We're talking about an unhappy man who drowned himself just thirty years ago. Without good reason, including the story feels in bad taste. Cheap. I'd like to think we're better than that, and honestly? I don't think we need it. What we do have is strong enough already." The biscuit vanished in a single bite.

He washed it down with a sip of tea then said, "We have Crow's Cottage's former owner being an expert in the occult. We have the Longwood Society angle, which is gold, as is the attempt to resurrect it. We have the rumoured recreation of the Arcane by a few of that group's core members, and proof they did recreate it after it was found hidden in the cottage. We have the background story of the original Arcane, what Charles discovered about this Andrea Fiorentino guy, who might have been the device's inventor who was burnt at the stake in the legend, and then the question of whether the replica was based on authentic drawings or just clever fakes. And let's not forget the cherry on the Crow's Cottage cake: multiple sightings of an apparition haunting the property, perhaps linked to the device being unearthed. And numbered among its witnesses? No less than our own Chloe and Charles.

"What's more, we can cover ninety-nine percent of all this material and scarcely name any names at all. We can mention Len Arkin's suicide, I think that's fair, but in passing. Ultimately? I don't think it should be the focus of the episode. Anyone feel differently?"

No one did. They all knew urban myth was undeniably, deliciously schlocky in all the best ways. Once they took a step back though, they couldn't escape it centred upon a man killing himself, a man with friends who were still around, a man known by most people for his music rather than the nature of his passing. Ray was right, without a scrap of evidence to support it, leaning into the 'two party revellers unwittingly summon a demon with an occult device' story to fuel the episode felt cheap, and would likely come across that way to fans who enjoyed *Where the Dead Walk* precisely because they tried to approach their investigations with rigour.

Moreover, even if they had more time, maybe succeeded in tracking down Jessica Simm, wouldn't that just confirm the story was total bunkum?

Better to focus on the Longwood Society, the Mephisto Arcane and the apparition. Who knew, if they were lucky they might even capture video of it and nothing else would matter. The episode would be legendary.

Chapter Thirty-Three

Behind the camera, Mark kept pace with Chloe, who was facing him but casually walking backwards, talking into the lens. They were almost lost in shadow, the day blocked out by foliage to either side of the track and the trees above.

"Our investigation this week brings us to a house," Chloe said, "frequented by aristocracy, mediums, occultists and magicians, a one-time meeting place for a group of individuals called the Longwood Society, brought together by a shared interest in the paranormal. It's a place steeped in mystery, which has seen tragedy, where an item believed to be a recreation of an infamous occult device designed to commune with the dead was recently discovered after being hidden away for thirty years. Since its discovery, an apparition has been witnessed on several occasions, including by Charles and myself on our first visit here. Is there a connection between the device and the apparition? Was the entity roused by its discovery? And who knows what other secrets this location might hold?

"During the next twenty-four hours, we will delve into some of the building's rich history and seek to learn some of its mysteries. Join us as we enter yet another place where the dead walk." Chloe continued to backpedal, to where the track curved and the trees above thinned. Dappled light broke through, danced over her until she emerged into full daylight and the building swung into view. She paused at the prearranged spot she and Mark had agreed delivered the most dramatic framing of the property, whereupon she held out an arm and said, "Welcome to Crow's Cottage."

She maintained the pose for maybe three more seconds, and asked, "We good?"

Mark lowered the camera. "We good."

-

Chloe, Charles, Mark, Keith and Giles Langley were gathered in the cottage's low-ceilinged lounge, Mark behind the camera, Keith checking everyone's wireless mics. Mark had explained and run through the shot and Giles' part in it. It was to present Chloe and Charles entering the cottage, as though for the first time, show them walking through the entrance and inside into the lounge where they would encounter Giles, as though they had somehow rocked up, all casual like. Once edited together it would form around ten seconds of complete pantomime. They had already covered the exterior shot of them entering the cottage, the interior one showing their passage through the door from the inside, and just finished the one showing them entering the lounge. Now they were about to film the part where they encountered and introduced themselves to Giles Langley.

It was exactly the sort of thing Chloe had never deconstructed as a viewer because in the context of the show it all seemed perfectly natural, but her first time filming the series of shots required to assemble such a transition had felt ludicrous. Outside shot. Stop. Let Mark through the door to set up to capture them walking in. Stop. Let him move up ahead to capture the next few metres of the journey. Stop. Set up with two cameras to get the chest and headshots with the owner or caretaker from both sides... What looked casual and spontaneous took a lot of preparation.

They had, of course, already met Giles, more than once, had seen him already this morning as it happened, gone through what they needed from him regarding material for the episode and keys to access the property when he departed.

The viewer didn't need to see any of that, but they did need a representation of the important bits. And as artificial as filming it might feel, the result worked.

Chloe's guerrilla-style approach on her YouTube episodes featured no such intricacy or shot choreography. She had filmed everything with a single camera which featured a night vision setting, and additional video from friends' phone cameras. Almost everything was done chronologically, with no fancy inserts or even voiceovers. Planning usually consisted of a little research, and determining how to get into where she intended to film. Even the most off-the-cuff portions of *Where the Dead Walk* were produced dozens of times more slickly.

Once Giles was straight on what he had to do, Mark gave them the go. There wasn't a great deal that could go wrong. The shot would run for around three or four seconds, and then Mark would move them quickly to the next.

In the final edit, a to-camera of Chloe would be inserted between them walking up and shaking Giles' hand and the following brief conversation. In the insert, Chloe would explain how "Giles Langley is the current owner of Crow's Cottage. He has requested our help to determine what might lie behind the recent paranormal activity Crow's Cottage has seen, and how peace might be brought back to a beautiful cottage whose history stretches back to the reign of James the First."

Then the scene would transition to the twin camera shot of the meeting and greeting; Mark would film from behind Giles, capturing Chloe and Charles, out of frame of Keith's shot which was covering Giles.

Charles and Chloe got into position, standing casually next to each other, as though they had just finished shaking Giles' hand a second ago and not the approximately ten minutes it had taken to get everyone in position and prepped.

They exchanged greetings, and Chloe asked Giles about the activity reported and witnessed.

Giles was great value, all the things one envisioned when it came to English aristocracy, posh, dignified, a little bit eccentric, and frightfully, frightfully earnest. Chloe liked him. He answered within the bounds discussed, not strictly rehearsed, but close. "I inherited the property a short time ago when my uncle passed away," Giles said. "Sadly, he had not been in contact with our family for a long while, which meant I never had the chance to meet him myself. I was delighted to discover he had thought of me. As you can see, the cottage is a charming building. I planned to carry out some work, so my wife and I might use it as a second home."

"But something happened?" Charles asked.

"Yes. Some of the tradesmen working in the cottage claimed to witness a dark figure. I confess, I was somewhat sceptical to begin with, until I saw the figure myself."

"Could you describe it for us?"

"It was very dark, almost like a shadow or silhouette, only present for a moment, before it stepped out of sight. When I gathered my wits sufficiently enough to follow, it was gone."

"Could you take us to the spot where you saw it?"

"Of course."

They all began to move as though to head to the stairs, and Mark said, "Great. Let's go get ourselves set up on the landing. A few more minutes, Mr Langley, and we'll have everything we need from you."

-

The next hour was spent filming Ray's delve into the building's history, mostly set in the rear garden with the back of the cottage and the large Georgian extension providing a backdrop. It was, as usual, meticulously scripted and well-researched, covering the history of the cottage's construction and later architectural embellishments, and some of the people who had lived in it or may have visited it.

In more recent times, this meant Damien Faulks. Ray expanded upon what they had learned about the resurrected, if short-lived, Longwood Society, and closed with the tragic suicide of Len Arkin, although he didn't go into this aspect in too much detail. Instead, he focused on the newly discovered Mephisto Arcane, and recapped the legend surrounding the supposed original.

After this, they moved on to Charles' and Chloe's daytime walkaround, and then took a break, ate and prepped for the nighttime vigil.

Crow's Cottage looked terrific in the dark captured in night vision. The eighties vibe immediately became less apparent; desaturated and draped in shadow, the more traditional architecture of the building became dominant. The crew paired up and investigated different locations throughout the building's three floors and many rooms.

Chloe and Charles spent a while in the attic rooms and were rewarded with an intermittent scratching which could have been a restless soul, a tree's foliage grazing the roof, or vermin. The Mephisto Arcane moved between pairings, as they swapped spaces and partners.

It was a decent vigil, and would be entertaining enough when later edited into a whole, Chloe felt. She had been involved in enough of them now to get a sense for which would, but compared to the promise Crow's Cottage had presented, it fell badly short. Off camera Charles quietly confessed he wasn't receiving any distinct or particularly strong energies from the house.

Still, the cottage mustered some reasonably eerie and atmospheric moments, and Charles handled them well. They had chatted too, Chloe serving him up questions, affording him the opportunity to expand on the formation of the original Longwood Society, and voice his admiration for the Bartleholms and the group's purpose.

She quizzed him about the use of devices like the Mephisto Arcane to engage with spirits and the device's supposed link with the occult figures of Fiorentino and Agrippa. It was all good stuff.

The rest of the crew had hopefully got some similarly respectable moments too, making the most from the usual bumps and creaks, and the questionable 'voices' discernible in the white noise of Keith's EVP recordings. As the final hour approached, and hope of capturing video of the apparition haunting the house dwindled, however, it was hard not to feel deflated.

It wasn't like Chloe had expected the apparition to greet them at the door with a cheery 'Woohoo!' and a tray of party nibbles, but she had allowed herself to believe they might capture something, even if only a glimpse of it on camera. Now, with the vigil almost over, she was less optimistic.

They had one last thing to do, something that would play well even if the apparition continued to resolutely ignore their presence in its house: the séance. They had briefly discussed how they might incorporate the Arcane. In truth, Charles had no idea how exactly it was meant to be used. Eammon hadn't either, and he suspected neither had Hubert, Faulks or Needham. They had decided the best option was to use it as the focal point, set between the quartet of candles Charles commonly used.

They conducted the séance in one of the guest rooms on the second floor, finding a table there large enough to accommodate them. Chloe briefly wondered if it had been the same table Edward Needham had used thirty years ago. It was certainly feasible. They gathered around it, she, Charles, Claire, Ray, and Keith making up the circle.

Charles settled, drew in a series of low, fulsome breaths, and closed his eyes.

"I call any spirit with a connection to this place to draw closer. Use your energy and draw on ours, find the light and warmth of these flames, use them to see us more clearly. Find us here, speak to us, make a sound if you are able, move something if you are able, let us know you are here with us…"

Almost at once the candles flickered. The stroke of flame dancing at their wicks trembled. Chloe felt something in the room with them. A glance around the table and the expressions she saw told her she wasn't alone. Something had joined them, something which hadn't been present a moment before. It had prompted Charles to open his eyes.

"Spirit?"

The candle flames seemed to lurch and glow brighter for an instant.

"Are you the spirit tied to this house, the apparition who has shown itself?"

The candle flames bulged, brightened and wobbled again.

"Can you share something with me, an image perhaps, or a word? I can feel your presence, but you must make contact if I'm to help you." Charles' eyes met the group, he looked perplexed. While there was something in the room, they all felt it, it clearly wasn't sharing any more with him than it was with the rest of them.

"If that's difficult for you," Charles soothed, "perhaps you might show yourself to us, here, now?"

The candles flickered again, a sudden whip. One was extinguished. Charles pursed his lips.

Claire looked to him. "Should I relight it?"

He shook his head. "No, it's trying, but I believe it's struggling, unable to focus itself." He tried again. "Are you one who has a connection to this device, to the Mephisto Arcane?"

The remaining three candles again flared and performed a sharp whip as though a gust of wind had swept through the room, only it hadn't. The room was still as midnight. Chloe felt almost frozen in place too, unable to move.

The second of the candle flames went out.

The room was further dimmed.

Charles seemed poised to speak again when, with a similar flare and lick, the final pair of candles was extinguished and the room was suddenly plunged into darkness. For a moment no one could see a thing, but they weren't deaf. They all heard something atop the table move. Chloe felt it shoot past her and reached out to grab it in the darkness, but only grazed it in passing. Whatever it was, and she was fairly sure she knew, it hit the floor hard with a crack.

An instant later Mark hit the lights.

They all saw what had happened.

The Mephisto Arcane was on its side on the floor. The base had taken the brunt of the impact, and come away slightly, or looked like it had. As Chloe looked closer, she saw that it wasn't broken. It had popped open, as it now appeared to be designed to. What she was looking at was a compartment, a secret compartment, with a tiny sliver of something white inside peeking out.

-

The Mephisto Arcane was back on the table. It was more evident now it had suffered only minor damage, and even this was largely confined to the mechanism which secured its secret compartment. The catch had sheared off. Hinged from the inside, the base now yawned open to reveal a felt-lined space approximately four inches square and an inch deep.

Looking at the interior the mechanism was exposed. It seemed something on the base's crisscrossed decoration was involved in disengaging it. It was an interesting discovery, but nowhere near as interesting as what they found inside. At this point Ray had asked Mark to quit filming.

Five Polaroid pictures which spawned a whole bunch of questions. Three were of a mirrored door, capturing what it reflected remarkably clearly, and what was reflected was a man tied to a bed, his wrists cuffed with fur-lined handcuffs secured to the headboard. He was naked, blindfolded and in his mouth, a red ball-gag secured in place with black PVC straps. Sitting atop him, straddling his groin, was a red-headed woman, most of her face obscured by the Polaroid camera taking the snap. The last two were of the man in close up. His face and chest.

It was difficult to be one hundred percent sure with the blindfold covering his eyes and the ball-gag distorting his mouth, but the man in the Polaroids and the Len Arkin they had seen in pictures and video clips looked very similar.

"So... what the hell does this mean?" Chloe asked.

"A good question," Ray replied. "If that's who I think it is then Len Arkin had a more eventful evening than we thought."

"A kinky encounter with Jessica Simm?"

"We're looking at a redhead. Jessica Simm was a redhead. That's a hell of a coincidence."

"And these are, what?" Charles asked. "Mementos?"

"Intended to be, perhaps. Len Arkin got into something, enjoyed it at the time, but maybe not so much when it was over? He was a quiet guy, usually buttoned up, a bit repressed even, then it all escapes one night? Maybe afterwards he felt ashamed, mortified in case this Jessica decided to tell everyone about the big record producer she had enjoyed a kinky tryst with? If he was depressed, prone to dark mood swings, the fear of that, the embarrassment, the shame, tipped him over the edge?"

Chloe could see Ray was thinking something else too.

"Or...?" she prompted.

"Maybe the pictures were what Jessica was after. It seems a stretch to believe this encounter, these pictures, aren't in some way connected to Arkin's decision to kill himself. What if the real story about Len Arkin and a missing redhead has nothing to do with black magic, and everything to do with blackmail?"

Chapter Thirty-Four

"Bringing these to light…" said Richard. "You'd be opening a right old can of worms, Ray."

"But if they shed light on the reason Arkin decided to kill himself, especially if it raises the question of blackmail?"

"An even bigger can. They might, but it's quite possible they're totally innocent and just show a guy having a good time."

"Got yourself a set of furry cuffs and a ball-gag in the bedroom cupboard do we, Rich?"

"Maybe I do." Richard smiled. "Look, all I'm saying is a little bondage, and a few snaps to document the fun is fairly tame, right at the novice's end of the deviancy yardstick. I don't even want to think about what the guys in obscene publications have to deal with these days. I doubt the internet has made people kinkier, but it's done a fair job of demonstrating the breadth of what some people get off on. If these pictures enter the public domain the press will definitely be interested, even thirty years later, but a police investigation might not even get off the ground."

Ray wasn't at all sure what to do with the pictures. He had brought them to Richard to get his opinion, having taken the precaution of bagging them up first, after Chloe had taken scans. If Richard thought they warranted police attention Ray wasn't about to argue. Ray was happy to defer. He used to be a copper, Richard still was one.

"I'm just saying a few pics of Arkin cuffed, blindfolded and gagged isn't exactly a smoking gun as proof of blackmail," said Richard. "The guy was wealthy, famous, at a party. This Jessica Simm, she may have spied a potential a sugar daddy, or if it's true she was an escort... Maybe she was on the game too? Maybe these just show Len Arkin getting exactly what he paid for and intended as a souvenir to take home?"

"So how did they wind up in a secret compartment in the Mephisto Arcane?"

"Okay, maybe Arkin wasn't aware she had taken the snaps. Maybe she intended to send them to him later to remind him she was still up for more fun, then got scared when she heard he had topped himself? She may have felt guilty. Unlikely to be keen to speak to the police, especially if Arkin had paid for what he got. Or... if she was an on-off friend with benefits with Damien Faulks, maybe he got off on being cuckolded by his girlfriend? She stored the photos in the box so he could take a gander later?"

"Or she took them to squeeze money out of him after? Showed him one and told him she had others hidden away?"

"If so, why not simply pay her off? Why kill himself?"

"Embarrassment? Shame? If he was already in a vulnerable state of mind, maybe the realisation he had been taken advantage of hit him hard. Maybe a blow hard enough to make checking out seem easier than dealing with a blackmailer and the fear of the pictures winding up on the front of a tabloid newspaper?"

"Maybe, maybe. That's the problem though. If these come to light Arkin's reputation is going to get a blast with the shit hose, an unwelcome turn of events for anyone who cared about him. Even if they are evidence of blackmail, this Jessica has vanished, and the guy is dead. Who gains from reopening a thirty-year-old crime where it seems no one actually benefited? And how would you go about proving any of it? Sounds harsh, but is it even worth the bother?"

Ray thought back to what Bob Vickers had said to him. *If you were to suggest the case was in some way ineptly handled, I would take that personally. I still have a reputation to maintain.*

Had Vickers conducted a slapdash investigation? With the press and his superiors watching carefully it seemed unlikely.

"Do you think our Bob Vickers could have missed something at the time, apart from these?"

"Funny you should ask," said Richard. "I did a little more asking after Bob Vickers since you spoke to him. A dedicated career climber apparently. Got an early start in the Vice Squad, before moving over to CID. You know how it goes, if you want to please, the bosses like nothing better than a fast and tidy result. If suicide looked obvious, and to be fair it did, and the press was in the mood to whip things up, Vickers wouldn't have wanted to extend the investigation further than absolutely necessary. Be seen to do due diligence, but don't dally too long to make it look like you've found something worth dallying over. I reckon he did his job, but not every stone went unturned."

"I suppose you can't blame him for missing the pictures," Ray said. "They were hidden in something that had also been hidden. Someone didn't want them found, whatever their reason was."

"You can't be thinking of using them in your show?" said Richard.

"No, of course not. I'm not even sure whether to share them with Giles Langley. I've asked for another night at Crow's Cottage."

"What? You hoping your mate Charles can get the ghost of Len Arkin to give him a first-hand account of what happened?" Richard wasn't being serious. He still confined himself to the sort of things one could prove in a court of law. Ray had seen things which had broadened his outlook somewhat.

"Trust me, Rich," he said. "Stranger things have happened."

Chapter Thirty-Five

Chloe woke early. The vigil at Crow's Cottage had meant an afternoon nap and an early night, which had played havoc with her body clock. She would try to grab a nap before they returned to shoot at the cottage again later. She couldn't wait to get back. Something had shoved the Mephisto Arcane off the table. Something had wanted them to find what was hidden inside it.

She pulled on a hoodie and a pair of sweats and took her coffee and her laptop out to the roof terrace. It was cool, but not yet late enough in the year to be cold, even at this early hour. She pulled up the scans of the Polaroids. Ray had the originals, but the scans were good, hi-res and crisp.

The man in the pictures was Arkin. She had scoured the internet for any picture of him she could find, and ended up with a folder containing dozens. Even with his eyes obscured by the blindfold and his mouth wrapped around the ball-gag, she was beyond sure. The hairstyle, colour, the shape of his face and ears. It was him.

Was the girl Jessica Simm?

Chloe pulled out her phone and dug out the snap of Maxine Needham's photos, compared the girl next to Maxine with the big red hair, then did the same with the selfie-style one of the two woman in the back of a car, and finally the one of them in bikini tops and shorts outside a beach bar. This last one showed Jessica's face clearest.

In the picture, the bar's sign above the women's heads was cropped, but the bottom half of the letters 'Zakyn' just peeked out. Zakynthos then? The Greek island was a popular holiday spot. Maxine and Jess had been on a girly holiday then, sunbathing, dancing, maybe finding a couple of guys for a bit of romance before the day came to board the plane back home. They looked happy.

Chloe moved her eyes from her phone to the scans on the laptop screen and back again. Was the woman definitely Jessica Simm?

Who else could it be? While her face was partially obscured by the Polaroid camera, the red hair and curvy body were on display, and close enough to peg Jessica for Polaroid girl in Chloe's book.

Ray had encouraged them to put forward and discuss theories. He told them he had taken the snaps to a friend he knew, a detective in the Metropolitan Police, and what his take was. Involving the police might not even lead to an investigation, but it would increase the likelihood of the pictures entering the public domain, something Len Arkin's surviving friends or family would be unlikely to welcome. If blackmail was a factor in Len Arkin's decision to take his own life, it still wasn't murder or even manslaughter. Even if the police managed to track down Jessica Simm and attempted to prove she tried to extort money from Arkin, a substantial undertaking in itself, without solid supporting evidence the Crown Prosecution Service would be unlikely to feel the case was substantial enough to bring to court, and even if they did, and the prosecution was successful, the most severe penalty was apt to be a few months in prison. More likely was a suspended sentence.

It was a pragmatic, sober and sensible perspective, but didn't take into account how they had discovered the pictures. Surviving friends or family may not welcome them coming to light, but the spirit haunting Crow's Cottage seemed to want them to. It had found a way to send a message. Chloe believed it wanted to expose the photos, and because they were the source of its unrest.

She returned to the first of the pictures, which showed the couple on the bed. She zoomed in and scrolled around, trying to discern any other details. There was a swatch of blurry curtains, a dresser on the far side of the room—

Something stopped her dead. She zoomed out, and then in again, feeling her mouth go dry. The photo was not directly of the couple like the selfie style one was. This picture was of their reflection in the set of mirrored wardrobe doors. Had something else, someone else, been captured too?

On the dresser on the far side of the room, behind the two figures on the bed, resting on the dresser top, almost lost out of frame, was one half of what looked like a hand.

She squinted, blew the picture up more, but the resolution tapped out. All she got was a brace of chunky pixels. She thought for a moment and fired up her ancient copy of Photoshop, the one she had used to make tempting thumbnails for her YouTube shows.

She imported the picture and went through a selection of filters and adjustments. She tweaked the hue, the contrast, she sharpened and tried anything else which might highlight the elements on display in a way that isolated the tiny pale spot she was interested in.

What she ended up with was a multi-coloured mess, but what looked suspiciously like the outline of half a hand and three fingers, middle, ring and pinky. Something straddled the ring and pinky. It was indistinct, by this point close to a mosaic of pixels, but Chloe was almost sure in her bones it was something she had seen very recently, on Damien Faulks' left hand. Two conjoined silver rings.

The doorbell rang, almost making her jump out of her skin. She got up and went back through the flat to go see who was there, and was greeted with the sight of Nick Spokes, holding a cardboard caddy with two lattes and dangling a paper bag that smelt of bacon.

"Fancy sharing a late breakfast before I start my shift?"

"Come in. I want to show you something."

-

"It could be, I suppose." Nick studied the picture again. "Do that thing you did with the contrast."

Chloe swung the contrast slider up, and huge swathes of the image suddenly vanished into solid black, but some parts of the edge of the hand came to the fore. Chloe had given Nick a brisk account of the last few day's events.

"We think this guy on the bed is Len Arkin, the guy who drowned himself, and the woman is the one who vanished?"

"Jessica Simm," said Chloe through a mouthful of bacon sandwich.

"So, what are you thinking?"

"I'm wondering if what we're looking at here," Chloe tapped the screen, "is Damien Faulks' hand. If we are, and he was there, and Arkin was blindfolded, did Arkin know he was there?"

"Hard to know," Nick said. "Seems to me the kinky road has been trodden a bit here already hasn't it? What if Damien Faulks liked to watch? Got off on seeing his girl with someone else? What if this Len Arkin *liked* to have someone watch? It doesn't prove anything shady was going on."

"It proves Damien Faulks knew more about what Len Arkin did in his last few hours than he told the police."

"True, but it's not difficult to imagine why he might have opted to keep this to himself. Let's play devil's advocate. You said the true purpose of his parties was to further his career, develop contacts, win friends in the business, get him closer to his dream of a TV show... If the story became about this, what he and his girlfriend got up to with Arkin the night he went on to kill himself," Nick glanced at the scanned photo, "hard to imagine his TV show dreams wouldn't be blown to kingdom come, isn't it? No matter how consensual and legal what they got up to was. Arkin's suicide was tabloid-worthy already, toss in a kinky threesome and it would be a bonanza. Faulks knew he'd be finished, and telling the police wasn't going to bring Arkin back."

"Or maybe they had pushed him into it," Chloe said, "and he left upset, distressed? Maybe he felt used, exploited and ashamed?"

"That's possible too."

"Or maybe the whole thing was a honey trap? Maybe the photos were intended to encourage Len Arkin to use his influence and connections to help Faulks get his TV show?"

"All possible, if what we're looking at is Damien Faulks' hand," Nick said, bringing things back down to earth with a thump, "and not a pair of knickers or something else that landed on the top of the dresser in just such a way as to look like it."

Chapter Thirty-Six

"The important thing to remember," said Ray, "is what we already have is more than enough for a show. I know we're here hoping for something more, but Keith's motion-sensing cameras have been here since we left and they haven't caught a thing."

They were in the main lounge of Crow's Cottage, and Ray seemed determined to manage expectations. Chloe had no doubt the last couple of days had been a nightmare for him. They would have been into crunch territory in any case around now, finishing up the show for broadcast, and Crow's Cottage had already doubled the workload. Now he was dealing with the fire and the impact of losing their workspace too.

It would be a shorter vigil than usual, just six hours, from ten until four in the morning. They would conclude with another séance. They had debated simply starting with it. A second séance felt like their strongest card, but for that very reason it seemed rash to play it too soon. They might be lucky enough to capture video of the apparition during the vigil first. Charles also said they couldn't know for sure that their extended presence in the house hadn't been instrumental in drawing the spirit out last time.

Chloe knew it was dangerous to get her hopes up. She was trying not to, but it was hard. She knew something was haunting Crow's Cottage, they all did. The last séance had confirmed it beyond doubt, but the presence wasn't making it easy for them. On their first visit, she and Charles witnessed it, and the previous night it had pushed the Mephisto Arcane right off the table, but those incidents aside, they had seen nothing else.

"Should tonight leave us exactly where we were walking out of here last time, I'm afraid that's just too bad. Time has become a luxury we just can't afford. We can't justify sinking any more of it into chasing answers to questions which aren't going to lead to a forty-five-minute episode television show. I'd love to know exactly what happened that night thirty years ago too, but we have more pressing concerns. We have a show to deliver.

"The Mephisto Arcane needs to go back to Giles Langley, and the photos too. They're technically both his property, and his to decide what to do with. My advice to him will be to do nothing at all. I say let people remember Len Arkin for his bloody awful tunes, rather than his proclivities in the bedroom."

"Hear that, ghost?" Chloe said. "If you want to drop by it's now or never!"

Everyone laughed. It was showtime.

-

In the event, Ray had been wise to temper expectations.

The following five and something hours passed in a similar fashion to those of the previous vigil. A few interesting moments which might look okay on camera but amounted to nothing of genuine substance, questionable results of electronic field detectors, Keith's EVP recordings, the usual subjective garble of white noise, pops and clicks, and Charles waxing lyrical about sensing different energies. An even harder thing for viewers to gauge the veracity of. It was all okay, but nothing truly additive.

Their time in Crow's Cottage was almost up. They prepared for the second séance.

The arrangement was similar to the one they had used before, but with a couple of differences. To begin with, they had moved the table to the bedroom in the photos. It had taken a bit of study to work out which room was the correct one, but Chloe felt confident they had got it right. The second difference was that while the Mephisto Arcane occupied the centre of the table as before, surrounded at four points by candles, the Polaroids which had been hidden inside it were now distributed among the séance's five participants. One each for Chloe, Ray, Claire, and Keith and Charles. Chloe felt hers beneath her right hand, which was flat to the table, pinky fingers in contact with Ray to her left and Claire to her right.

Mark was behind the camera as usual. The participants had been instructed to keep their Polaroids out of sight. Whatever happened, they couldn't appear in the final edit.

Charles settled himself and began.

"Spirit, we invite you to join us here at this table, seek out the light from these candles…"

Chloe tried to relax, to prepare herself to detect the same sensation she had experienced last time, but not reach for it. She watched the candles. Any movement in their flames was imperceptible. They appeared untroubled, infuriatingly at rest.

Charles continued, "Cleave to the light and the flame, join us in the room, at this table…"

Chloe imagined Len Arkin at Edward Needham's séance, one of a series of events making up his last night alive, one of many, beginning with completing Gary Swift's new album, the decision to go out to celebrate, winding up at Damien Faulks' party at a cottage in the middle of Surrey's greenbelt, being roped into a séance, and indulging in a little racier than orthodox sex with a stunning redhead, and what then?

Was he struck by the realisation none of it had caused him to feel excitement, pleasure or contentment? Had he been struggling with depression for some time, hiding it like so many do? Had the struggle suddenly ceased to feel worth the effort?

Leaving Crow's Cottage, sliding into the seat of his car, intending to head home, did another option present itself, a drive to the coast and the oblivion of a dark, cold ocean? Was the only real explanation that for some life becomes intolerable, and they don't want to go on?

Charles was still speaking. The hour, the dark, the hypnotic quartet of flames at the centre of the table all enticing Chloe to zone out. She caught a slice of her reflection in the polished metal plate atop the Arcane, softened by the dull surface, and then she both saw it and felt it.

She twisted, stared back, and found herself looking at it.

Everyone else must have sensed it as well, or seen her look around, because they were looking too. Charles stopped talking.

"Are you all seeing what I'm seeing?" she said.

There was a garbled, hushed mush of agreement, as though everyone was afraid the figure would be frightened off.

Then came one dissenting voice: Mark.

"It's not showing up. *I* can see it, but it's not here in the viewfinder..."

The figure moved to the doorway. Chloe had almost anticipated it and was instantly on her feet, reached the landing to find the figure at the far end. She kept moving, aware she wasn't alone. As she advanced, the rest of the group was close behind her. The figure moved again, tuned down to the staircase, as it had when she and Charles had seen it last. Only this time she reached the head of the stairs in time to see it disappear around the corner. She plunged down the steps two at a time, in hot pursuit, to the lounge, where she saw it enter the kitchen, and then feared she had lost it.

Then Claire said, "Look, out there."

They all stared through the window into the garden and the grey light of nascent dawn, seeing what Claire had seen. The figure stood at the foot of the garden by the gate leading to the woods beyond, almost lost among the shadows.

Ray was madly sifting through the keys Giles had given him, looking for the one with the tag which read 'rear garden'. He located it and rushed to unlock the door. They spilt out, but there was nothing there. Hurrying to the gate, they stared into the trees and the gloom. Mark switched on the camera's flashlight, swept it through the trunks, boughs and branches.

"There," Ray said. The figure was moving deeper into the woods. They filed quickly through the gate and followed.

And then it stopped near the foot of a tree. It appeared to be staring down at its feet. They inched forward.

The figure raised his featureless black face, stared at them and promptly vanished.

They spread out. Phones were switched back on and their tiny flashlights used to sweep the area, but the figure was gone. Chloe already knew it had, she felt it. Perhaps they all did. Ray was the only one not to have moved.

He remained at the spot where the figure had stopped. When the group came back together, they found him staring at the ground there, much as the figure itself had. He brought out Giles' keys again, searched one out and handed the set to Keith with it pinched between his fingers and the rest of the bunch dangling below.

"This should open the shed out by the side of the house. Go see if there isn't a shovel in there will you?"

-

Dawn was breaking. It was still gloomy in the woods, but it was becoming possible to see now without the need for flashlights or phone lights.

Mark appeared through the trees, carrying a shovel. Ray reached for it, but Mark hesitated. "Hey, shouldn't we…"

"What?" Ray asked. "Call someone?"

For a moment they all collectively had the chance to imagine exactly how that would play out. Mark handed Ray the shovel.

He glanced around, shared an uncharacteristically nervous smile, and said, "Look, I'm sure there's nothing to find."

Chloe didn't believe it, and she could see by their faces no one else did either.

Ray started to dig.

Clearing away the surface mulch of dead leaves away revealed a bed of dank, knotty earth. A small mound started to build to Ray's left as he deposited each shovelful of soil there and the hole got both wider and deeper. It was a job of work. A few of them offered to take a turn, but Ray waved them off, assuring them he would ask if he needed to take a rest.

Soon he was required to raise the shovel and throw some force behind it in order to cut through the tangle of roots fanning out from the tree, and the deeper he went the thicker the roots became. The pile of dirt and the hole continued to grow. A couple of feet down he encountered something more stubborn and stopped.

He set the shovel aside and dropped to his knees, cleared more dirt away, but carefully now. This was more than root. He had hit a different type of barrier. He brushed and clawed away more soil. What emerged looked like a sheet of canvas. It was possible to make out a weave in the material.

Ray retrieved the shovel and began to work around the outside of the hole, exposing more of the sheet, trying to find an edge, and eventually, he did. It was braided. He cleared more earth away and tugged at it, working it backwards, breathing quite heavily from exertion now.

With more of the material peeled back, it was possible to identify what it was or had once been: a rug. There was no chance of making out either a pattern or colour, it was too clogged with soil, but the weave left little doubt.

Ray teased the dirt out from underneath the portion he had uncovered until he came upon something else. He continued to pick and brush away the soil. What emerged looked like a rock, pale and pitted. Ray scooped away a clump of dirt and suddenly stopped.

They all stared down, understanding what lay before them.

They took in the portion of pale plate, a ridge which plunged sharply into a cavity, beside which the material flared out to meet another smaller cavity...

The object wasn't a rock.

Rocks didn't have eye sockets and nose cavities.

Skulls did.

If Ray had continued, he would have found teeth just an inch or so below...

But Ray wasn't going to continue. He stood up, his knees cracking loudly in the woodland which had also served as a burial plot, and would soon become a crime scene.

He removed his phone, and the screen lit up his face, bathing it in a wash of blue light as he dialled a number and asked for Detective Chief Inspector Richard Daley.

Chapter Thirty-Seven

Within hours, the woods behind Crow's Cottage were a hive of activity, policemen and folk covered head to toe in plastic onesies, all focused around a tree and a big white tent.

The *Where the Dead Walk* crew had been interviewed, Ray had submitted to a DNA swab so they could eliminate him from any material they gathered at the site, and finally, they went home. Richard was running the investigation.

Ray had told everyone to answer any questions honestly. The police were clearly wary of the crew's role in the discovery. It was understandable, Chloe supposed, when the truth of how they had uncovered skeletal remains in the woods behind the house was that an apparition had led them there. One that, of course, had resolutely failed to appear on Mark's footage, despite everyone present having seen it with their own eyes.

DCI Richard Daley had the advantage of knowing and trusting Ray not to be pulling some sort of stunt. Whatever had led to the discovery of the remains, they, and Crow's Cottage, were going to be subject to the sort of scrutiny their paranormal investigations couldn't even come close to.

It was a measure of how exhausted Chloe was that, once home, sleep came easily. The second her head touched the pillow she was gone.

She was roused around eleven the next morning by her phone. The Wilhelm scream might make for a kitschy and fun ring tone, but it wasn't something to wake up to feeling sleep deprived and befuddled. She groped for her phone, knowing it was there somewhere on the bedside table, almost knocked the lamp over and eventually found it, pulled it in front of bleary eyes, thumbed the call answer icon and brought it to her ear.

"You okay?" said the voice on the other end. Nick's voice.

"Yeah, eventful night. I mean, really, really eventful night."

"I can imagine. Have you seen the news?"

"No."

"That cottage you were at is all over it. The're saying human remains were discovered buried there? Some local reporter got wind of it and the police have been forced to issue a statement. You were there last night, weren't you?"

"We were."

"Did you find the body?"

"Yep, we did."

"Are you okay?"

"Yeah, I'm fine."

"What the hell happened?"

And so she told him, all of it, even the bits she had skimmed over before. Around halfway through she realised it was as much for herself as it was him. The discovery of the remains had put everything in a new context. As she spoke, several pieces took on a new appearance, some more meaningful, some considerably more sinister. It settled on her that Crow's Cottage was no longer simply a story about a cool urban myth, the Mephisto Arcane, the Longwood Society, a magician, a medium or an

275

occultist, or indeed a man who had committed suicide and a girl who had vanished.

It was a story quite possibly about a murder, and concealment of that murder for thirty years.

Chapter Thirty-Eight

Bob Vickers entered the sleek curved pavilion entrance of the Metropolitan Police's new home on Victoria embankment; the former Whitehall police station was certainly grander than the tall, bland windowed box he had served out of in Broadway.

Things looked bad. He had seen the news before he had received the call. A body, or what remained of one, had been found behind Crow's Cottage. No one was saying who it belonged to yet, maybe the lab bods were still awaiting confirmation, but he doubted it.

Bob reckoned someone related to Len Arkin had been asked to provide a mouth swab recently. He guessed the result was behind the request to interview him.

Could he come in and answer a few questions?

He could hardly say no.

He took a deep breath, and was about to present himself to security when he recognised a couple waiting in the large stylish foyer. A second later one of them noticed him.

Maxine Needham was sitting beside her husband Edward Needham. Bob was good with faces, and this one had worn well enough over the decades since he had last seen it to deliver an unpleasant jolt. In the scant seconds they shared eye contact, Bob saw she recognised him too. What did they say about history repeating itself?

The Needhams were clearly waiting to be interviewed. Unless they already had been and were waiting for a cab to leave?

Maxine averted her gaze first.

Had the body been found by the bloke he had agreed to chat to, Ray Darling, and his paranormal TV show filming at the cottage? It had to have been. Paranormal investigators. It would almost be funny, were his reputation not about to be put through the wringer.

Only, paranormal investigator or not, Ray Darling hadn't struck him as naïve or stupid one bit. Like Bob, he'd been a cop, a detective, a DCI no less, and Bob knew even the luckiest dim copper couldn't fail that far upwards. He was about to meet a few more of the clan, and he knew no matter how cordial and relaxed their questions, he would be under close scrutiny.

He had screwed up thirty years ago, and people were going to want to know how and why. The night everyone believed Len Arkin had walked into the sea and to his death was going to be the focus of a lot of attention. Everything was going to be raked over and put under the magnifying glass. He expected a body wouldn't be the last thing to be unearthed.

How long would his and Maxine Needham's secret survive?

Chapter Thirty-Nine

Ray was back at Richard's place, and it was late. Richard had been busy handling what was shaping up to be a murder investigation sure to attract a lot of media attention, and his anticipated shift had run on until long after midnight.

He had briefly spoken to Ray earlier in the day, but things had progressed somewhat. Before falling into bed, he wanted to hear more of what Ray thought off the record, and not over the phone. They both knew Ray sometimes acquired information in ways, and from people, he wouldn't be inclined to disclose in a statement to the police. Some of these ways were not, strictly speaking, legal. They relied on longstanding contacts who knew him, respected him and trusted him well enough to bend the odd rule or take a peek at something in a record somewhere and pass a few details along. The way Richard shouldn't have really checked on Bob Vickers or into the missing woman Jessica Simm, and shouldn't be sharing what he was with him now.

The remains belonged to Len Arkin. DNA results had confirmed it beyond doubt. They had conducted preliminary interviews throughout the day.

"Spoken to Giles Langley," said Richard, speaking as quietly as he could. It was long past midnight and his wife and kids were asleep upstairs. "Got some more background on the property. Spoken to Edward Needham and his wife. Bob Vickers was about as helpful as I'd anticipated. On paper, it looks like he did his job. He missed something, maybe a lot of things, but that doesn't necessarily prove he botched the investigation through negligence. He made sure to come across as friendly and eager to help…"

"But?" Ray prompted.

"Something about him… He presented as agreeable but…"

"He wasn't actually all that helpful," Ray said. "Told you nothing that wasn't already right there in the records?"

"Exactly."

"He can't have been involved though, surely?"

"No, I think he's just determined to cover his arse. If he had suspicions something wasn't adding up back then, but let it go, he's not about to say so now. I'll be speaking to him again, you can be sure of that."

"The Needhams?"

"Told me essentially what they told you. We're trying to build a list of guests who were there that night. They were able to name some for us, that might prove helpful. I'll be talking to Gary Swift and Leslie Wilkinson tomorrow." Richard paused, and said, "I spoke to Dave Moore today. A very illuminating conversation."

"Arkin's partner."

"Yeaaaah… The discovery has hit him hard. He looked like he's been crying since the story broke, looked ready to most of the way through the interview. I haven't mentioned the photos to anyone we've talked to yet, but given Moore probably knew Arkin best, I risked probing a little in that direction, asked if Len Arkin was into anything kinky, maybe had a taste for BDSM, liked being tied up by women during sex?

"No, says Moore. Absolutely not. Seemed very confident. So, I asked him, how could he be so sure? Even good friends don't always share that sort of stuff. Moore was adamant: Len wasn't into being tied up, and he wasn't into women."

"Arkin was gay?"

"Yep. Deep in the closet. Moore knew. He's bisexual himself, a blokes and gals chap. Has a history of monogamous relationships with both sexes—including Len, who it seems he cared enough about to accept his demand they keep their relationship secret. Arkin and Moore weren't just partners, they were *partners*."

"Which sheds more light on why Arkin left Moore his entire estate."

"And puts those Polaroids under a different light, eh?"

"You're not kidding."

"I'm beginning to wonder if the real reason I still can't reach Damien Faulks is he doesn't want to be reached. The staff at his club were told he'd be 'away on business', which doesn't strain credibility, but his phone being powered off does. A story is suddenly all over the news about a body being discovered behind his old gaff, and he just so happens to be out of town and incommunicado. That's some coincidence, no?"

Chapter Forty

The room he had spent the last day in reminded Damien of the ones he'd stayed in touring clubs and small theatres early in his career, when money was tight. Old hotels and bed and breakfasts, cheap, tired, second—no, third rate. Peeling wallpaper, worn carpets, fusty wardrobes and beds with mattresses broken by the bodies of a thousand guests whose budgets also only stretched to such a room.

He hated it, but it hadn't been his choice, although yesterday it had seemed a good deal more attractive than a police interview room, and infinitely preferable to a prison cell. As somewhere to stay it was depressing, as somewhere anonymous to vanish for long enough to think and get his story straight it had its merits.

Just a day before, the suggestion to run and gain some thinking time had sounded good, smart even, in the midst of near panic, with police crawling all over Crow's Cottage, and statements on the news about human remains being discovered in the woods behind the property. Now he wasn't so sure it had been a wise move.

The clock was ticking. The longer he left it before speaking to the police the more suspicious they would be.

There was a rap on the door. Finally.

He rose from the sagging bed, opened the door, admitted the thorn in his side.

"You took your time," Damien said. "Have you managed to find out anything useful, or am I just busy making things worse for myself here? Have they identified the remains yet?"

"If they haven't, it won't be long before they are. DNA test."

"What?"

"They'll find a relative, see if there's a close match."

"What about my bloody DNA? Could any of that still be there after thirty years?"

"Hard to say."

"Well, that's very comforting."

"Calm down."

"Calm down? I feel like a fugitive already. This is all your doing. I meant what I said before, if I wind up spending the rest of my days in prison, I'll make damn sure I see you there too."

"I'm going to fix things. No one's going to get caught. No one's going to prison. It's not about what anyone thinks happened, it's about what they can prove, and after thirty years that's not going to be easy."

Damien wanted to believe it, he did. But how could he?

He studied his visitor's face and had to admit it looked remarkably confident. Maybe there was a way out of this nightmare after all.

Chapter Forty-One

The city of London sprawled out before him, filling the large picture windows. On this particular morning, however, Bob Vickers was struggling to appreciate the majesty and grandeur of it all. A pigeon had landed a bullseye on the centremost pane, depositing a white streak of shit with a dark greenish lump at the head a full three feet down and across the view. The bigger issue wasn't the bird shit, though.

The prestigious corner office, the huge windows facing the city, on any normal day these things were a comforting reminder that he had made it. He had worked hard for these markers of success, earned them, and until very recently he had mistakenly assumed they would be his for a while yet.

To most of KSHF Security's key clients, he *was* KSHF security. He had got to where he was through a lifetime of building valuable relationships, winning favours and getting the job done. He had accrued friends in government and the police, who respected him, trusted him, owed him, and were ready to stick their necks out for him. But he also knew any man's personal currency only extends so far.

He had taken a call earlier from a detective he knew, one who had been successful in obtaining a place on the team investigating the remains found at Crow's Cottage. What he had to report wasn't good.

Polaroid photos of Arkin had come to light, showing Arkin blindfolded, gagged, and cuffed to a bed, straddled by a redhead. It seemed there may have been someone else in the room too, a room identified to be one in Crow's Cottage. The Polaroids were believed to have been taken on the night Arkin died, and they confirmed the investigation he had conducted at the time had been less than thorough. The discovery of the body made a mockery of the scenario he'd so confidently packed the case into. If Len Arkin had ditched his car and clothes on a beach and walked into the sea, what was he doing buried behind the cottage?

The bad news didn't end there.

As if things needed to look any worse, it transpired Arkin was gay. Len Arkin and Dave Moore were a couple, which cast the Polaroids in a more sinister light.

Bob's man said blackmail was being considered as a possible factor in the events leading to Arkin's death.

Arkin had not driven himself to the coast after the party, had not ditched his car at the carpark, had not removed his clothes, nor left them on the beach where they were found with his wallet and other personal items. Arkin had not waded into the sea to kill himself.

Arkin, it seemed, had not left the party at all, although at some point during the evening he had been blindfolded and tied to a bed naked, and climbed upon by a redhead who took snaps of the episode and then seemed to have vanished around the same time his apparent suicide was discovered.

The body, the attempt to conceal it, the efforts to make it look like suicide, the photos, these were hard facts, inescapable. They also made it look like he had done a spectacularly piss poor job of investigating Len Arkin's death. A thirty-year-old case was in the process of shafting his reputation, and to add insult to injury, it was the cast of a TV fucking ghost hunting show who had brought it all to light. Somehow, three decades after the event, they had discovered a body he had missed when the dirt had hardly settled over it.

He had been hungry back then, maybe even at risk of cutting corners, and had exercised poor judgement once or twice. His time in vice had invited him to make a particularly careless one.

While questioning the guests who attended the party at Crow's Cottage, the sight of one of them had given him a nasty shock. When Maxine, the black girl from the escort agency in West Brompton, had walked in, his face must have been a picture. She clocked who he was immediately, just as he had her. Twelve months out of the Met's vice unit hadn't just seen him moving onward and upward, but her too, it seemed. She had been dating Edward Needham, the medium.

Bob wasn't the first vice cop to mix business with pleasure; the higher-class outfits viewed it as part of the game, sound business, a small price to pay for keeping the law's attention trained on grubbier outfits. Bob wouldn't have thought himself stupid enough to take advantage of such a perk, but he was single at the time and, as it turned out, all too human.

Any bloke presented with some of the girls who worked for the classier outfits would be tested. Most could have been glamour models. Maxine could have. He passed up the offer of an evening with one a few times, but in the end, it was hard to say no. One discreet date and some action afterwards. That's all it had been. He knew it was dumb to sleep with her and told himself he wouldn't do it again, and he didn't. His move to CID a year later removed the temptation entirely.

Faced with Maxine, he'd been keen to sidestep a sticky situation, and thought he had. It didn't take a genius to work out Maxine hadn't informed her new boyfriend about how she used to make a living. So, he interviewed her just as he interviewed the rest of Damien Faulks' party guests. A quiet word afterwards confirmed Maxine wouldn't welcome their past association coming to light any more than he would. There was no reason to screw things up for her, and she was good enough to repay the favour. There was no reason to because Len Arkin's death was as straightforward and simple a case of suicide as they came. In the next few days or weeks, his body would probably wash up somewhere and confirm it.

In the meantime, he set about doing what had served him well and seen him advance quickly. He got the job done, got it done fast and got it done efficiently without wasting undue resources. The brass liked nothing better. Burning lean police budgets on some maudlin millionaire record producer who had topped himself benefited no one.

The discovery of Len Arkin's body changed everything. Now it looked like he had failed to investigate a murder properly, and who knew what details were going to come under the microscope?

His name was going to be dragged through the mud.

He was still gazing at London's picture postcard skyline through the huge windows when his office phone rang. He wasn't to be kept waiting long, it seemed. He picked up.

"Mr Gilroy," he said, still gazing out the window.

The conversation was brief. Warren Gilroy, the CEO of KSHF himself, to his credit, kept things professional. Bullshit was minimal. The bastard had contacts of his own in the force, of course, far more than Bob did, and with more clout. Whatever he had managed to learn about the investigation into the remains discovered behind Crow's Cottage, Gilroy knew it all, if not more.

Bob listened, struggling to focus on the view, his gaze drawn irresistibly back to the epic streak of bird shit. He made the occasional noise to indicate he was listening. Gilroy was busy telling him he was screwed while making it sound like it was no big deal, just something to deal with in the short term. Company image. Reputation, blah, customer confidence, blah… An extended sabbatical until the dust settled. Did he think Bob was a moron? When the muck settled it would be all over Bob as squarely as the pigeon crap on his window. None would settle on KSHF Security or Warren Gilroy.

"Of course," he said, once Gilroy was done. "I'll make sure Derek has access to everything he needs before the end of the day. I do. Of course. And you sir."

Bob set the phone down and resumed staring out of the huge picture windows, past the bird crap, while he still could, before it became someone else's office.

Chapter Forty-Two

Ursula knocked and waited a few seconds, then knocked again for good measure. It was never good to walk in on someone, even in the afternoon. It could be embarrassing. She would rather not know what some guests got up to. Cleaning up the aftermath was bad enough.

Dedra, who had worked in hotels half her life, told the most outrageous stories. She claimed she once cleaned a room where half a dozen humongous sex toys had been lined up in the bathroom by the basin, accompanied by a note that read 'Please Wash' with a twenty pound note tucked underneath. Dedra decided to forego the tip, and the task.

Confident the room was empty, Ursula let herself in and was about to wheel the linen cart through behind her when she saw she was wrong and it wasn't.

A man was on the bed, fully dressed, but lying down facing the window. He was dozing, but perhaps had not intended to, as the curtains were still open and the sun was streaming in. Ursula began to quietly backtrack when she was struck by a dark thought. The man was very still.

She stopped, and watched for a few seconds to see if she could spot the rise and fall of him breathing.

She couldn't.

Leaving the cart where it was, she moved closer, crept to the end of the bed and around to the far side where she could see the man's face. First, however, she saw the needle and syringe. The face came a second later.

It was hard, and blue around the lips. His eyes were open but blank and dry. Ursula stumbled back. She had never seen a dead person before. Was the man a junkie, the victim of an accidental overdose?

That was when she saw he had something in his hand, a piece of paper folded into four.

Chapter Forty-Three

DCI Richard Daley was exhausted. It was late, and the end of a long day saved only by what appeared to be some resolution. Len Arkin might not have committed suicide thirty years ago, but the man responsible for his death had, approximately twelve to fourteen hours ago, according to the pathologist.

Damien Faulks had bid the world goodbye via a massive intramuscular injection of morphine, enough, in the pathologist's own words, 'to kill a sturdy elephant'.

He had left a note. It made for illuminating reading, one close typed sheet which read as part apology, part suicide letter, but added up to a neat and tidy explanation and a confession all in one.

Long day or not, and despite the fact tomorrow would start early, Richard had still made a call before heading home, followed by a short visit to see an old friend he trusted to keep his mouth shut until the whole business became public.

Chapter Forty-Four

Ray, Chloe and Charles were in Ray's kitchen. He had called them first thing and asked them to come over. He had something to share, but before doing so he impressed on them the importance of keeping what he was about to say to themselves until it was released to the press.

Then he told them what Richard had told him.

"Faulks killed Arkin. Not deliberately, but he killed him all the same."

"Faulks confessed?" asked Chloe.

"In a fashion," said Ray, in a way that struck her as slightly odd.

"When did the police interview him?"

"They didn't. He was good enough to put the confession in writing, the whole ugly mess. Damien Faulks is dead. He was found in a hotel out near Southend on Sea. Topped himself, a lethal dose of morphine."

Faulks' suicide note was coherent, fulsome, and very transparent regarding the events surrounding Len Arkin's death thirty years ago, including his responsibility for it. It was a story of ambition, opportunism and greed, ending in manslaughter and a cover-up and, if Faulks' remorse was genuine, years of regret for a crime which always haunted him.

Afraid the truth would come out, and faced with spending his autumn years in prison, and his winter ones upon eventual release labelled a killer, Faulks had opted instead for a swift and peaceful end.

Where he had obtained the morphine was a mystery one that would be looked into along with everything else, but it had got the job done. A guilty conscience, disgrace and incarceration were perhaps not the only factors in play. Faulks also confessed to being almost broke. He had fallen back into the habit of gambling, and not fared well. He had loans taken out against his house and club, and stood to lose both.

"I think it's fair to assume our investigation rattled Faulks," said Ray, "especially the discovery of the Mephisto Arcane. Rich says in the note Faulks insists Arkin's death was an accident."

"How?" Chloe asked.

"Remember Leslie Wilkinson's opinion the parties were about more than just fun? He was right," Ray said. "Damien was trying to secure a deal for his own show, and he reckoned appearing successful was part of the game. Meeting Hubert through Needham and the reprised Longwood Society was the stroke of luck he was waiting for. Hubert had a lot of what Faulks needed.

"He had connections, he had standing, he had money, and he had a passion Faulks knew he could exploit. He turned out to be correct, much to Edward Needham's frustration. Through Hubert, Faulks wangled the use of a very impressive home and gained access to Hubert's old boys' network. Leslie Wilkinson said it best, these were simply the type of people at the top back then, everywhere, including TV. People who could make Damien's dreams of a TV show a reality. So, with Hubert on the hook with the Mephisto Arcane project, he started throwing the parties at Crow's Cottage and encouraged Hubert to invite his friends to them.

"The plan worked, Faulks began to make connections, but not fast enough. The parties cost money, and so did the lifestyle he was projecting. Damien Faulks was living way beyond his means.

"Then an opportunity presented itself, one which celebrity magician Damien Faulks may have let slip by, but a cash strapped grifter who had once gone by the name of Ronny Turpin couldn't resist. One of Hubert's posh pals, some privileged, upper-class, titled wonder, got himself good and drunk at one of the parties, staggering drunk, blackout drunk. Damien got Jess, who he had drafted in as an unofficial hostess along with Maxine, to quietly shuffle the guy into one of the guest rooms to sleep it off. Whereupon they both promptly forgot about him until the rest of the guests were long gone.

"Even by then the guy was still drunk as a lord, and who knows, maybe he was one? Damien had an idea. All the note says was he knew the drunk was wealthy with a reputation to maintain. He was also unconscious. Damien and Jess peeled off his clothes, draped a blindfold over his eyes and tied his hands to the bed. Jess stripped down to her lacy underwear and climbed on top of Rip Van Drunkle. A few snaps with her favourite toy, a Polaroid camera, and several appropriately compromising pictures were in the bag. Faulks stowed them in the hidden compartment of the almost complete Mephisto Arcane for the time being, where no one would find them, removed the blindfold, untied the guy's hands, and left him to wake up the next afternoon to the hangover of all hangovers.

"Faulks called him a cab and sent him on his way, assuring him he had nothing to apologise for. Didn't everyone need to cut loose now and again? He just hoped he had had a good time…

"A few days later," Ray continued, "Jess contacted him and presented a couple of the Polaroids, and bluntly demanded a payoff for them not to end up in the hands of a Fleet Street reporter she was friendly with. The guy paid up. Faulks was able to continue to present an image he really couldn't afford, for a little longer at least.

"He threw more parties, only now, without consulting Jess, he made sure he'd be ready if a similar opportunity presented itself. He'd been terrified, that first time, that the guy would wake up, and he didn't intend to take that risk again. So he decided that from now on he'd introduce an insurance policy. He'd spike their drinks – just a little – with sedatives, and he'd be able to work the rest of the game safe in the knowledge that the victim wouldn't be waking up at an inopportune moment. He'd move in when the effects began to show, guide them, with Jess's assistance, to a guest room, lock the door, and wait until they were out for the count. Once they were, they would grab fifteen minutes to pose everything and get the snaps, and Faulks would return to the party before anyone even knew he was gone. Jess could tidy up before doing likewise, leaving the guests to sleep the sedatives and booze off."

"Arkin fitted the bill, a millionaire record producer, famously private and shy?" said Chloe.

"Only something went wrong," Charles added.

"Faulks spiked his drink and the sedative worked its magic. Arkin was quietly shuffled to the room, and the door was locked. A few hours later when the party was winding down, they checked and found him solidly asleep. Even a few healthy nudges failed to rouse him. They got to work, Faulks undressing Arkin and posing him, while Jess got herself looking appropriately scandalous. Then they took the pictures. The whole thing took minutes. Faulks was about to return to the party, leave Jess to tidy up when they noticed something was wrong.

"Perhaps Arkin had an issue with his lungs. Asthma, maybe? Whatever the cause, he had stopped breathing. Jessica freaked out. Faulks tried to resuscitate him. He performed mouth to mouth, chest compressions, but it was no good. Arkin wasn't coming back.

"Jessica was no use, in fact, she was hysterical. Faulks told her to keep quiet while he put on his game face and set about shifting the last of his party stragglers off home and out of Crow's Cottage."

"Faulks knew how deep a mess he was in. The sedative meant manslaughter. He needed to cover up what he'd done, and had an idea how to, only he couldn't do it alone. The plan he had in mind required someone to drive Arkin's car to the coast while he drove his. Jess couldn't drive, so he had asked Hubert to stay until after the other guests left. He had something for him, he said. The Mephisto Arcane was complete.

"Except what he actually presented Hubert with was Arkin's dead body, naked, blindfold, cuffed to the bed, ball-gag dangling under his blue lips. He told Hubert exactly how Arkin had ended up that way, and that Hubert was going to help him to cover it up. He assured Hubert that if he didn't help, and he, Faulks, ended up facing charges of blackmail and manslaughter, he and Jessica would swear Hubert had been in on it too, just for kicks, not even for the money, just for the thrill of it all, and to watch them take the pictures.

"They were looking at a dead man, a famous record producer, who had died after being snapped appearing to have kinky sex not just at a party Hubert had attended, but in a house he owned. As far as the tabloids were concerned, Arkin would have died at Hubert's party. The situation threatened to destroy both of them unless they took steps to avoid it. Fortunately, Faulks had a way out. He just needed Hubert to make a short drive, that was all.

"Hubert was probably in a state of shock, had had a little or moderately more to drink, and was being persuaded by a skilled performer who bamboozled people for a living."

"He coerced Hubert into assisting in the cover-up," Charles said.

"Faulks rolled Arkin's body up in a rug, dragged it out through the house in darkness and left it in the woods to bury on his return. Then he drove Arkin's car to the coast, with Hubert tailing him. Once there, they dumped Arkin's car in the car park, left his clothes and wallet on the beach and drove back together.

"I've no doubt Faulks worked on Hubert the whole way back, making perfectly sure he understood he was now fully complicit in a crime. What Faulks hadn't expected was to find Jess gone when he returned.

"She left a note, warning him to not come looking for her. She had cleaned out all his ready cash, the remains of their first blackmail. The Mephisto

Arcane was gone too, along with the photos hidden inside it. Without knowing how to open the secret compartment she just took the whole thing."

"She didn't though, did she?" Chloe said.

"No," said Ray, "I guess she thought carting something like that around might call attention to her. So she hid it in the cottage instead, and just let Faulks believe she had taken it."

"Why did she take off, though?" Charles asked.

"The most obvious reason is she knew Faulks well enough not to trust him. When Faulks had told Hubert about the sedative, Jess had learned about it too, realised Arkin wasn't simply drunk. She hadn't known the full picture, and understood Arkin's death lay far more at Faulks' feet than hers. Maybe she was even afraid he would view her as a liability, a loose end? Or maybe she believed Hubert would crack under pressure, confess to the police once people started asking about Arkin's apparent suicide and his movements at the party? Decided to get a head start in case the law came knocking?"

"Or maybe she felt Damien had exploited her, and landed her in a mess he had created?" Chloe said.

"Maybe," Ray said. "Whatever the case, she was gone. Things would never be the same with Hubert either. He swore to Faulks he would never willingly set eyes upon him again. For his own sake, he said he would take his part in the cover-up to his grave, but was sure it would haunt him to his final breath."

"We know Hubert kicked Faulks out of Crow's Cottage soon after," Chloe said, "and for obvious reasons probably visited the place rarely, and never again rented it out."

"Until Hubert died and Giles inherited the place," Charles said.

"And we started asking questions."

"And Faulks started to get twitchy. The discovery of the Mephisto Arcane alone must have given him sleepless nights. He knew the photos were still hidden inside it."

"Which explains the final confession his letter contains," Ray said. "He admits to taking steps to prevent the truth from coming out."

"The fire?" said Chloe. "He was the bastard who torched our offices?"

"To derail our investigation, and hopefully destroy the Mephisto Arcane. He thought that's where we were keeping it. He had assumed Charles had it first, and come up empty-handed."

Chloe didn't follow, and she could see Charles didn't either.

Ray explained. "Your attempted burglary, Charles. I think the person you saw beating a hasty getaway was Faulks. You said the police were unable to find any sign of forced entry?"

"Yes…"

"I don't think Faulks had to force his way in. I think he lifted our keys when we met him at his club. Including the keys for Bennett White. I'm assuming the additional security there meant just keys weren't sufficient. He'd have needed our security codes too."

Chloe saw Charles was doing the same thing she was, rerunning their encounter with Damien Faulks at The Effectary in his head. The card trick, the hearty two-handed handshakes, too close, too intimate, perfect if he wanted to hide the fact he was busy dipping into their pockets. Calling over a member of table staff to pass the keys to, so she could briskly duplicate them all out back? It seemed elaborate, but then, wasn't everything a magician did, cards tucked up sleeves, artfully marked decks, mirrors and misdirection…

"Once the body was discovered he knew the game was up," Ray said. "The prospect of a trial and almost certainly a prison term was too much for him. Maybe he knew it would all come out, the important bits, what he had done and how he had covered it up, and wanted to come clean, and, for once, to reveal himself how the illusion had worked. The evidence looks to support his story. Richard said the pathologist confirmed Arkin's remains showed evidence of broken ribs and sternal fractures consistent with the application of CPR, supporting Faulks' claim he did at least try to save him."

"Where does this leave us?" Chloe asked. For all the death and sadness they had uncovered, there were still practical matters to consider. "Do we still have a Crow's Cottage episode?"

Ray shook his head. "I don't think so. Not for a while. The police will need to conduct their investigation, confirm what they can, the authorities will have to reach an official verdict on Arkin's death... Depending on that, they might try to track down Jessica Simm. Hey, we wanted answers as to why something was haunting Crow's Cottage and why the Mephisto Arcane was hidden there, and we got them. Now the truth is going to come out, maybe Arkin's spirit will finally be at peace. Giles and his wife can eventually look forward to weekend breaks at Crow's Cottage without worrying about unnerving encounters with a shadowy apparition."

Chloe heard what Ray was saying, but couldn't help feeling it was all slightly anticlimactic. Ray must have noticed.

"Come on, we did good work," he said, "helped solve a thirty-year-old mystery. At some point people will get to hear about it, just not in the immediate future."

Chapter Forty-Five

"Give it a rurr-ruurr-rest will you?" Eamonn grumbled.

Harriet's spirit was back, a frequent visitor, and easy enough to ignore when Eamonn felt rested, but the wind off the sea had been uncommonly fierce last night and had woke Eamonn on at least three occasions. He was tired, and consequently, his defences were more fragile than usual. Sometimes he was sure Harriet could sense when his armour was thin, and used the opportunity to double her efforts to gain his attention. A few other spirits had come to burble a chorus too, but none as loudly or persistently.

In life, Harriet had been the daughter of the keeper stationed in the lighthouse up the coast. In death she was a nuisance. Eamonn tried to have sympathy, but Harriet was a talker, not a listener, a trait which had to great extent been the source of her demise.

Harriet's father had taken pains to warn her about the danger the sea presented. After catching her out on the tip of a peninsula a short walk from the lighthouse, dangling her legs into the spray crashing off the rocks, he had vigorously and loudly explained how much peril she had put herself in.

The sea and the surf could be beautiful and hypnotic, but deadly as a bed of knives too. He had described how easily an unexpected wave could sweep her off the rock and into the sea. Harriet, contrite, polite, and eager to shut her jabbering parent up, had assured her daddy she would never ever do it again, and then continued to do it as often as the mood visited her.

She died the following spring when a freak wave dragged her into a turbulent sea which proceeded to smash her teenage body into the unforgiving rocks before playing with it for a day and tossing it up on a nearby beach after high tide.

In death, Harriet seemed to want only one thing, to return home to her father, who had sadly passed away, and on, approximately a century and a half ago. Eamonn had tried to do what he could to help her move on too, but thus far his efforts had been as futile as her father's attempt to keep her from the water.

Eamonn was just passing through the lounge, near one of the armchairs, when he spotted a flash of white beneath one. He slowed, squinted, and finally clomped over. Crouching, he reached under the armchair to pick up the item lying there. It was the playing card Charles had shown him, a joker bearing his friend's flamboyant signature, slipped into his wallet by Faulks as part of a trick. It must have fallen from Charles' pocket when he got up to leave.

When Eamonn's fingertips connected with the card he felt the familiar wallop and sudden disorientation he often experienced when garnering something by means of psychometry.

The resulting image was brief but remarkably vivid.

He rubbed the card between his fingers, but like a static shock discharged on contact, whatever energy the card had carried was now gone.

Chapter Forty-Six

Charles strolled down Ray's drive with Chloe, toward their cars parked on the road outside. He knew he should feel relieved. On a practical level, with the Crow's Cottage episode temporarily on hold, the current series was close to complete. What he actually felt was like the rug had been pulled from beneath them all. The facts of Len Arkin's death had been explained, but it was hard to feel triumphant given how the final pieces of the mystery had come out.

He was about to bid Chloe goodbye when his phone rang. He fetched it out, and held up his finger for her to give him a moment. The caller was Eamonn.

"Eamonn?"

"Faulks—"

"You heard already?" Charles was surprised. "Was it on the news?"

"What?"

"Faulks' death."

"Faulks is dead?"

"Yes."

"So, he was surrr-sick? Well, I suppose that explains it."

"It does?"

"Yes, the doctor or ssss-surgeon or whoever it whuh-was."

"Sorry, Eamonn, can we perhaps back up a little?"

"The playing cuh-card you showed me the other durr-day. It must have fallen out of your p-pocket. I just found it under the chair. I picked it up and got a strong impression fuuur-from it."

"Go on."

Charles listened, but couldn't really decipher the impression any better than Eamonn could. He furnished him with a lean summary of the last twenty-four hours.

"So, no, Faulks wasn't sick," Charles said. "He killed himself. I'm not sure what your vision means, but I'll give it some thought. Thank you, Eamonn, and take care. I'll call tomorrow, yes?"

Charles put his phone away.

"What was that all about?" Chloe asked.

"Good question. Eamonn got something from the playing card Faulks put in my wallet. The joker?"

"Really? What did he see?"

"An image, of Faulks, and standing at his shoulder, casting a shadow over him, a doctor or a surgeon."

"Weird. What do you think it means?"

"Right now, I haven't the foggiest. Is it possible he was sick? Something nasty he was afraid of?"

"I guess the autopsy will find out, right?"

"I suppose it will."

Chapter Forty-Seven

Chloe was driving home, still digesting all Ray had shared with them. She thought about Len Arkin's body buried behind Crow's Cottage all that time, thought about Damien Faulks and Hubert Langley living with the knowledge for thirty years. Jessica too, wherever she was.

Secrets have weight, carrying them takes a toll.

Had Damien Faulks felt the burden of his secret grow sharply after receiving a call from Ray, a producer on a paranormal investigation TV show asking to talk about Crow's Cottage? Had learning about the discovery of his Mephisto Arcane and reports of an apparition increased its heft? Did it grow heavier still with their investigation, the knowledge they were asking questions about what had happened thirty years ago, turning over old stones, particularly regarding a story relating to Len Arkin and a missing woman?

Had Faulks' secret grown too heavy to bear? Had it grown heavy enough to crush him?

How could it not, knowing they were tramping around his old home, Len Arkin's remains such a short distance away, reduced to bones, but bones with the power to erase his freedom and reputation in an instant, quicker than a coin vanishes from a magician's hand? Poof. Gone.

The note he left behind may have spoken of regret, but his first instinct had been to save his skin, hatch a scheme that got him into Charles' home, so he could presumably remove the Polaroids from the Mephisto Arcane, and when this failed, he had taken the more drastic step of torching the Bennett White Production offices.

Chloe didn't doubt Faulks felt regret for what he had done, but how much of it came from what it might cost him rather than what it had cost Arkin? It certainly wasn't a deep enough regret to embrace facing justice. When a reckoning looked inescapable, he had instead performed his final trick and left the stage.

Faulks had spent a lifetime keeping secrets, confounding, concealing, bamboozling. Maybe any confession from him at all, while alive or once dead was surprising? It would almost have felt more in keeping had he bowed out taking the details of his most audacious illusion with him: fooling the world into believing Len Arkin had committed suicide. It didn't feel in the nature of a magician to reveal his method, even after the final curtain came down.

Secrets were heavy, Chloe knew it only too well, but they perhaps weighed more on some than others. For some, the temptation to unshoulder the ugly cargo might grow irresistible. They might find an old and damning truth, that a man had died, and that they had helped conceal it from the world, left his body to rot in a shallow grave for decades, too much to carry anymore.

Damien Faulks had spun a whole life out of secrets, lies and illusions, but Hubert Langley hadn't.

Hubert Langley had spent his life looking for truths, the occult, 'knowledge of the hidden'—Chloe remembered the Latin.

Chloe parked up outside her building, turned off the engine.

How might Hubert have felt at the end, as cancer spread through his lungs, shortened his breath, robbed him of strength and exchanged it for discomfort and pain? Death had not been a choice for Hubert. Death had not crept up and taken him by surprise. It had marched slow and steady in his direction across a desolate expanse, leaving him ample time for reflection. Nursed through a long illness with no hope of recovery—

Chloe had been about to get out of the car, but slowly slid back into the driver's seat. She was thinking now about Eamonn Lister's phone call, and the image he had received from the playing card: Damien Faulks, the shadow of a doctor looming over him, or a surgeon. That was what Charles said. A doctor or a surgeon.

How exactly would Eamonn know he was seeing a doctor or a surgeon?

Maybe because the man in the vision was wearing scrubs?

Doctors and surgeons wore scrubs, but they weren't the only ones, were they?

Nurses wore them too, surgical nurses, or maybe just nurses who worked at posh Knightsbridge hospices whose uniforms were artfully designed to evoke the image of scrubs.

Had Hubert shared all near the end, everything, including his fears Damien Faulks might have had a greater hand in Len Arkin's death? Perhaps Hubert's long-ago friend, Faulks' first blackmail victim, had tried to warn him about the parties, and only later had Hubert made the connection.

Had he told it all? Had he told it to Nick? If so, what had Nick chosen to do with Hubert's secret?

It had never reached the authorities, if that had been Hubert's wish. Had Nick kept it to himself then, to preserve Hubert's reputation, believing there was nothing to be gained by tarnishing a dead man's standing? If so, what impact had the show's investigation had on his decision?

She thought through the possibilities.

Was this why Nick had asked her for a date in the first place, after their meeting in the park? Had Hubert's disclosure been on his mind as he walked back to the hospice to work? Was he really thinking about how he was attracted to her, or was he thinking about how a bunch of people were about to dig into the events surrounding Crow's Cottage and the death of a famous record producer? After they had gone out, maybe he had found himself genuinely attracted to her, and simply accepted whatever would come out would come out?

Or had he done something else entirely with Hubert's confession?

Nick was buying his mum a house. He had over half the asking price ready to put down in a lump sum. What if this hefty deposit wasn't the result of years of diligent scrimping and saving, what if it had been extracted from a cornered Damien Faulks in exchange for keeping quiet?

It was hard not to see the irony in such a turn of events, and maybe a perverse type of justice too. After all, morally speaking, how guilty should someone feel about blackmailing a blackmailer? What would the truth do for Hubert or Len Arkin? Both were dead and gone. For someone who had no

309

time for spirits, ghosts, or an afterlife, they were beyond harm, oblivious to anything at all the moment their brains ceased to function. Nick might even have eased his conscience by telling himself he wasn't just punishing Faulks, but righting a wrong done to his mother?

Was this all she had meant to Nick? A source of information, a window into whether he needed to worry the truth was coming out?

With every second the dark worm of suspicion burrowed deeper.

It wouldn't have stopped here though, would it? Not as things progressed.

Faulks would have paid good money to secure his secret.

As Chloe told Nick about the investigation he would have become increasingly concerned. Hearing who they were talking to, and what they were learning, what Charles was doing with the Mephisto Arcane, the dubious picture steadily forming around Arkin's death, and then the photos discovered hidden inside the Mephisto Arcane's secret compartment. Had he grown scared enough to intervene? If the truth came out then surely Faulks would seek solace in seeing him ruined too?

She immediately thought of Charles' attempted burglary, and with its failure the more drastic step of the fire. She tried to recall where Nick had been the night the Bennett White Production's offices were set ablaze. It took a moment or two, but she remembered his last-minute call to cancel because he had been asked to cover a shift at work.

She didn't like the way it all fit, didn't want to acknowledge how well it did.

Nick Spokes had made her trust him, open up to him. How much of what he told her was even true? The sob story about his gambling dad and heartbroken, destitute mum, was it all bullshit? Did she know Nick Spokes at all?

She wanted to hear his voice, needed to, to ask him a question and listen to his answer, alert to the words and the tone, ready for the ring of a lie. Aware she wasn't really thinking things through, acting on impulse, but somehow unable to stop herself, she pulled out her phone and called him.

He answered almost immediately, must have seen it was her.

"Chloe? What's up?"

"Quite a lot as it happens. You?"

"Erm, yeah you could say that. Everything okay? You sound... Is something wrong?"

"Tell me again how you got the money to buy your mum's new house."

There was a pause. Chloe tried to keep her head and not read too much into the delay that followed, but it was hard not to.

"I saved it," Nick answered, after what felt like far too long.

"Years of scrimping?"

Another pause.

"What's this about?"

"I was just thinking how that's a lot of money to save."

"I guess it is."

"Hubert tell you anything important before he died?"

"What?"

"Just answer the question."

This time the pause was even longer, and she was sure. Suddenly she wasn't uneasy, or confused or hurt, she was angry.

"No," Nick said. "Not unless you tell me what you're getting at."

Her intention only to fish for hints went out the window. "Did he maybe tell you something which allowed you to get the money for your mum's house a little more easily?"

"What would Hubert have told me? Honestly, I don't have the first idea what you're on about."

"Don't you?"

"No. Look, Chloe, I'm busy here. I have a very sick patent waiting for me to assist her in getting through what may be her last day with the living. She's in a lot of pain, her family are understandably upset, and right now my major concern is making her as comfortable as possible, so if you've got something to say please just come out and say it."

This time the pause was on her end. Suddenly his irritation birthed a stab of doubt. Was Nick being evasive, or was he just under pressure, and simply wondering if his girlfriend had lost her marbles? Before she could marshal a response, Nick's voice, flat and blunt said, "Fine. If you want to throw riddles at me, you'll have to wait until I finish my shift."

Then he cut her off.

At a stroke, Chloe felt lost. The once-plausible scenario she had rapidly brewed up was beginning to feel a bit outlandish, more so by the second. She felt her face flush with embarrassment as it dawned on her how she must have just sounded to Nick. If not plain crazy then plain rude. Why hadn't she called

Ray, sounded her mad conspiracy theory out? She knew why. It was the fear she actually meant nothing to Nick at all, nothing more than a way to help him save his hide.

A bit of clear-headed thinking was required, to empty her crazy head and start over. See how things stacked up, and then maybe she would call Ray.

She got out of the car on autopilot, unlocked the door to her building and began to climb the five flights of steps to her flat. She let herself in, shut the door behind her, took off her coat and pulled off her boots, wandered to the kitchen. She needed to *do*, not to think, just for a short while. So she made lunch to busy herself. Something nice and normal. She chopped up some ham and cheese and whisked a couple of eggs. Made an omelette, grabbed a fork and started to eat.

It looked decent enough, but trying to consume it was like munching on cardboard. She had zero appetite. She binned the lot.

Okay then, what were the facts? She tried to assemble them in her head, eye the fit. Could Nick really be involved? Technically he could, and why had the thought slid so easily into her mind and taken root so powerfully? Was it just what Charles' friend Eamonn had seen, or was something else there? Nick... She didn't want to believe him capable of something like that. If he had extorted money from Faulks, it would explain where he got enough to buy the best half of a house, and the magician's sudden 'gambling debts', although so would gambling debts and years of saved wages.

Most of all, having called Nick, heard his voice, and asked the question, his reaction wasn't what she had expected. He hadn't sounded guilty, just irritated, stressed and baffled. But then how would a guilty Nick have responded? What exactly had she expected, that just the question alone would trip him up and he would betray himself, confess to being a blackmailer and possibly a house intruder and an arsonist?

Now she had gathered her wits and tempered her emotions, she knew she should have waited. She'd had time, all the time she needed to think it all through before she did anything, but instead, she had gone off half-cocked, let her anger get the better of her, run her mouth off like an idiot. Just like with Kara. She had no excuse for not knowing better…

She set the kettle to boil. A double strength mug of black coffee would help get her brain limber. She grabbed a mug, dumped two heaped spoons of instant coffee and one heaped spoon of sugar in, added boiling water and gave it a quick stir.

She carried the drink out with her to the roof terrace. Distracted, she took a sip and promptly burnt her top lip. Cursing, she set the mug down on the small garden table.

The decking behind her creaked. Before she had time to turn and look, two arms clinched around her and a hand fastened over her mouth. She tried to break free, but her arms were pinned and her feet suddenly lifted from the ground.

A voice hissed into her ear, "Couldn't leave it alone, could you?"

She knew the voice, and knew also she had been both dead right and horribly wrong at the same time. The initial shock of being grabbed was followed by a more profound fear.

Hubert *had* told all near the end then. To ease his conscience, expose Faulks, or just to get out from under his heavy secret, she couldn't say, but he had told all.

It hadn't been to Nick, though.

The voice was thick and close in her ear. She could hear the desperation and frustration in it. "Poor Nick. If you knew him at all you'd know he could never do what I've done. When you called, he hadn't a clue what the hell you were talking about, but I did."

'You killed Faulks,' she wanted to say, 'wrote his suicide note, his confession,' but the hand fastened over her mouth prevented it, and calling for help.

"I made the mistake of telling Faulks what you'd found out. The wily old bastard turned the tables on me. Set me to work tidying up his mess. Get the photos, and failing that just fucking destroy them. I'm sorry, I'd rather not have to have to do this, Nick's my mate, but I don't much fancy the idea of prison."

James Barlow moved towards the guard rail.

She struggled, but her feet just thrashed the air. Barlow was big and he was strong. When they reached the railing, she jammed her legs out, bracing them against the rail, but, as she applied force, the rail began to bend. She had been wise never to trust it. She stopped pushing, but Barlow didn't, he took over, planting a foot on the rail and bending it further forward until finally it gave way. The whole section snapped at the bottom and toppled off, landing with a clang five floors below.

He wound back to throw her off, down to unyielding paving and a low brick wall.

She felt him swing forward and let go, felt herself thrown forward, about to die in what would no doubt be taken for an accident.

She twisted in the air, grasping for whatever she could. Temporary salvation came in the form of a jutting stub of railing bar, a remnant from where the rest had snapped off. She jerked to a stop, a flare of pain in her shoulder as it took her weight and the weight of the fall. An instant later she swung down and slammed hard against the wall, but kept her grip. She looked up to find a panicked looking Barlow bearing down. He began to peel her fingers free.

She had to hold on, at least until someone saw or heard what was happening. Barlow had clearly aimed to make her accident quick and quiet and beat a brisk getaway, but now it was taking longer and making a hell of a lot more noise. Surely someone had heard the railing strike the ground?

She started to yell for help.

She didn't see his fist coming, but she saw the stars. Boom. Her head felt like it had been smacked by a bat and then dunked underwater, the sound of her pulse beat thickly in her ears. She was vaguely aware he was drawing back for a second blow.

She threw an arm up, grabbed for the leg on his scrubs with her free hand, seized a fistful of fabric, her shoulder still screaming in agony.

Boom. Her head rocked back, more stars, deeper water…

She held on, but knew she wasn't going to weather too many more hits. She had to do something while she still had the strength and the wits. She scrambled at the wall and hauled herself up some more, enough to hook her arm under Barlow's thick meaty calf.

She kept going, until she was close enough to sink her teeth into it.

He yelled in pain and suddenly she was dragged forward and up. Her chest and stomach scraped painfully across the remains of the guard rail, sharpening her head. Barlow was pulling back, trying to shake his leg free, but she clung on, a chunk of him still between her teeth. She bit down harder. He kept backpedalling, and she finally lost him.

Far from safe, but still with the living, she crawled the rest of the way up and rolled back onto the terrace, scrambling for the wall, as far away from the edge and Barlow as the small space allowed.

He was blocking the doors back into the flat, the route out, and nothing but a cheap garden table lay between them, a pathetic barrier considering her wiry frame and the slabs of muscle packed into James Barlow's scrub style uniform.

He looked as freaked out as she must. He knew he had to finish the job and fast.

He came for her.

But she was ready. She scooped up her coffee mug from the table and hurled the scalding black contents right into his face. Barlow screamed and tried to barrel into her, but she ducked awkwardly under him. They collided, but the connection was glancing. Chloe spilt one way and Barlow the other. She crashed into the wall, he veered towards the edge of the terrace. She saw him try to fight momentum, and fail. His foot landed clumsily on one of those jutting stumps of rail bar. His knee buckled, and he plummeted over the edge.

There was no dramatic Wilhelm-esque scream, just a clipped sort of yell, the kind someone trapping their hand in a doorjamb might make, as much an exclamation of surprise as of terror.

Chloe tried to sit up, but all at once every inch of her felt like it had taken a beating. One of her eyes was closing fast and her nose and mouth felt twice their usual size. The impact of the last two minutes smashed into her like a tidal wave. Shock, pain and adrenaline converged at once, causing her to shake violently.

Was she safe?

Gingerly, she crawled to the edge of the terrace and peered over.

Below, James Barlow's hulking frame hung over the low wall fronting the building, folded into a shape no body should take. His eyes were open, but past seeing.

"Almost killed," she said, her rapidly swelling lips turning the words into mush, "by a bloody nurse."

Epilogue

Chloe eased up on the gas to negotiate a bend approaching on the lean winding road climbing into the village, just a slight drop in her speed: any more and she might not make the hill. This area of the island's roads were both steep and twisty, although no steeper or twistier than those their coach driver had happily sailed a vehicle eight times the size of her dinky rented jeep around at speed during their transfer from Zakynthos airport to their hotel a few days ago.

She passed a series of traditional whitewashed Greek homes with red tiled roofs, one or two with the familiar iron rods jutting out, ready for another floor that would likely never come, and arrived at a junction. She glanced down at her phone to check the directions and peeled off to the right.

In the aftermath of the Crow's Cottage business, when the dust had mostly settled and the picture cleared, she had returned home for a weekend to visit her mum. There was something she had to do. While the prospect was daunting, recent events had illustrated all too well that the things people do don't go away just because they keep them secret, and their attempts to keep them hidden can be more damaging still.

James Barlow was dead, but even without him the authorities knew what to look for; there was ample evidence to put the important pieces together. Between interviewing Nick, data extracted from

Barlow's phone, records from his network provider including GPS data, CCTV recordings in the area close to the Bennett White offices on the night of the fire, and Damien Faulks financial transactions, the police investigation assembled a picture which was as close to complete as anyone needed.

Hubert had told all at the end. Perhaps he had intended to share his ugly secret before he died but felt that moment was always one more day away. When it arrived, death no longer a dark spectre on the horizon but a stark presence looming at the foot of his bed, he found the only ear available belonged to James Barlow. Perhaps he would have preferred Nick to hear his confession, but Nick wasn't around.

Hubert had been in poor shape for days. He was dying, but in such situations, it can often be difficult to predict exactly when the end will come. Nick had stuck around for as long as he could, but after a lengthy shift on the back of several similarly lengthy shifts, he had finally handed Hubert's care over to James, instructing him to call if his condition worsened. James did, around six hours later.

When Nick returned, he found Hubert was still with the living, but beyond talking, and oblivious to his surroundings. As his pain and discomfort had increased so had the meds to deal with them. Enough morphine to allow him to meet his end peacefully.

He died two hours later. Nick and Barlow were there when the end came.

Barlow did not share what Hubert told him with Nick, or with the authorities. Hubert's confession had not prompted a search of the woods behind Crow's Cottage. No remains were located. The police did not beat a path to speak to the man Hubert said was responsible for putting them there.

Barlow had taken what Hubert had told him, dug into the events, and arrived at a different decision. He had approached Damien Faulks and used the information to blackmail him for over half a million pounds. Faulks' financial transactions showed he had cashed in practically all the investments he held, and then re-mortgaged his club to raise more. This had been the sum required to avert spending his final years disgraced and in prison. It should have been an end to it. Len Arkin's body would continue to occupy a shallow grave wrapped in a thick rug for who knew how many more decades, if it was ever to be discovered at all.

Only Hubert had a will, and Crow's Cottage moved into the hands of Giles Langley. A strange box was discovered hidden there, followed by sightings of an apparition, which had, in turn, led to an investigation conducted by a paranormal investigation TV show. When Chloe had gone to chat with Nick Spokes, Nick had told James Barlow about it. Nick had also happened to make a comment about how attractive his interviewer had been. Likely uneasy about this new turn of events, Barlow had nudged, or as Nick put it, shoved him into giving her a call and asking her out on a date. It was a long shot, but if she bit, James might be able to discover more about what was going on.

Chloe said yes to the date, but Barlow wasn't ready to trust in second-hand information, so crashed the date instead. Chloe and Nick's subsequent relationship must have been a gift, making it possible for him to quiz Nick as events unfolded. What he heard made him nervous enough to pay Damien Faulks another visit. Perhaps he had hoped to enlist Faulks in derailing the investigation, but if so, he had miscalculated badly. It seemed Faulks, while equally keen to keep things hidden, decided the best way to achieve that was by counter-blackmailing Barlow. After duplicating the keys to Charles' house, Chloe's flat, Ray's house and Bennett White, if not the alarm code, he handed the job of dealing with the photos from the Mephisto Arcane to Barlow, first by gaining access to Charles' house when he was supposed to be out, and then by torching the Bennett White Production offices.

When both interventions failed and Len Arkin's remains were discovered, and it looked like Damien Faulks was about to answer for what he did, Barlow knew Faulks would take him down with him.

Barlow could see only one sure fire way out: deal with Faulks in a fashion which would bring an end to the whole mess, and allow him to hang onto both his blackmail money and his freedom. He urged Faulks to get off the grid for a spell, just long enough for them to think, make a plan, assess what the police could actually prove. If there were incriminating loose ends which could be tidied up, Barlow would see to them.

This was how Barlow manoeuvred Faulks into an anonymous hotel room, paid for in cash, isolated. Barlow arrived, having taken care not to be seen, packing a fake confession letter and a syringe full of morphine, a lethal dose. When he left, Faulks would be on the bed, appearing to have chosen death and confession over a trial and prison. The police would have the villain of the piece and an explanation for everything in one tidy package.

The road levelled out and then began to fall. The whitewashed, red-tile roofed houses gave way to hills dotted with wizened olive trees. Beyond lay an impossibly blue swatch of the Ionian Sea. Chloe glanced at the map on her phone and saw she needed only to follow the coast road for a minute or two longer to reach her destination.

Things had been awkward with Nick; admittedly he had been left with a whole bucket of stuff to wrestle with. James Barlow had been his friend, colleague and flatmate, landlord technically. Nick had been lodging with him, renting Barlow's spare room while he saved and saved and saved.

Chloe knew he found it hard to reconcile the person he knew with the things he had done. Perhaps like Damien Faulks and Jessica Simm, Barlow had only intended to commit one crime, and the consequences had spiralled beyond his grasp. Perhaps like Hubert Langley, he found himself trapped and doing things he would never have believed himself capable of. One bad deed compounded by another in a desperate effort to conceal the last…

Chloe felt her share of guilt too. While he would never admit it, she knew she had wounded Nick by believing him capable of Barlow's crimes. It had only been for the briefest of crazy moments, really, and she had been half right. Her misguided suspicions were excused to some extent, given Nick had been totally blindsided by Barlow's crimes.

Still, it was something they were awkwardly negotiating. She wasn't sure where they would land, but she hoped they could get past it, even if they never quite reached a stage where they could laugh at that time she had suspected him of being a blackmailer, arsonist and murderer.

How different things could have been if Nick had been the one to hear Hubert's confession, if Hubert hadn't been cheated out of his dying wish.

Charles now believed they had made a false assumption from the start. The first sighting of the apparition seemed to coincide with the discovery of the Mephisto Arcane, but it had been in the house all along, and Len Arkin's remains had been buried behind Crow's Cottage for thirty years too. Granted, Crow's Cottage had been largely unoccupied during these years, but not completely vacant. It had received regular, if infrequent, visitors in the form of staff who spring cleaned the property, who carried out repairs in accordance with the maintenance provisions Hubert had set in place. If Len Arkin's restless spirit had been fighting to lead someone to his remains, it had been remarkably relaxed about it until recently.

So, had finding the Mephisto Arcane really been the catalyst behind the apparition's appearance, and had the spirit been Len Arkin's at all?

The apparition had appeared after Giles Langley had inherited the cottage, which had of course been in the wake of Hubert Langley's passing. Hubert Langley, whose dying wish had not just been disregarded, but used by someone no better than Damien Faulks for his own gain. Despite confessing all at the end, Hubert Langley had been robbed by James Barlow, left with unfinished business, haunted beyond his last breath.

They had seen Giles just a week ago. Hubert's eternally affable nephew was pleased to report there had not been a single new sighting, or any other unexplained phenomena since their last visit.

As for the show, the Crow's Cottage episode was on hold for the time being, at least until the police investigation was fully wrapped up, but it would make a hell of a splash when it did. They had secured new production offices, and the series had been edited and finalised. It was due to air at the start of autumn in a few weeks. They would be on the promotion cycle for a spell when it did, but in the meantime, they were enjoying a well-earned break.

Chloe had asked her mum if she could take her on holiday, a couple of weeks together, some quality mother and daughter time. Her mum had been surprised and thrilled.

Chloe felt only trepidation.

She had ulterior motives. Secrets were corrosive, and if you wanted to be free of them, whatever the consequences, it was perhaps wise not wait too long.

She booked two weeks on the Greek island of Zakynthos. The intention was to say what she had to on the first day, and have the rest of the fortnight to deal with the fallout, if her mum didn't simply book a flight home. In the event, it was harder to do than she anticipated. It was her mum who tackled her eventually, four days in, demanding to know what was troubling her. She knew something was troubling her daughter, despite the sunny front Chloe was putting up.

So Chloe came clean. Once she started, she kept going, wanting, needing to get it out. She told her mum to sit down, and then admitted to something she had kept from her since Kara had vanished, something that had never been far from her mind since.

In the days before Kara vanished, she and Chloe had argued. It had been a bad one, although at the time it had felt like just one more bad one on the top of the last bad one and the inevitable next bad one. It had seemed familiar enough, featured the same elements, the same patterns. Kara had done something which perfectly demonstrated she didn't give a crap about anyone but herself, on this occasion borrowing Chloe's hairdryer, breaking it and simply tossing it back onto the floor of her room like it was Chloe's problem to solve.

Chloe had discovered the broken hairdryer and tackled Kara about it. Kara had explained, in the way one might to a simpleton, how it had obviously been about to break anyway so what difference did it make who had been using it when it did? As far as constructive dialogue went this had been the high bar. Things rapidly degenerated from there on in. Each was likened to unintelligent genitalia, various species of the animal kingdom and the like.

Chloe and Kara were sisters. Sisters argued. Sometimes they even fought, slaps and scratches, but commonly love creates a buffer, love pulls the punch, love throws a leash over some words, reins in some insults, some accusations, holds certain retorts far enough out of reach for their damage to be temporary, and wounds never more than skin deep, quick to heal.

The problem was, Chloe wasn't sure she still loved the person her sister had become. Kara was always difficult and often mean, but had become so much worse, caused too much pain, too much worry, showed ever dwindling evidence to suggest she still cared for anyone beyond herself. It had grown difficult to recall a time when she had ever been different. Arguments had become so common there wasn't time for resentments to fade or wounds to heal before the next assault. The love she felt for her sister was harder to locate, its power to prevent lasting damage overwhelmed. Kara had long since quit pulling her verbal punches, but Chloe began to find it harder to hold back her own.

So, on this particular afternoon while their mum was at work, and Kara had crashed in to make use of her increasingly vacant room, an argument about a hairdryer somehow became an argument about everything. Kara had spat the usual venom, and Chloe had spat right back. Vile things were said at a volume which ensured both would be hoarse the following day. The game became who could wound the other deepest. It was a game Kara had developed a talent for, one their mum was reluctant to play, and one Chloe was sick of playing with one hand tied behind her back.

It wasn't the last thing she had said, and not at the greatest volume, or embellished by the most colourful of adjectives, and had not signalled an end to the fight, but Chloe had said something which had crossed her mind on more than one occasion but she had never actually given voice to before.

"I wish you'd just fuck off," she told Kara. Her sister smiled back at her. "Seriously. Just fuck off and don't come back."

These were the exact words she had used. She clearly remembered saying them, especially later. She had selected them precisely for the sharpness of their edges, hoping they might cut through Kara's belligerent and selfish hide and inflict maximum pain.

She may even have meant them.

Back then.

She had never honestly expected Kara to vanish though, and even before berating herself later she knew it wasn't what she honestly wanted. What she wanted was for her sister to be more like she used to be, capable of caring, that was all.

Kara had fucked off though, and not come back, and as the weeks and months rolled by and her mum grew more distraught and desperate, looking her in the eye became more and more difficult. Secrets grew heavy. Hubert Langley would have understood.

Then, out of the blue, like a rope thrown to a drowning mariner, she had been contacted by Ray, offered a job, and an escape. This, coupled with liberal doses of deflection and self-justification, helped for a while, but only so far. She knew she needed to come clean, whatever the consequences.

Her mum listened to what she had to say, never once interrupting, or saying anything at all. Afterwards, she was silent for what felt like an age but was likely only seconds. Then she sighed, like the air had suddenly gone out of her. Chloe was afraid to look into her face, scared she had just wrecked what remained of the tiny Harker family unit, but forced herself to. She had to know how much damage she had done.

Her mum got up, closing the distance between them, reached out and took her in her arms and said, "All this time you've been carrying this around with you? Afraid you're responsible for her not coming back?"

Chloe nodded.

Her mum sighed. "Sweetie, since when did your sister *ever* do what she was told? You didn't make her leave, no more than you made her act the way she did, or say the things she did, do the things she did. I don't know why she left, but if she chose to it was because she wanted to, or maybe had to."

"Where the hell is she, Mum?"

"I don't know. I think maybe she did something, got herself into some trouble, landed herself with a debt she couldn't pay back, did something bad, had to leave. I just don't know, but if it's any of those things I hope she's found somewhere safe, far away from whatever it was. It helps me to imagine she's more like the old Kara there, maybe even better or wiser, and one day she might be able to come back."

"Do you really believe that?"

"Sometimes. If I try very hard."

"I miss her."

"I never doubted you did."

-

Chloe slowed the jeep again. The road had dropped more sharply, sweeping downward toward a stretch of sandy beach beside an expanse of clear blue water. Her mum was back at the hotel, by the pool, almost certainly reading one of the half dozen paperbacks she had brought with her. They had fallen into the routine of the last week, eaten breakfast, applied sun lotion, found a couple of sun loungers near the pool, and then when her mum had looked settled and comfy, Chloe had suggested hiring a jeep to explore the island for a spell.

Her mum had started to get up, but a little reluctantly as Chloe had hoped. That's when she had said she quite fancied going alone, just a few hours, a gentle bite-sized afternoon adventure. She had her phone to navigate and intended to simply follow where the roads took her for an hour or so before setting back. Her mum remained beside the pool.

In truth, there was more to the outing.

There was still one loose thread dangling in the wake of the whole Crow's Cottage fandango, and one thing connected to it that nagged at her. It was a Polaroid photo. Not one featuring a gorgeous redhead astride a blindfolded, ball-gagged man tied to a bed, but another.

It was not difficult to find where she was searching for once she really set about trying. In a pre-internet age, like say, the late 1980s it may have been, but those five letters on the bottom of the sign – Z, A, K, Y, N – had narrowed things down drastically. A Google Maps search and a little poring over street view had finally located the place in question. The sign was different, but the wall outside, the beach in the background, and the olive trees were almost identical to their equivalents in the Polaroid. When she looked up the name of the bar's registered proprietor it definitely warranted a second glance.

The sand and sea rolled past to her right until the arrow on her map app and the dot denoting her destination converged. She pulled in and brought the little red jeep to a stop. The bar from the Polaroid and her detective work on Google street view lay ahead. She left the jeep and walked to the entrance, taking in the sign. It now declared the establishment was called Breeze Beach Bar.

It made for a perfect place for tourists and sunbathers to grab a cold drink, an ice-cream or a snack. A few patrons were doing just that, amid company of a furry four-legged kind. This was something else Chloe had gleaned from her street view search. The pictures had all featured a liberal number of cats, lazing on the wall outside. The explanation lay in the next building along, a cat sanctuary linked to the bar, owned and run by the same proprietor.

Chloe had pulled up the sanctuary's basic but functional website. Stray and abandoned cats were rescued, rehabilitated and rehomed. Many were dotted around now, basking in the sun like royalty, or dozing in the shade, one or two sauntering lazily about. Despite their regal repose, several were worn and weathered, bits of ears missing, one or two limbs or tails, some with shaved patches of fur, female felines who had clearly been recently spayed. Chloe was familiar with the existence of cat cafés, but felt perhaps this bar functioned as one purely by accident.

One cat sat by the entrance, like a maître d'. Chloe stroked its head as she entered, its snooty bearing immediately evaporating as it pushed to bunt its head against her palm and started to purr. She saw a couple under the shade of some olive trees, one sauntering through the bar like it owned the place.

Chloe passed a calico with one eye and parked herself at the bar. A man with greying hair, a healthy belly and dark Mediterranean skin spotted her and came over, smiling at her from a big kind face.

"Drink?"

"A Coke please."

The man nodded. "Ice?"

"Yes, please."

The man fixed the Coke and set the glass in front of her. She handed over a ten euro note and accepted her change. She sipped her drink, enjoying the sea breeze and the shade. Looked casually about the bar, to anyone looking probably appearing as relaxed as the cats were.

Chloe had assembled a story in her head. She had no idea if she had all the details right, but she was willing to bet many of them were.

When Jessica Simm had fled Crow's Cottage, while Damien and Hubert were busy depositing Len Arkin's car, clothes and ID on a dark coastal beach, she had realised she needed help, from someone she felt she could trust, a friend, perhaps the only true one she had made since arriving in London. She had arrived at this person's door and told her some or all of what happened, and that she had to disappear, far enough away it would be hard to find her. Jess had taken what remained of Damien's share of the blackmail money, but she needed more: what remained of hers, and all her personal ID from her room in Lisa Gastrell's flat. This friend could get both without fear of being found.

What she did not have was the Mephisto Arcane or the photos locked inside it. A strange, large occult device wasn't exactly the sort of item she relished putting through airport security. It might attract unwanted attention, be memorable enough to stick in someone's mind should the police start asking questions. She realised she didn't actually need to take it. She just needed Damien Faulks to believe she had. So, instead, she hid it in Crow's Cottage and left a note warning him she had taken it. Hopefully, it would be sufficient to make him think twice about coming after her. If they came out, they would do far more damage to him than her.

She had, however, taken her Polaroid camera, the one she had taken the pictures with. Why wouldn't she? A camera in the possession of someone travelling abroad would scarcely warrant a second glance.

Jessica's flight had landed on a Greek island, perhaps not this one, perhaps she had hopped between them a little for good measure. Jessica Simm ceased to exist, if Simm was her true name in the first place, and not the latest she had chosen after skipping the last town for the next, trying to lose the part of her that was a magnet for trouble, or outrun a past which had long, strong legs and never seemed far behind.

Perhaps she was at last far enough away to achieve escape velocity. Things would be different this time, maybe because she knew they had to be, and she had money. Not enough to live a life of leisure, but enough to buy a bar, enough to build a life, one happy enough for her still to inhabit thirty years on, having married a Greek man with a healthy belly and a kind face, and become Jessica Georgiou.

Chloe had begun to wonder about the Polaroid in Maxine Needham's memory box, the one of two beautiful young women in front of a bar by a beach, Maxine and Jessica on holiday. She had naturally assumed it was from sometime before the business at Crow's Cottage had turned everything upside down. A girls' holiday the previous summer.

She still had the snap she had taken of the Polaroid on her phone, and had studied it in greater detail. Something, in particular, had caught her eye, and it had nothing to do with the two beautiful women in the foreground, but a man behind them in the bar. He was wearing a t-shirt featuring an album cover Chloe was familiar with. It was one her mum had owned, among the tower of CDs next to her old boom box at Nan's house. The album's title was *The Stone Roses*, by a band of the same name. The cover type was bold and orange, atop a squiggly green and white background. The 'O' of 'Roses' was a slice of lemon.

When Chloe googled the album's release date, she found it had come out in 1989, one year after Len Arkin's death, one year after Jess had disappeared.

Chloe let her eyes wander around the bar, while she unhurriedly enjoyed her drink. She had emptied the glass of all but ice and was about to request another when a woman with red hair, liberally threaded with grey, appeared from the direction of the sanctuary. She neared and then walked behind the serving area with the liberty of someone who had every right to, and shared a few words in Greek with the man tending it. The man smiled, nodded, and strolled off in the direction of the beach.

The woman caught Chloe's eye, spotted her empty glass and smiled.

"You okay there?"

"Could I get another Coke, please?"

"Coming up."

"Name's Chloe," Chloe said, extending a hand to the woman behind the bar.

"Jess," said the woman, shaking it while reaching for a fresh glass.

"It's lovely here, right by the beach," Chloe said. "Yours?"

The redheaded woman nodded, set the drink down. "The bar is, the sanctuary next door. The strays? Well... Does anyone truly own a cat?" She smiled, set a fresh glass of Coke in front of Chloe. "We take them in, lost, hungry, injured, feed them up, fix them up and try to find them a home. Somewhere they'll be loved, and feel safe."

"Strays are only strays until they find a place they belong, right?"

Jessica Georgiou agreed.

Chloe didn't hang around long. She had seen what she had wanted to see. She finished her Coke and left, but only after she had insisted Jessica Georgiou accept her remaining folding cash, around seventy euros, as a donation to the sanctuary.

It was a beautiful day.

She intended to spend the rest of it with her mum.

The End

335

Did you enjoy this book?

PLEASE, PLEASE CONSIDER LEAVING AN AMAZON REVIEW!

It's no exaggeration when I say reviews are vital to authors, and especially to independent authors like me. Without the support of a big publisher they are without doubt the biggest reason other readers will try my books.

Thanks for reading.

John Bowen.

You can find me at:

https://johnbowenauthor.wordpress.com

Find me on Facebook at:

JohnBowen – Author

Or contact me directly at:

johnybwrites@gmail.com

Also
by John Bowen

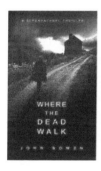 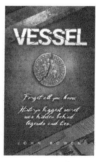 

Acknowledgements

Thank you to my wife Caroline and my kids, Henry and Freya,

to my mum, Carol Thornton, my stepdad Tony Thornton, and my dad, John Bowen snr, and to Richard Daley who sufferers my daily ramblings.

Thank you to all those who helped out by enduring the janky beta versions and offered valuable feedback and corrections. Author Sharn Hutton, Kath Middleton, Jacqueline Bickley-Parton, the spooktacular author Shani Struthers, and Kelli Mahan, Andy Coldham, your keen eyes amaze me and saintly patience boggles my mind.

Thank you to the wonderful people who helped the book get out of the gate with extra oomph, my own advance review group, the incredible Tracy Fenton, Melanie Preston and Helen Boyce at Facebook's best book group, the amazing THE Book Club, and Compulsive Readers.com for an amazing blog tour. I am once again greatly in your debt.

Finally, thank you to kick-ass thriller author, Joel Hames, and my brilliant editor Joanna Franklin Bell (trust me, any mistakes you may find will NOT be hers).

Your contributions, friendship, faith and support mean so much.

Cheers guys.

Printed in Great Britain
by Amazon